Hunting Bernie Weber

Books by Matthew J. Flynn

Bernie Weber: Math Genius Series
Book 1: Milwaukee Jihad
Book 2: China Code
Book 3: Hunting Bernie Weber

Revenge Series
Book 1: The Court of Last Resort

Coming Soon!
Book 2: American Dawn
Book 3: The Peasant of WalMart

Hunting Bernie Weber

CIA Hunts Local Math Genius
Small-Town Milwaukee Protects Him

Matthew J. Flynn

SPEAKING VOLUMES, LLC
NAPLES, FLORIDA
2024

Hunting Bernie Weber

ISBN 979-8-89022-145-2

To my wife, Mary

Acknowledgments

I wish to acknowledge, with thanks, the efforts of my agent, Nancy Rosenfeld; my editor, David Tabatsky; and my publisher, Speaking Volumes, in the publication of this book.

Chapter One

When I comb my hair each morning, I imagine my head is a planet. I use precisely 50 strokes of a comb to arrange the vegetation on the planet so circling observers can tell it's inhabited.

I'm Joe Weber, Masters in Poli Sci at the Community College of Milwaukee, presently receiving unemployment compensation. I'm the least obsessive member of my family. My Uncle Dan used to count the license plate numbers of every 20th parked car on his way to work, and he multiplied them by two to see which plate could get closest to one thousand. One morning, a car pulled out into traffic, and the decision to count it or not distracted him. Uncle Dan died when he crashed into a telephone pole.

You have to understand something about Milwaukee. We're pickled in Schadenfreude. You breathe it in the air and drink it in the water. People here are obsessed with letting you know when you do something wrong.

We do things here better than anyone else, and we know it. Arizona is a securities fraud in progress. The culture of Texas is homicide. Even their sanitation policy. Don't mess with Texas. A zoo in South Carolina will have a small, weathered sign that says "Alligators" on a short fence that a child could climb over. A traffic light in Indiana will hang from a wire and blow in the wind, not firmly bolted on bright yellow poles, one on each of the four corners. We once sent our County Executive to prison for using office stamps for personal mail.

A Milwaukeean will gently point out your faults, sticking his finger in your eye to the knuckle as he does it.

"Your child was killed in a bicycle accident? I'm so sorry! Was he wearing a helmet?" or "Oh, your husband died of lung cancer? I'm so sorry! Did he smoke?"

"Do not mention the rope in the house of the hanged man."

This proverb is unknown in Milwaukee.

Our city has no sense of nuance. We are the most literal people on the planet. My girlfriend, Frannie Ferraro, is from out East. She's a Teaching Assistant in the Spanish Department. The students laugh at her serious points and write down her jokes. Once, while explaining how to use the masculine ending when both genders are referred to, she said, "The feminine follows the masculine, but only when it comes to matters of grammar." A weak joke, but it appeared as an answer on three exam papers.

Our newspaper, *The Journal*, reports garage burglaries. If someone from Milwaukee is mentioned in *The New York Times*, *The Journal* will report it as news. If someone from Milwaukee appears on national TV, *The Journal* will write an article about it.

Milwaukee is the hardest city in the country for an actor to get a standing ovation. In New York, you see them at almost every Broadway show. Here, you have a better chance of seeing an actor fly off into space on his own power than witnessing an audience rise to its feet. Why? Because we're afraid we might get it wrong! We're afraid someone will laugh at us. We're afraid we might praise someone who didn't deserve it.

In fact, we clap slowly even for the best performances. Unless you're *famous*. If a famous actor stumbles into Milwaukee to perform, he gets a standing ovation *because he's supposed to*! Because he's been ratified by someone else. He could lurch onto the stage, trip, and hit his head on the piano stool, and the audience would still rise to its feet to applaud. *The Journal* would review him favorably because someone who knew what he was doing had approved him somewhere else!

There is no litter on the streets of Milwaukee. We will stand on the sidewalk for a light to turn green at four in the morning when it's 20 below zero and there are no cars in sight.

"Joe! Joe Weber!"

"What?"

I snapped out of my daydream and looked over at Frannie, my girl-friend, in the passenger seat. Frannie has short dark hair and gorgeous grey-green eyes. She has more common sense than me or anybody in my family, and she frequently lets me know it.

"Joe, are you counting stripes again?"

"No, I'm not counting stripes."

I never should have told her about what I do when I'm driving.

"Are you counting license plate numbers?"

"No."

"Are you counting parked cars?"

"No."

We pulled into the parking lot of Curtin Hall, with its neo-riot architecture from the late 60's. In 1969 the students carried the dean out of the building, tied by his ankles and hands to a pole, like a deer. All the new construction at the college was concrete, with slits for windows like gun turrets.

It was a cold, clear evening in early January 2010. About two feet of snow lay on the ground. I looked up at the clean white points of light spread across the horizon, starlight beaming through my windshield from billions of years ago.

"So, tell me about this, Joe. What's this thing we're going to after my class?"

"Jimmy and Bernie are in a program being presented by the Math Department. It's about how to get kids interested in math again."

Bernie and Jimmy are my brother's boys. Bernie's a sophomore at Riverside High School. Jimmy's a freshman at Fordham University. Got a full ride. He was home on Christmas break.

"Jimmy's eighteen, right? And Bernie's what?"

"Bernie's sixteen."

I held the door for Frannie as she got out of the car. She wore a starched blouse and tight blue skirt just above the knee. She looked really good.

"So, what are they going to do? They're cute little buggers. I know they're smart."

"It's a Math Circus. You give Jimmy a day and a year and he can tell you what day of the week it was. You tell him July 18, 1582, and he'll tell you it was a Friday. I mean, I don't know if it actually was a Friday. But Jimmy can tell you."

"How about Bernie?"

"Something with numbers. You'll see."

"Okay. Are you going to sit in, or should I meet you there?"

"I'll sit in the back. We can go over together. Which class is it?

"Golden Age. I'll let them go early."

There were about 25 kids scattered around Frannie's third-floor classroom in Curtin when we got there. She arranged some things on her desk while a few more students straggled in, dropping their backpacks on the floor.

"Hello, everybody."

Frannie beamed at them.

"Our extra credit question for today comes from beyond the course curriculum. This one's from the twelfth century. Give me one significant attribute of Alfonso the Chaste. Anybody?"

4

They stared like trout on ice.

"Come on. For a point on your final grade. Jason, what can you tell me about Alfonso the Chaste?"

"Alfonso the Chased."

Jason enunciated it like a home-schooled spelling champ.

"Alfonso the Chased was chased by a king, I think like from France, or maybe another nobleman, who wanted his land and stuff. I think he perhaps chased him over the Pyrenees, or some adjacent place."

"That's not quite right, Jason."

None of the other trout moved or blinked.

"Alfonso the Chaste was a poet. But was Alfonso celibate, as his name implies?"

Not a sound or a blink at a question so far from their experience.

"Well, he wasn't," said Frannie. "Okay. Today we're discussing the great 17th century play Fuente Ovejuna, by Lope de Vega. And we're going to relate it to modern America. Ashleigh, it's your turn to present. Tell us about the play."

Ashleigh shifted in her seat. She smoothed her long blonde hair and crossed her legs.

"Fuente Ovejuna means the sheepwell? It's the name of a town? An evil nobleman came to town, and like ravaged some maidens? And the villagers like killed him? Then the soldiers came and they like tortured the villagers to find out who killed the nobleman. But they wouldn't tell, and they just like yelled 'Fuente Ovejuna did it' when the soldiers tried to make them tell who did it?"

"That's not bad, Ashleigh. Did you have the same reaction I did when you read it? I actually cried at the villagers' heroism. To endure abuse and stand together as a village against unjust authority. What lessons does that have for us today?"

5

No one seemed to think it had any lessons to offer. No one had ever met a nobleman, or a maiden. The room was silent.

"Let me put it another way. Today, if the federal government came to Milwaukee in force and tried to impose its will on us, could we beat them? Are we strong enough? Are we smart enough? Milwaukee against Washington. Who wins?"

Frannie endured a long silence.

"All right. Think about it for our next class. Would we be as strong as the villagers of Fuente Ovejuna? Would we be as smart and resourceful to stand up to an overwhelming outside power? You're dismissed early today. Use the rest of the hour to start reading *La Vida Es Sueño* by Calderon. Meghan, you'll present next class. Dismissed."

There were maybe a hundred people in the first-floor auditorium of Curtin when Frannie and I walked in. I recognized some of the faculty. A meeting of college professors is like a reunion of royal families, with each reduced to driving taxis or waiting on tables but obsessed with his stature. A roomful of Hapsburgs, Bourbons, Isrids, and Romanoffs, all with bad haircuts and ill-fitting clothes. A faint odor of resentment lingers in the nostrils. Cash is a problem.

Xeno's First Paradox is still unanswered.

"If I'm so smart, how come I ain't rich?"

I saw Bernie in front of a bulletin board. It was 20 feet wide, with many announcements for lectures, concerts, and meetings, such as "The Influence of Ruben Dario," "Womyn's Herstory II," and "The Quaga: Why He Disappeared." The notices were fastened by thumbtacks with long colored plastic handles. Some were doubled up, so they flopped to one side. Some were simply posted over other notices.

Bernie was arranging the notices so that they were perfectly spaced. Vertically, two inches apart. Horizontally, one inch apart. Each had its own thumbtack. Bernie carefully folded the extra notices on the floor in a pile.

"Hey, Bernie."

"Hey, Joe. Hey, Frannie."

Bernie kept arranging the notices in straight vertical lines.

"How you feeling, Bernie? Ready for tonight?"

"Yup."

"What are you going to do?"

Bernie looked at me and rolled his eyes.

I saw my uncle walk toward us. Professor Frank Weber, associate professor of chemistry. He was a handsome man, tall, with thick grey hair and kind blue eyes. He wore a pink cardigan sweater and slippers that day. Slippers! Plaid, from Wal-Mart. None of his fellow royals even noticed.

"Joe, did you see the playoff game? Buffalo against Cincinnati?"

"No, I didn't. Who won?"

"Buffalo. It was a great game. They played hard. But you know, they claim they never go for the groin."

Uncle Frank's a great perseverator. Instead of lining things up or counting them, he tells the same five jokes and uses the same phrases. He hasn't ever spoken about a pro football game without saying, "they claim they never go for the groin."

This is an insight that he feels bears repeating. Sometimes, he'll also point out the obvious, that the reason they don't do it is a fear of retaliation. Like enemies outlawing poison gas.

A man with a weedy beard extended his arm into our conversation.

"Professor Weber? Do you remember me? Bruce Nichols? I did my master's degree with you five years ago. I'm teaching chemistry at Marshall High. Freshman and Advanced."

Frank shot him a radiant smile and stared at Nichols. But there was absolutely no connection. The question barely penetrated.

"Oh, yes, good to see you Bruce. Do you have any good students? Do they ask any interesting questions?"

Nichols fumbled a reply until Frank wandered off to take his seat near the front. Nichols stared at him as he walked away.

"You know, you can't lay a glove on that guy. I studied with him for two years. I've seen him lots of times since then. He always asks me if I have interesting students, and if they have any interesting questions. The identical two questions, every goddamned time! One time, I told him I had a kid who'd discovered a new element, just to see what he'd say. He just said that was great and walked away."

"Attention. Ladies and Gentlemen. Attention."

Carl Gripentrog was wrestling with a microphone at the podium. I excused myself from Nichols and saw Frannie sitting in the front row with Sharon, Bernie's mom. They were saving me a seat. Sharon isn't too fond of the Webers. My brother Jimmy Sr.'s sick and hasn't spent much time with his own wife and kids. I think Sharon blames the whole family. She didn't smile or say anything when I sat down.

Carl called again for attention. He was an assistant professor in the Math Department, a basic Badger dressed in a red Rose Bowl sweatshirt that he probably bought at a gas station from a rack where they sell plastic roses and beef jerky.

Carl explained the juggler and dancing bear approach to Math that the evening represented.

"It's a circus! A magic show! Math is stranger than magic! And now, ladies and gentlemen, it gives me great pleasure to introduce our guests, the two math rappers, Dr. Kalen Darr and Pryme Knumber!"

Carl started to clap, leading the crowd. When he claps, instead of tapping the tips of his fingers on one hand into the palm of the other, he slams his palms together, making his elbows flap like the wings of a flying goose.

Jimmy and Bernie made their entrance wearing capes, and Bernie had a pair of oversize green ears. Jimmy tipped his aluminum foil beanie to the crowd. The screams from their classmates filled the room.

"So, now, let's start with Dr. Kalen Darr. Doctor? What are you going to do today?"

Jimmy beamed at the audience. He had thick, auburn hair, freckles, and a smile that widened as shouting erupted.

"If you give me a date, I can tell you what day of the week it is . . ."

"Doctor!"

"My man!"

"The Dick Smith"

"The Pecker Checker!"

The howls from his friends drowned out the rest of the audience. Carl stared triumphantly.

"In other words, Doctor, if I said to you, 'April 4, 1789', what day of the week was that?"

"Tuesday."

Maniacal applause exploded in the section where Jimmy's friends were sitting. An old fellow in a tattered parka stood up. I remembered seeing him hanging around the student union during the winter, staying warm all day on a single cup of coffee.

"How do we check it out? How do you know the kid's right?"

"You can check it out in the library. The reference desk. Anyway, I've heard him do this before, and he's always right."

A woman stood up in the third row.

"How about October 3, 1947?"

"Friday," said Jimmy. "It was a Friday."

"That's right!"

The woman was excited to be part of the show.

"That was my birthday. My mom delivered at three a.m. I was a breech. I was a third child. I . . ."

"Thank you very much," said Carl. "Next date, please."

A little man with a thin moustache sat directly behind me. I heard him chuckle as Jimmy nailed date after date without a single mistake.

When Jimmy's classmates threw dates at him like July 14, 8947 B.C., Carl disallowed the question to avoid a fight over calendars. After Jimmy's half hour was over, Frannie cheered wildly. Frannie has a whistle that could crack windshields in the parking lot. Jimmy bowed deeply from the waist in all directions.

"And now, ladies and gentlemen, I want to introduce Pryme Knumber. Mr. Knumber, what are you going to do?"

Bernie shrugged.

"Whatever you want. Maybe we should start with cube roots. Ask me a cube root."

"Okay, what's the cube root of 27?"

"Three," said Bernie.

"What's the cube root of 125?"

"Five"

Carl surveyed the audience.

"All right, I'll ask Bernie one more question and then you can all try it. Bernie, what's the cube root of 1,331?"

"Eleven."

The man with the moustache behind me raised his hand. He smiled slightly as he stood up.

"What's the cube root of 6,859?"

He spoke with a foreign accent but enunciated clearly. Bernie didn't hesitate.

"Nineteen."

The man stared at him and sat down. Frannie jumped up to whistle. "Frannie, sit down."

Bernie was shy. I didn't want to throw him off. He sat up there with his round face and bushy brown hair, staring solemnly at the audience. His cape was open, and one of his ears had slipped back slightly. He looked like a trick-or-treater dressed in discards.

"Okay," said Carl, "we'll have one more cube root and then we move on. Who has one?"

The man in back of me raised his hand again.

"How about the cube root of 18,191.447?"

The crowd was silent. Frannie glared at him.

"What a dirty rotten thing to do. He's trying to make Bernie look bad."

"26.3," said Bernie.

He didn't even move a muscle on his face. The crowd was silent, and the man continued to stare.

"Okay, okay", said Carl. "Let's go on to the next part. Bernie, what have we got next?"

"Prime numbers. You give me a number, and I'll give you its prime factors."

The crowd was silent again.

"What's he talking about?" said Frannie.

I didn't explain.

"Shh, let's watch."

"A prime number is any number that is only divisible by itself or one", said Carl. "Okay, Bernie. 377."

"Bernie looked bored.

"13 and 29."

I heard a thud. I looked around to see the man behind me pick up a book off the floor. He couldn't hide his agitation.

11

"2,993." said Carl.

"41 and 73."

The crowd remained silent. Slowly, very slowly, the man rose.

"This is interesting. Very interesting. Can I ask the young man how large a number he is capable of factoring?"

Bernie shrugged.

"Pretty large. Pretty much any number."

The man stared at Bernie.

"23,843."

"113 and 211," said Bernie.

Then he yawned and smiled at me.

"That's good. Very, very good. And now let me ask you another one. 2,695,417."

Frannie glared at him.

"Why do we let them in the country?"

"1,913 and 1,409."

Once again, a profound silence filled the auditorium.

It became a dialogue between the man and Bernie. He asked Bernie numbers in the millions, and hundreds of millions, and then billions. When his examples could not be factored into primes, Bernie told him. Carl finally stopped it.

"I guess that's the end of our program, folks. Doctor and Mr. Knumber, thanks for your terrific work. And remember, Math can be fun. Not lucrative, but fun."

Chuckles swept the hall. Carl's fellow threadbare royals appreciated the gallows humor. We stood and cheered for Bernie and Jimmy as they came off the stage. Frannie gave them both a hug.

I didn't notice the man with the moustache until he'd wormed his way right into our conversation and stood a foot away from Bernie.

"I just want to meet this remarkable young man," he said.

He extended his hand. Bernie gave it a polite shake and drew back.

"Both of you, too, of course."

He pretended to smile at Jimmy, then looked at Bernie.

"But tell me, how did you do that? Did you ever think about how you did that?"

"Did what?"

"The prime factors. Not the cube roots. The prime factors."

Bernie shrugged and looked embarrassed.

"Yeah, sort of. I'm trying to put together a program that can do it. It's hard to explain. But I think I can."

The man stood as still as a mime. Not a muscle moved in his face, his arms, his legs, or anywhere. It was strange.

"That's very good. That's very good indeed."

His accent became more pronounced as he got excited.

"Do you suppose I might see a copy of that program when you're finished?"

"Look," I said, "I appreciate the interest, but this is a family thing. Thanks for joining us. We've got to be going."

The man didn't move.

"Where are you from?" said Frannie.

The man didn't answer. He nodded slightly, then walked away.

"Okay, guys, we're out of here. Jimmy, Bernie, where do you want to go?"

"Pizza," said Jimmy. "Let's go to Lisa's."

We all left together. Frannie, I, Sharon, Jimmy, Bernie, and Uncle Frank. I saw the man take out his phone as we left.

Chapter Two

The man dialed.

"Hello."

"This is Nizip."

There was a pause.

"The population of Nizip?"

"30,219."

"Where?"

"Milwaukee."

"Go ahead."

Nizip spoke urgently, and too quickly. He skipped words. The man on the other end never interrupted.

"So that's it. You won't believe it. He factored every number I gave him."

"Did you record it?"

"Record it? How could I? I didn't know it was going to happen. I went there by accident."

"The boy said he was writing a program?"

"Trying to. He said he's trying to."

"Come home immediately. I'll see you at ten tomorrow morning."

The phone went dead.

Nizip woke frequently that night, dreading the ridicule he knew he would face. He was a Turk, masquerading as a graduate student in mathematics at the Community College in Milwaukee. In fact, he had been placed there in a joint operation between American and Turkish intelligence agencies to see if he could penetrate security at Avionics, a top-secret defense contractor in Milwaukee that had no knowledge of his existence.

Turkey still had a bad image in the U.S. government, especially at the CIA and NSA. The unstated impression was of an army in pajamas and turbans pitching tents outside of Vienna and trying to disembowel everybody in the city with swords shaped like croissants.

Now, Turkey was important, knocking on the door for admission to the European Union, a dike restraining Iran, Iraq, and the Muslim states to the East.

But the Turks had to be trained.

They were in the dark ages of espionage and everything else. What better place to train them than in Milwaukee, the espionage backwater of the universe, the quietest, safest spot on earth, a wading pool to teach an infant to swim? The rudiments of a joint operation, the management, the protocol: all done in perfect safety. If Nizip succeeded, fine. Like hiring a hacker to break into your own computer, to show you where you had problems. And if he didn't succeed, that was fine, too. It was a first baby step toward more involved cooperation.

Nizip reflected on all this as he stared up at the ceiling. He wished he had never attended what he thought would be a lecture.

At ten the next morning, he stood before a three-story townhouse in Georgetown, waiting for the door to finally open.

"Yes?"

A woman stared at him. She was perhaps 65, with impeccably groomed hair and a small birthmark on her cheek.

"I am Nizip."

"Come in."

The interior of the first floor looked like a private library of a wealthy recluse. Fresh gladiolas burst from a vase on the mantle over the marble fireplace. The floors were polished hardwood, covered by antique Persian carpets. Walnut bookcases lined the lower half of every wall. Silk brocade drapes, drawn tightly, covered each window, so the only light throughout the interior was artificial.

Nizip stared at the rugs. All Bakhtiari. Importing them was illegal. He admired the cone shapes of the pistachio trees on one, and the royal profile in the center of the largest. At least an 18th century.

"They're waiting for you upstairs."

The woman nodded at the carved walnut staircase that wound out of sight to the second floor. She did not follow Nizip as he ascended the stairs.

"Good morning, Nizip."

Three men sat around a table and did not rise as Nizip entered the room.

"Good morning, Wayne."

Wayne Hawkin gestured to the two men at his side.

"These gentlemen are my colleagues."

He didn't introduce them further.

"I told them about our conversation. Tell us what happened."

"I don't know. I thought I was going to a math lecture. I sat in the auditorium, and a couple kids started doing tricks. I was about to leave, but the smaller kid said he'd divide numbers into prime factors. I couldn't believe it."

Hawkin glared at Nizip.

You told me on the phone he was wearing green ears, too. You sure they weren't his real ears? You incompetent scoundrel. You've done nothing but waste our time.

"Nizip," Hawkin said, "you were sent to Milwaukee to gather some intelligence on Avionics. It's not a difficult assignment. It's our first joint operation of this kind with your government, and we hope it goes well. Turkey is one of a few Muslim countries that share our objectives.

And now you expect me to believe that a 16-year-old kid can crack every code in the world in his head. Is that right?"

Nizip looked uncomfortable but said nothing.

"All modern cryptology is based on trapdoor functions," said the man closest to Hawkin.

He was Maynard Gieck, senior mathematician to the NSA.

"It's easy to fall through the trapdoor. It's impossible to go back the other way. Every government on this planet sends messages in coded numbers. Computers can easily break those codes. You understand that, don't you Nizip?"

Nizip nodded but said nothing. He wished he'd never made the call.

"What every government does is multiply the code number by a very large prime number. Only we know the prime numbers we use. When the receiver of the message gets it, he multiplies it again by his own very large prime number and sends it back to us. We divide by our prime number and send it back again. The recipient divides by his prime number, and he has the message. Even if it's intercepted, no one could understand it because they don't know our prime numbers. It would take a computer thousands of years to factor out all the prime numbers we use. And you say a kid in Milwaukee can do it?"

"I'm not saying anything. I'm just staying that I saw him up on the stage doing cube roots. He could do pretty big cube roots. Then, he said he could do prime factors. I started asking him numbers, and he started giving me prime numbers. That's all I know."

"How big?"

Gieck leaned forward.

"Pretty big. We got in the millions, maybe the billions. The kid didn't hesitate."

"You taped it, of course?"

Nizip slumped in his chair and looked at his shoes.

"I didn't have a tape recorder."

The three glared at him, ready to flog the Turk.

The skinny little mustached idiot! We send him to Milwaukee to spy on a domestic defense contractor to see if a prototype operation can be accomplished with the Turkish government, and this is what happens. Inspector Clouseau shows up at a community college and comes back with a story about a kid who can crack any code in the world in his head!

Nizip sensed their displeasure.

"Why should I bring a tape recorder? I was out for the evening."

"You took notes, of course."

Nizip squirmed some more.

"No notes. I had no pen."

"How do you know if the kid isn't faking it? You give him some numbers, and he throws out some answers, and the crowd in Milwaukee claps. Isn't that possible?"

Nizip shrugged.

"It's possible. He said he's writing a program that will do what he can do in his head. I asked to see it, but his family told me to leave."

Gieck leaned back in his chair and stared at the ceiling.

"There have been prodigies. There was the German idiot, Dase, who could multiply any two eight-digit numbers in his head in less than a minute, or two twenty-digit numbers in six minutes. There was Aitken in Edinburgh. But there's a big difference between that and factoring out prime numbers in your head."

He leaned across the table to glare at Nizip.

"Are you sure that isn't all it is? Are you sure it isn't some prodigy doing cube roots?"

Nizip shook his head.

"The kid's brother could give you the day of the week for any date in history. It was amazing. But this kid Bernie could do primes. Believe me."

Gieck shook his head.

"There have been other prodigies who could give you days of the week. You could write that computation on the back of a matchbook. The computation for factoring out prime numbers hasn't been written. There isn't a computer in the world that can do it."

Hawkin opened a folder on the table in front of him.

"We ran a check on the family. Joe Weber. Masters in Poli Sci from Milwaukee Community College. Obsessive compulsive. By the way, they're all obsessive compulsives. Very interesting family. You could write a case study about them."

He referred back to his folder.

"Frank Weber. Associate Professor of Chemistry at the Community College. Wrote thirty-two papers. Some weird titles, but our people say they aren't bad. Like, 'How Did Chemicals Manage to Combine Themselves Into a Chemistry Professor?' Jimmy Weber, Senior. Paranoid schizophrenic. Presently in mental hospital. Father of Jimmy Jr. and Bernie."

Hawkin looked at Nizip.

"Bernie's the kid who did the primes, right? And Jimmy Jr. is the kid who did the dates?"

Nizip nodded.

"Some of the others were probably there. They all left together."

"All right. Here's what we're going to do. We're going to get the kid out here to talk to him. We'll see if he's for real."

"How will you get him out here?" said Nizip. "He's a kid."

"We'll find a way. Scholarship. Prize. Class trip. And you find out what you can. Especially if the kid's writing a program. You may leave, Nizip. Thank you."

The three men said nothing until Nizip had been escorted out. A bottle of sherry stood on a small antique Japanese table at the side of the desk, along with a platter of cheese and a silver bowl of crackers. The third man motioned to the table.

"Gieck. Hawkin. Will you join me?"

"Not me."

Gieck rose to leave.

"I've got to go, Willis. I'll take a rain check."

Lathrop Willis waved at him as he picked up the phone.

"Can you stay, Hawkin? Just have to leave a message."

Hawkin poured a glass of sherry and sipped as he looked at the man on the phone. Willis had a full head of white hair and deep brown eyes. He was quite elderly. If his hair were dyed, he could have passed for 15 years younger.

Willis finally hung up the phone. He also poured himself a glass and gestured to Hawkin.

"To your health, Z."

"To yours, Z," said Hawkin.

There is a class chasm inside the Central Intelligence Agency that is slow to close. Willis and Hawkin were a generation apart at Yale, but on the same side of the chasm. The Agency recruited heavily at Yale, and especially at Scroll and Key.

Nine senior societies are established at Yale, each with about 15 members who dine and meet several times a week. Their members are tapped from the junior class at the end of the school year. Scroll and Key is the literary society. Its 15 members meet every Thursday and Sunday during their senior year to read essays and stories each has written, and to critique and debate. To support this, Scroll and Key has an endowment larger than that of some small colleges.

Each evening starts with sherry and cheese in the poculum, then dinner in the dining room of the society's main building. Afterward, port, Madeira, and cigars. The building is a massive stone structure with no windows, and vault doors. A staff of attendants prepares and serves the meals and maintains the building. Dean Acheson was a member. So were Cole Porter, Benjamin Spock, John Lindsay, Cyrus Vance, Gary Trudeau, a Mellon and a Rockefeller. The members entertain themselves by singing Cole Porter songs that no one else has ever heard, written while he was at Scroll and Key.

The society was founded in 1842, influenced by German romanticism. The founding group assigned a name to each member. The butler is called Wamba. These names, drawn from mythology and history, have been passed to the incoming group of 15 for more than 160 years. The leader of the group is called Zanoni, or Z for short. Willis and Hawkin had each been Zanoni.

Willis had been with the agency since its founding. He had worked with Donovan and Dulles, becoming much like Admiral Rickover in the Navy. Willis ran covert operations, just as Rickover had run nuclear submarines. As with Rickover, Willis had strong supporters on Capitol Hill. No matter who headed the agency, no one interfered with Lathrop Willis.

"What's up?" Hawkin finally said.

"We captured an Al Qaeda man in the Congo. In Isangi."

Willis typed on his laptop. A map appeared.

"He had a disk on him. With a very large number."

"Has he talked?"

"Of course. But he's just a messenger. Doesn't know beans about what it means. The damned thing is thousands of digits long. Gieck's sure it's a message. But we can't factor it down."

"What can we tell from the location and the identity of his handler?"

"Gieck will keep working on it. Hawkin, I want you to oversee this project. Make sure Maynard and his people have all the resources they need. Come at it from every direction, not just the number crunching. Everything. Understand?"

"Yes. I'm glad to be part of it."

"Good. Please tell me, Hawkin, what is going on with this boy in Milwaukee? It's hard to believe Nizip's report."

"I don't think it'll turn out to be anything. Nizip didn't record it. We'll follow up, but it sounds farfetched."

"Right. Listen, Hawkin, there is one other thing I want to talk about. Allen Barnes."

"Barnes? He's still in the hospital, isn't he?"

"He is. But I got a call from his doctor. Depression seems to be under control. He's a good man, Hawkin. His father was a classmate of mine. Allen Barnes is a legacy. He can retire in a few years. I want to bring him back and give him some projects. I want him to go out with his head high."

"Willis, do you think that's wise? Barnes is a friend of mine, too. But we could sick leave him out right now at full pay. He can take early retirement in three years. Why risk a project?"

"He tapped you, didn't he? For Keys? He's one of us, Hawkin. We take care of each other. I don't want Barnes's boy thrown over the side for depression. He needs his work, and he needs us. Don't give him anything sensitive. Make something up if you have to. But make sure he feels as if he's part of it again."

"Alright. For starters, I'll put him on Nizip's find in Milwaukee."

"Fine. And give him some intercepts to work with. Gieck can give you some material from the morgue. Make him feel part of it again, Hawkin."

"I will. When can he be released?"

"Right away. I'd consider it a favor, Hawkin, if you'd go up there personally to bring him back."

"I'll be glad to."

Hawkin returned to his office. As his secretary called for airline reservations, he picked up a photo he'd clipped from *The New York Times*. The top half of the photo showed a view of a plain on Ganymede, one of Jupiter's moons. It looked like a large ax, with evenly spaced knobs on the handle, laid out across the plain. The bottom half of the photo showed a plain on Europa, another of Jupiter's moons, covered with striations. They looked like thousands of ridges clustered in small groups. Hawkin had an amateur interest in astronomy and clipped frequently. Now, he had Barnes's first project.

Chapter Three

The sign said 53 more miles to Madison. I looked over at Bernie as I drove. He was holding his hands up to the windshield and measuring something.

"What are you doing?"

"See that overpass?"

"Yeah."

"See that blue car going across it?"

"Yeah."

"I think we'd hit it. Except that it's going over us."

Bernie was right. Just as we went under the overpass, the blue car was exactly overhead.

"So what?"

"There was a guy driving it. Let's suppose he came from Beaver Dam, and he had a banana for breakfast."

There's very little Bernie says that surprises me.

"Okay."

"And let's suppose he left home at 11:13 this morning."

"Okay."

"What are the odds we'd hit a blue car at this exact spot at this exact time when the driver started from Beaver Dam at 11:13 and then had a banana for breakfast? Say you had to have all those factors."

I shrugged.

"Pretty slim."

Bernie stared out the window.

"Say you had to compute the odds of everything that moved in the universe for the last billion years. Like every car against every car. And every animal against every animal. And every atom against every atom. It would never have happened *exactly* the way it did."

"But it did."

"But it never would have if you tried to predict it starting out."

"Look, Bernie, when was the last time you saw your dad?"

"Three months ago."

"How do you feel about seeing him?"

"It was okay."

Bernie kept measuring the overpasses. When we got to Hartland, we stopped for cheeseburgers at McDonalds. Bernie was unusually quiet when we got back on the road.

"Those were some rations, hey Bernie?"

Bernie didn't answer.

"Alright, what's the matter?"

"I saw him."

"Who?"

"The guy who asked me the questions last week. You know, the one at the college."

"Oh yeah. The guy in the audience. So what?"

"What are the odds he'd be here? He's following us."

"Come on. It's just a coincidence."

"He was parked on the side. He didn't get out. He looked at us."

I checked the rearview mirror.

"Where is he now?"

Bernie looked around.

"I don't know. Maybe he's staying back."

"Come on, Bernie. It's okay. It's just a coincidence."

We got to Madison about two o'clock. Visiting hours for my brother Jimmy at the mental hospital were from two to four.

There was a short line at the check-in desk when Bernie and I got there. I signed for us both. The guard motioned us to the metal detector.

"Everything out of your pockets."

A girl in front of us put keys and change in a plastic bucket. She stepped through the detector. The alarm sounded.

"Do it again. Take off your shoes."

She stepped through barefoot. The alarm sounded again and the guard smirked.

"Do you have any metal in your bra?"

"Of course not. I'm not bringing anything in."

"No. The strap. Support panels. Go to the bathroom and take it off. Then try it again."

As the girl left the line, Bernie stepped through. The alarm sounded.

"Take off your shoes."

"But they're Reeboks," I said. "There's no metal in them."

"You'd be surprised. They all have metal."

Bernie took off his shoes and walked through in his socks. He passed. I did the same.

A guard showed us down a corridor to the visiting room at the end. Clusters of plastic chairs were arranged in groups, so that individual visitors had some privacy. A guard sat at a desk in the front of the room, watching everyone. A few children played on a plastic jungle gym set up in the corner, while their mothers visited their fathers.

Jimmy was sitting in the back of the room by two empty chairs. He grinned and waved as we walked in.

"Hey, Bro. Bernie. How're you doing?"

I shook his hand, and he hugged Bernie.

"Sit down, sit down."

Jimmy spoke with exaggerated voice and gesture. He was dressed in a sweatshirt and jeans. I could see the fluphenezine dancing in his eyes. Bernie sat quietly without reacting.

"So how are you doing, Jimmy? What are you reading?"

"Fine. I'm reading the Bible. Deuteronomy. You should read it."

"Great. I'll have to."

"Yup. Say I've decided what I'll do when I get out. I shall open a restaurant and serve fish and fowl. Or I may join the Marine Corp."

"Great. Maybe you can be the food editor over at *Guns and Ammo* magazine. Listen, how are they treating you?"

I watched Bernie while Jimmy talked. The pain he felt didn't show. He sat like an adult, without expression, listening to his father.

"I want to show you my painting. It's your portrait, Joe."

Jimmy walked up to the guard's desk, and after they spoke, we were escorted down the corridor to another room. It held an easel, a stool, and a set of paints. It had no windows. The guard stayed with us as I stared at the painting.

"That's you, Joe. How do you like it? I did it off a photo."

It was a painting of a man in a short-sleeved shirt, leaning on a golf club. He had a Chinese face and green skin.

"Do you like it?"

Jimmy stroked his chin, sizing me up.

"Yeah, it's different."

"That's a five-hundred-dollar painting, Joe."

"No, it's not. It's a fifty-dollar painting. That's it."

I sometimes buy paintings from my brother when he really needs money. He's too proud to take gifts. Fifty dollars is my limit, and he knows it.

"Done. It's yours. What do you think, Don?"

Don, the guard, who looked about 25, stood silently at the door. He was about six feet five inches tall, must have weighed 250 pounds, and wore a thick red beard. He had the personality of a turnip.

"I don't like who flung the dung art. I like nature scenes. Animals."

"Ducks? Mallards, right? Velvet tigers? Let's go back, Don."

Don was stung by Jimmy's taunts.

"So, how many tiles are there on the floor there, Jimmy? I'm surprised you haven't counted them already. How many?"

I looked down at the floor. It was inlaid with miniature tile. The main part of the room was square, with a rectangular section bending off to the side.

"Tell him, Bernie," said Jimmy.

Bernie's Sherlock, but Jimmy's Mycroft. Jimmy's always a step ahead of everyone else, but totally incapacitated.

Bernie studied the floor, obviously counting the perimeter squares. He examined the rectangular section.

"19,476."

"19,476?" said Jimmy. "Look again."

Bernie looked again.

"Oh yeah. 19,474. There are two missing in the corner."

"God," said Don. "It runs in the family. If I drop a box of matches, you guys gonna shout 'one hundred and ninety-eight' or some bullshit like that? You guys ready to go back?"

"Yeah, let's go," I said.

"Hey Bernie, why don't you get a soda in the lobby? Don can walk you out. I'll be out in a few minutes. Is that okay, Don?"

I knew Bernie had had enough, and I wanted time to talk to my brother alone.

Jimmy seemed despondent when he returned to the visiting room. We sat by ourselves in a corner at the back. He wouldn't look at me.

"Jimmy."

He still wouldn't look at me.

"JIMMY!"

He was older than me, and I'd never spoken to him like that in my life. He looked at me, startled.

"Jimmy, you know why you're in this time, don't you?"

He grinned at me without any humor in his eyes.

"Failure to conceal."

"You were walking naked down the street. Why'd you do it?"

"It was hot. You know, the end of summer."

"And you remember why they put you in last time?"

"I don't."

"Yes, you do. They caught you sneaking into the Art Museum with one of your paintings. You fought with them when they caught you."

"I was just going to hang it on the wall. It's better than most of the shit they have there."

"Look, one of these days they're going to let you out again. Why don't you concentrate on doing something really different? Something new. Change your life around."

He hung his head.

"I feel bad. I feel bad that Bernie has to visit me here."

"Listen, it's not too late. Remember Ulysses Grant? He was in his 40's, working on his father's farm, not doing anything, and the Civil War came along. You're only 36. Something could happen."

Jimmy glared at me.

"Ulysses Grant. You're comparing me to Ulysses Grant?"

He jumped up and hit me as hard as he could. Caught me right on the nose, and I fell to the floor.

I still remember the guard blowing a whistle and a swarm of other guards ran into the room. I propped myself up by the chair, sitting on the floor. They grabbed Jimmy and carried him out, a guy on each arm and each leg.

"You better go now," said the guard.

I held a handkerchief over my nose as he walked me to the lobby. Bernie was sitting with a can of soda, staring out the window toward the parking lot. I stuffed the handkerchief into my shirt pocket.

"Ready to go, Bernie? Your dad says goodbye."

I saw the guard at the front desk pick up a phone as we left. He didn't take his eyes off of us.

"They're leaving, Sir."

It was faint, and I might have been mistaken, but I heard what I heard. I was getting as jumpy as Bernie.

To pass the time, I played chess with Bernie in our minds on the way home. It's his favorite game. The trouble is, he can keep the board straight a lot longer than I can. Our games never end in mate. They end when I announce a move, and Bernie tells me there's already a piece on that square, or the file is blocked.

"Rook to f4."

Bernie looked exasperated.

"You know you can't do that. Your own knight is in the way."

"Oh, yeah. Then knight to e3."

"You can't do that. You're taking your own pawn!"

"Well, I give up. Listen, Bernie, why don't we go by your dad's apartment? We have to move his stuff out or get rid of it. Let's see what's there."

We got to Jimmy's place after dark. He rented an apartment on Michigan Avenue in Merrill Park. It was once a nice neighborhood. Most of the houses have great natural woodwork, with ten-inch oak or walnut moldings, and mullioned windows. Some are three stories. But now, it was one of the worst in Milwaukee. Prostitutes work in parked cars in the middle of the day. So do drug dealers. You have a very good chance of being jumped or shot just walking down the street.

I had trouble with the door. The key was bent. I hit the door a few times with my shoulder, and it finally opened. I heard a door open on the ground floor, and I looked over the railing.

"What you want?"

The woman spoke with an accent. She was short and quite plump. She wiped her hands in her apron as she stared up at us.

"I'm Jimmy's brother. Joe Weber. This is his son, Bernie. We're here to get his stuff."

The woman came up the stairs.

"I'm Rosa Martinez. Where's Jimmy?"

"He's sick. He's in the hospital. We're going to move him out."

She stepped into the apartment with us. At least 30 paintings were stacked against one wall, all oils with the canvas stapled to wooden frames. Some were self-portraits in bizarre colors. Some were designs, and some were cartoon characters. The sofa had a hole in one cushion. A card table and four chairs filled the kitchenette. The bedroom had a futon and no dresser. Jimmy usually just laid his clothes on the floor. We'd already gathered most of them and his books when he went back in the hospital.

"Rosa, take anything you want. Or the neighbors. Jimmy's not coming back. He'd want you to have it."

"I don't know."

She looked with disapproval around the room.

"The sofa has a hole in it."

The sofa has a hole in it! She's living in Merrill Park, with a woman's head in a guy's lap in the car across the street. With a guy selling dime bags on the corner, and the sofa has a hole in it.

"I don't know. I'll come back later. I have Jimmy's key. See what happens."

She went back downstairs.

Bernie started sorting through the paintings.

"Joe, I don't want them to be thrown out. Are these any good?"

"I can't tell. I went to a Matisse exhibition once in Chicago. Some of the paintings looked like some of these. The designs. But I don't know. Van Gogh cut his ear off and never sold a painting except to his brother. And now, they sell for millions. I've got fifty paintings by your dad in my basement."

"I hate to throw them out."

A knock sounded on the door. I opened it to see Rosa and two guys.

"This is Michael, and this is James. Michael lives next door. James lives downstairs. I told them they could take some stuff."

Michael and James eyed the apartment like cats in front of a hedge, waiting for something to pop out.

"Rosa," I said. "I need a pad of paper and some scotch tape. Do you have some?"

She left. The two neighbors carefully inspected the apartment.

"So, you Jimmy's bro. How you doin? And you his son. Righteous. You look like him. How he doin?"

"Not good. He's sick. He's not coming back. That's why Bernie and I came by."

Rosa returned with the paper and tape. I started to write.

"We be back. We be back. Thank you."

Michael, James, and Rosa had completed their inspection.

"You leave the tape here."

Rosa ushered them out ahead of her.

"I be back."

"What are you doing, Joe?"

I took the pages I'd written on. $2,000, $5,000, $10,000. Most of them were $2,000. There were a few fives, and one ten. I taped a price on each painting. The $10,000 went on the largest canvas, a field of oversized No. 2 pencil stubs. The pencils were actually quite good, each about three feet high and six inches wide.

"Let's go, Bernie. We'll rent a U-Haul and get what's left later."

Chapter Four

The plane landed at Logan at 10:30 in the morning. Hawkin rented a car and drove west from Boston on the Massachusetts Turnpike. He exited ten miles out of the city, heading north toward Belmont.

It was a cloudy, January day, with a few inches of snow on the ground. Hawkin turned into the drive of McLean Hospital and wound his way across the grounds to the administration building.

McLean has treated patients with mental illness since the early nineteenth century. It advertises itself as an affiliate of Massachusetts General Hospital, and a teaching facility of Harvard Medical School. What it does not advertise are the countless celebrities and officials who have been treated there, including entertainers who would surprise the public. When it became clear that Barnes was ill, the decision where to send him was not difficult.

Barnes was waiting for Hawkin in the lobby. They shook hands warmly. Barnes hugged him.

"Thanks for coming, Hawkin. Good to see you."

Barnes was tall, about six feet three inches, several inches taller than Hawkin. His face was puffy from medication, but still handsome, although he stared at Hawkin with unusual intensity.

"We can't go just yet," Barnes said. "Out processing. Let's take a walk while they finish up."

The hospital sat on an estate of several hundred acres. They stopped at a maple tree out of sight from the buildings. Barnes made a snowball.

"Remember in New Haven when I threw snowballs?" he said. "I threw five at Nathan Hale's statue from the middle of the Old Campus and hit it every time. I bet you ten bucks I can hit that tree five times."

He pointed to a tree about forty-five feet away.

"Okay. Go ahead."

Barnes threw the first snowball and hit the tree dead center.

"See?"

"Look, Barnes, there's a project Willis wants you to work on. It's potentially explosive."

Barnes made another snowball and hit the tree a second time.

"See! I still have it."

"Yeah, but you have three to go. Listen. This is important. We've found a kid in Milwaukee, a math whiz, who may be able to do some computations in his head, believe it or not, that we can't even do on a computer. Are you interested in getting involved?"

Barnes hit the tree a third time.

"What does Willis want me to do?"

"Bring the kid to Washington. Have our people question him. See if he's for real. If he is, figure out a way to use him. We found something in one of our photos from a space probe. Maybe he can help."

A fourth snowball smashed into the tree several inches off center.

"Four! That's four in a row, Hawkin. You're dead!"

Barnes bent over with the last snowball in his hand behind his back. He wound up and delivered a fastball into the middle of the trunk and raised both fists high over his head.

"Just like New Haven! Ten bucks!"

Hawkin fished through his wallet for a ten. They walked slowly back to the administration building.

"You know this really is a beautiful spot," said Barnes.

He stopped to look at the trees beyond a clearing.

"You almost expect a Minuteman to pop out with his musket."

Barnes flexed his knees and pointed his arms at an imaginary target.

"Barnes, I want to ask you something. We've been friends for forty years, but I've never asked you. What happened to you? You were near

35

the top of your class, captain of the golf team. You tapped me for Keys. Now you're here. What happened?"

Barnes kicked the ground, face flushed, and didn't look directly at Hawkin as he spoke.

"Remember forty years ago, Hawkin? The class questionnaire? Out of a thousand guys in my class, about two hundred thought they'd be president. Fifty thought they'd be editor of *The New York Times*. Most of the rest thought they'd win the Nobel Prize. Do you remember?"

Hawkin said nothing.

"It was all there! We were young. In the Agency. Right out of school. China, the Soviets, Viet Nam. We had everything."

He glared at Hawkin.

"And you know what happened? N*othing happened*! *Nothing! Not a godamned thing!* No one comes here out of Keys anymore. There's nothing left to fight! Who are we going to infiltrate? Somalia? Chiapas? Pakistan? Who cares?"

"How about Al Qaeda? There's plenty to fight after 9-11."

"They're disorganized. They have no technology."

"You're still a romantic, aren't you, Barnes? You loved sitting at the round table, a fire roaring in an eight-foot-wide fireplace behind you, leading the toasts in your own temple. It was all Wagner, Barnes. All theater and myth. You can't stand the fact that there're billions of light years of emptiness in every direction. Unspeakably cold with a few exploding stars along the way. You can't stand to be an accident. You can't stand to be alone."

"I'm a rationalist, Hawkin."

Barnes rolled his eyes.

I loved every minute of it. Sherry in the poculum, Served by Wamba. The dignity of the man. His ancestors must have been kings in Africa. The fireplace as wide as a wall, the round oak table 12 feet in diameter, each of us on a small throne. Cole Porter's songs, the port, the cigars, the debates. I wasn't alone, and I'm not alone.

"I've been divorced for ten years. I have no children, nothing. I lived at the wrong time. If you were career Army in the 1860's or the 1940's, you're part of history. But if you were career Army in the 1890's or 1990's, you're a fireman sitting at the station and the bell never goes off. And you can't control it!"

"So what?"

Hawkin shrugged.

"We do our best. You're born when you're born. We did it for the excitement. It turned out to be quiet on our watch. You can't roll back thirty years."

"Imagination, Hawkin! You need imagination! They're out there. Maybe you're right. Now, it's the Muslims. And some day, it'll be something else! We've got to be nimble. We *need* enemies to survive!"

Hawkin held his tongue.

"Look at the Aztecs. They fell apart. Couldn't react. That won't happen to us, Hawkin! Can't happen. We won't let it!"

Barnes inched closer to Hawkin.

"We're only a year apart, Hawkin. But it was the end of an age and the beginning of another. I was coat and tie, parietal hours, legacies, all men. You were Cambodia, Kent State, Black Panthers, women. Listen, I know what's out there. A vast universe of wogs, out to get us. Drag us down. It won't happen! *I won't let it happen*!

"Look, Barnes, let me explain Willis' idea. If this kid is real, it could be a huge breakthrough."

Hawkin put his arm around Barnes' shoulders as they walked back to the building.

37

Chapter Five

The street was almost deserted at six in the morning. Maynard Gieck turned into the driveway of a Georgetown town house and idled a few seconds. The garage door opened, and he slipped down a ramp into a large underground garage, much larger than anyone would have guessed from the exterior. The door closed behind him.

Gieck didn't bother to lock his car. A man sat on a chair near a door at the other end of the garage. Gieck nodded to him without speaking. He opened the door and stepped into an elevator.

When he arrived, Hawkin was alone inside the conference room, sipping a cup of coffee.

"All set?" he said.

"Yeah. But we're going to a lot of trouble, aren't we? I know Willis wants to make it easy for Barnes, but why not let him retire? Or put him on a desk? Review reports. Why this?"

"It's how Barnes *feels* about it. That's what's important to Willis. You can't just throw Barnes out or make him a clerk. He's got to feel like the old days. His own project. Proper briefing. Only thing is, he belongs in a hospital. But he won't stay there. We've got to give him an assignment that doesn't jeopardize anything or have significance. We've got too much to do. I don't want him getting in the way."

Gieck shrugged and poured himself a cup of coffee.

I'm getting tired of all this Yale shit. They all call each other by their last names. So, I do, too. They all think they're the Duke of Gloucester, or some such shit. Just like what old days? The eighteenth century? One of them'd lose his marbles, so they'd make him a bishop or an admiral and wonder how he felt, *for Christ's sake. Who cares how he feels? If I, Maynard Gieck, B.S., M.S., Phd, University of Rhode Island, flipped out, my ass'd be carried to the curb that afternoon.*

"Alright, here's the plan," said Hawkin. "I'll set the table and pose the assignment. If there are technical questions, you step in. Got it?"

"Fine."

"He can chase this kid in Milwaukee, give him a big number to break, and stay out of our hair. You see?"

"Right."

"The kid's a fraud. You said so yourself. And what if he's not? All the better. It's a perfect tree for Barnes to bark up. He can take the next two years. I don't care. I just don't have the time to babysit him. Let him chase his tail and leave with dignity. Willis has made up his mind."

Allen Barnes arrived a few minutes later. He had barely poured his coffee before Hawkin reached under the table and the lights dimmed. The wall opened to reveal a large television. An image appeared on the screen that looked like swirling gases.

"The Galileo spacecraft passed through the atmosphere of Jupiter a while ago and took these pictures of one of Jupiter's moons. Europa."

Hawkin sounded like a tour guide. Gieck rubbed his eyes.

For this I had to get up in the dark?

He watched Barnes take notes as he stared intently at the screen, eyes glowing.

You poor bastard.

"I thought the camera malfunctioned," said Barnes. "Mechanical error or something."

"The camera worked perfectly. I had it reported as malfunctioning because of what you are about to see."

A succession of still shots appeared, focusing more clearly on the moon's surface.

"Recall that Jupiter is the fifth planet from the sun. It's also the largest. It has four large moons and twelve small ones. It takes eleven years to circle the sun."

"Actually, it's 11.86."

"Thank you, Gieck. Europa is one of the four large moons. It's about the size of our moon."

The succession of stills continued. Europa's surface came more clearly into view, until the camera focused on what appeared to be a large icy plain, covered with striations.

"Now, look closely at these markings."

The camera focused even more until the striations came clearly into view. They looked like thousands of small ridges and circles, clustered in groups. Barnes could make out // ////// 0 //////// / /// /// / /// 0 // before they blurred. The plain was covered with them.

Hawkin restored the lights while the picture stayed frozen on the screen.

"Gieck, tell Barnes about NASA's conclusions."

"NASA doesn't have any conclusions. I told you that. They're ridges on the surface. Wrinkles. You could take an aerial shot of the rough on a Scottish golf course and it would look very similar."

Wayne Hawkin glared at Gieck, who looked away.

Better be careful.

"But of course," Gieck said, "no one knows for sure what it is. Meteor craters? Who knows?"

Hawkin handed Barnes a photograph. It looked like a huge ax with evenly spaced knobs on the handle.

"We photographed that on Ganymede, another Jupiter moon," said Hawkin. "It's a perfect ax, with a carved handle, hundreds of miles long. Some of our people say a broken-up comet formed it billions of years ago. They say the Europa pictures are the same thing. Others say they aren't sure."

"Where do we come in?" Barnes said. "The Agency, I mean."

"We've analyzed the photographs for months."

Hawkin rubbed his fingertips together.

"The markings may not be random. Of course, then again they may be."

"What is Jupiter?" said Barnes. "A couple hundred million miles from the sun?"

"483.4," said Maynard Gieck.

"So, there are some dents on a moon. Or ridges. It could be meteors, couldn't it?"

Barnes crossed his leg. Gieck saw an inch of colored cloth appear below the cuff. Pajamas! They were still under his pants! Barnes had gotten dressed in a hurry and hadn't bothered to take them off!

*How did I end up here? Why didn't I go to Microsoft? Maybe it's not too la*te.

"It might," said Hawkin. "But of course, we can't be sure what it is. We've analyzed the photographs for several months. It would be interesting to speculate that these markings are not random, that they comprise a very large number. And there is one coincidence that makes this worth further study."

"And what is that?" said Barnes.

"You could argue that a meteor wouldn't carve out a number several hundred digits long, the first ones being the same that were carved on the Ishango bone twenty thousand years ago. It would be like a meteorite crashing into Earth and spelling out the first chapter of *The Great Gatsby*."

They sat in silence.

"Bone?" said Barnes. "What bone?"

"About eighty years ago," Hawkin said, "a Belgian archaeologist found a twenty-thousand-year-old bone tool handle in the mountains between the Congo and Uganda in a place called Ishango. It's the most famous puzzle in paleontology. It had sixteen numbers carved on it in three rows. Groups of notches that can be read as numbers. 9, 19, 21 and 11 on the first row. 19, 17, 13 and 11 on the second row. 7, 5, 5, 10, 8, 4, 6 and 3 on the third row. No one knows what they mean. It might have been a primitive lunar calendar. But those are also the first sixteen groups of notches on what Galileo photographed on Europa."

"Hawkin, this is crazy!"

Gieck couldn't' restrain himself.

"We don't even have a complete picture of the Europa plain! Some of our mathematicians picked up on the Ganymede ax handle picture. They found some ridge clusters in the Europa photo that looked the same as the numbers on the Ishango bone and posted the two photos together as sort of a goof."

"Sure," said Hawkin. "But we need to use our imagination. We must anticipate. Anything's possible. Lathrop Willis wants this number broken down, and our people haven't been able to do it. Right, Gieck?"

Gieck was visibly annoyed.

My people haven't been able to do what? *This is pathetic. I'm not going to have my guys trashed so that Lord Buckingham can tickle the nuts of Lord Packingham with a turkey feather.*

As his mind wandered, more sober thoughts intruded. Thoughts of his pension, his salary, his job.

"Right," said Gieck. "We haven't been able to break it down."

"The kid in Milwaukee," Hawkin said. "The one I told you about in Massachusetts? We want to bring him out to see what he can do. Gieck will give you a stick with the Europa number on it. Have the kid look at it. See if it factors. Prime factors. If it turns out to be purely random, so what? We can use his technique on other files. Stay on it until he cracks it. Gieck, how quickly can we get Barnes the Europa number?"

"Right away. It's out at the morgue. With the dead files. Unsolved numbers. I'll get him one on a memory stick tomorrow. I'm gone the rest of today."

"I'll do it, Gieck." Barnes was excited. "I can get on it now."

When they were finished, Barnes drove to Agency headquarters in Langley. He joked with the guard while he verified his ID. The guard waved him through, and Barnes parked in a small lot behind where the complex jutted out in two parallel extensions. He was admitted through two more checkpoints until he arrived at a large room, much like a library reading room. Endless aisles of electronic equipment and closed cabinets extended to the back of the room on both sides. A warren of interconnecting rooms without doors lay beyond the aisles.

A man sat at a desk in the front.

"Hello, Mr. Barnes."

"Hello."

Barnes showed the man his identification.

"We need a number for an exercise. The Europa number."

"What do you mean, the Europa number?"

"I don't know. Wayne Hawkin said he was just out here. I need it on a stick. They might call it the Ishango number."

"Okay. I know the one."

Barnes followed, as the man walked back to a control area.

All these goddamned numbers, all these files. We spend our whole lives trying to break codes, and ninety percent of it's garbage. Trade deficits in the Ukraine. Crop figures in Bulgaria. Nothing. A lifetime of hide and seek, for what?

The man looked up from a screen.

"It's currently under review."

"It's under current review by me," said Barnes. "I'm the only one supervising the review. I want another copy. Log it to me and Wayne Hawkin."

"Level of security? Read only?"

"No. The mathematician I will use must be able to manipulate it. He won't need to copy it. Hawkin and I will be responsible."

The man said nothing. He disappeared into a back room and then returned with a stick in a plastic pouch and gave it to Barnes.

"Thanks."

Barnes left with the pouch.

Chapter Six

"Joe!"

"Yeah. Bernie?"

"Joe? I got a call from the principal. They want me to come down to the school. Jerry's giving me a ride. Can you come with?"

Jerry Piano's a cop who lives next door to Bernie.

I looked at the clock on the end table. It was eight a.m. I was sitting in my bathrobe with a cup of coffee, reading the paper.

"It's Saturday morning. Can't it wait until Monday?"

"I don't think so."

"When do they want you?"

"Nine."

"Okay. I'll be right over."

Sharon was still in bed when I got to their house. The door was open. Jerry was sitting in his car at the curb.

"Hey Bernie. Are you ready?"

"Just a minute."

Jimmy Jr. came in and reached for a clean bowl.

"When you going back to New York, Jimmy?"

"Couple of weeks."

"Listen, Frannie got tickets to a Bucks game on April 17. What day is that?"

"Tuesday."

He yawned as he poured himself some cereal.

"Let's go, Joe."

Bernie had his coat and gloves on and was shifting impatiently at the door. We got in Jerry's car and drove along Locust Street, toward Riverside High School, where Bernie was a sophomore.

"So, what's the story?" Jerry said. "Why do they want to see you?"

"I don't know. They called last night and told me to come in this morning. I thought Mom could take me. But she has the flu."

"Who called you?"

"The principal. Mr. Schneider. He didn't say why."

"Jerry, tell me what you think of this. Here's what happened."

I told him everything, from Pryme Knumber to the trip to Madison.

"So, what do you think?"

Jerry got serious. He loves to be asked for advice.

"You got to be careful. You got your . . . so, you think they followed you to Madison? We'll call over there. See if they know anything. Next time, they want to see you guys, you let me know."

Jerry drove past Jakes, the last deli in the inner city. We passed Marcus's Clothes, with no windows, and metal fencing around the door, and the open fields at 27th Street, originally cleared for an expressway that was never built, and where preachers give outdoor sermons and sidewalk merchants sell pictures of velvet unicorns.

Oprah Winfrey grew up in this neighborhood. Golda Meir moved there with her family, and eventually taught school a few blocks away. Sixteen blocks south, Liberace had played piano in bars under the name of Walter Busterkeys, near where Douglas MacArthur lived as Douglas McArthur before his family changed the spelling of his last name. Teddy Roosevelt survived a shooting there while giving a speech. Sometime later, Joe McCarthy pumped gas nearby to put himself through Marquette University.

The front door of the school was open when we arrived.

"That's highly unusual," said Bernie. "It's always locked. Even during school."

As we walked down the marble hallway to the principal's office, our footsteps echoed off the walls. The door was open, but I knocked anyway. There was no answer. I opened it slightly more.

"Hello? Hello?"

"Come in, come in."

Mr. Schneider introduced himself and showed us to a conference room off his office. I didn't recognize the men sitting at the table.

"Gentlemen, this is Bernie Weber and his uncle, Joe Weber, and their friend, Jerry Piano. This is the president of our school board, Mr. Stanton Stover, and Mr. Maynard Gieck. Mr. Stover, perhaps you would like to take over from here."

"Call me Stan."

Call me Stan? The guy's wearing a pinstripe suit and a red tie on a Saturday morning, and he wants to spend it with Joe Weber and a 16-year-old kid, and he want us to call him Stan. Right!

"This is a great day for Riverside High. For Milwaukee's schools. Bernie, Mr. Gieck here is from the National Cryptologic School. They asked your math department to recommend their best student, and they selected you. Based on a review of your grades, Mr. Gieck tells us you're a finalist. Is that right, Mr. Gieck?"

"Absolutely right. Bernie, you're a finalist in our National School Math Award competition. There's a test you must take, and if you score well, you win a trip to Washington for you and your parents. There, you'll take another test, where you can win a scholarship for college."

"Wait a minute," I said, "What is this? The Redheaded League? What's the National Cryptologic School?"

Gieck looked at me with unkind eyes.

"It's a mathematical unit of the Department of Defense. Like the Navy's language school in Monterey. Only thing is, we like to support promising students in mathematics."

"How come he got the call last night?"

"My plans changed. I was able to be in Milwaukee, and here we are."

"What kind of test does Bernie have to take?"

"It's right here."

Gieck handed me a document. It contained several pages of math problems stapled together. I gave it to Bernie.

"When do you want him to take it?"

"Right now. All contestants are given an hour to take it."

Bernie looked briefly at the first page.

"Can I use the bathroom first?"

Gieck looked impatient.

"Of course."

Bernie looked at me as he left the room. Jerry and I followed him.

"I'm afraid, Joe."

Bernie looked under the stalls in the bathroom to make sure we were alone.

"What are you afraid of?"

"I'm afraid they're going to grab me. It's too strange. What am I going to do?"

"They ain't going to do nothing," said Jerry. "Play along. See what happens. Do you think you can pass that test?"

Bernie didn't answer.

"I don't like it, Joe."

I had to admit I felt the same way.

"I'll tell you what. You stay in here a little while. I'll try to find out what they're after."

The three men were talking when Jerry and I reentered the room.

"Bernie isn't feeling too well. He'll be out in a minute."

"I hope he's alright," said Schneider.

Gieck looked at me as if he were dissecting an insect.

"You have an interesting family", said Stover. "Mr. Schneider was just discussing it with us. You all have mathematical abilities?"

"Pretty much. Yeah."

"Bernie lives with his mother, I understand?"

"Right."

"And where does Bernie's father live, if I may ask?"

"On Michigan Avenue. Merrill Park section."

"I see. That's a . . . changing neighborhood."

Guys like Stan pipe their subconscious right into my ear. Let's face it. *Everything everybody says is camouflage.* It's just that I filter it out and imagine the real words.

Gieck was restless.

"Is the kid ready? I mean, I hope he's alright. Maybe we better see."

"I'll check on him."

I went to the bathroom. Bernie peeked around the door of the stall.

"What are we going to do, Joe?"

"You know what? Take the test and nail it. Let's stick it to these guys. Show them what you can do."

"Okay, Joe."

Bernie limped out with me like Sir Lawrence Olivier, only better. Bernie loves acting more than math. I think he likes strapping on his green ears as Pryme Knumber more than factoring out primes.

Jerry and Schneider were deep in conversation about the Bucks. They all looked up when we came back in. Bernie stared sorrowfully at them, wincing absurdly at random. Gieck barely concealed his anger.

I spend my career breaking codes so Hawkin, Barnes and their kind can destabilize micro-cap governments. Channel away the lava flows of lascars, Rastafarians, sherpas, luz senderos, cong, Tamil, Afghans and God knows what other assorted nostril-piercing, reggae-chanting, loinclothed, turbaned, bodega-robbing, building-bombing, dog-snatching rabble that belch continuously from Africa, Asia, and South America and try to sneak into the country and this is what I get? To finally break the Japanese or German code and win World War Two? NO! No way! I get a Saturday morning in a Milwaukee school with an ungrateful kid and his uncle. What the fuck, over?

"Listen," I said. "Bernie's a little shaky, but he's tough. Give him the test."

"Good. Good!"

Gieck hurried over with some papers stapled together.

"Here's the test. And a blue book, and a calculator. Mr. Schneider said you could sit in his conference room and take it."

Bernie disappeared into the conference room. Jerry and Schneider had turned from the Bucks to the Brewers—their sorry record for 25 years, the pitching they needed.

Mercifully, or so he thought, Gieck's phone rang.

"Excuse me."

Gieck stepped out into the hall.

"Gieck?"

"Yes."

"Hawkin. Are you secure?"

Hawkin was angry.

"Sort of. I'm never convinced of our cell security."

"Have you read your mail?"

"No. I'm with the kid. Remember?"

"The hell with the kid. Barnes picked up the wrong number! The wrong fucking number."

"What do you mean?"

"It wasn't the Europa thing. The bullshit thing to keep him busy. He picked up something very much alive."

"Like what?"

"Come home as soon as you can. We can talk then."

Gieck stalked back into Schneider's office.

"So, tell me," I said. "What exactly do you do?"

"Oh, I do math. I'm a mathematician."

"What do you specialize in?"

"Number theory, actually."

"How come you're interested in Bernie?"

"His high school teachers say he's a very talented young man. We like to encourage talent."

He dodged some more questions. Jerry and Schneider had worked their way from the pitchers to the infield. About 30 minutes had gone by. Suddenly, the door to the conference room opened. Bernie came back into the room with the exam.

"I'm done."

"You have thirty more minutes," Gieck said. "I suggest you at least recheck your answers. Maybe give them a little more thought."

"That's okay."

Bernie handed him the stapled pages. Gieck pulled a pad from his briefcase and compared it to the exam. The rest of us were silent as he read. He finally looked up, over to Schneider's desk, and back at Bernie.

"There's something wrong here. Very wrong."

"What's that?" I said.

Gieck ignored me.

"Bernie, I gave you twenty problems. Very difficult problems. For instance, I asked you to give me the cube root of a ten-digit number. I asked you to compute the prime numbers in the first thousand-digit range above one hundred million. I asked you to give me the prime factors of a ten-digit number."

"So, how many did he get wrong?" said Jerry.

"That's exactly what's wrong. *He got none of them wrong*! And the calculator I gave him couldn't do those computations."

"I didn't use it, actually."

"Did you use a PC?"

"There's no PC in there," said Schneider.

Gieck got up slowly from his chair.

"I've got to leave now. That was very impressive, Bernie. You'll be hearing from us about the next test in Washington."

Chapter Seven

Carroll Dalton had thin brown hair combed down just above his eyes, which rotated around the room through rimless glasses, never blinking. He straddled the wooden chair with difficulty, looking back and forth among Lathrop Willis, Maynard Gieck, Wayne Hawkin, and Allen Barnes.

"Let us begin, Gentlemen. My assignment today is to brief you on the pathologies of two operation venues, Azerbaijan and Milwaukee. I will start with Azerbaijan. First, Leaders and Holy Men."

Willis looked at him with contempt. Obviously unfit for work in the field. Willis tolerated him on his staff because he presented first-rate research.

"Dalton."

Willis dragged the name out, as if it had three syllables.

"Start with Milwaukee. Barnes isn't concerned with Azerbaijan. He has to leave. And why must you describe all your research as pathologies? Haven't you ever discovered anything normal by accident?"

"Once," Dalton said. "I thought I'd discovered a Russian cabinet minister who didn't steal. Turns out I was mistaken. He was corrupt after all."

"Okay, enough. What about Milwaukee?"

"Very good. Leaders and Holy Men."

Dalton took off his glasses and tapped them on the table.

"I must say it is one of the most disturbing places I've reviewed. It is one of ours after all. Let's start with leaders."

He pressed a button, and a list of names appeared on a screen.

"LaFollette, Duffy, Wiley, McCarthy, Proxmire, Nelson, Kasten, Feingold."

Dalton read them all, back to Philetus Sawyer.

"These are all their senators for the last hundred and thirty years. Two were extremists, LaFollette and McCarthy. Kamikaze pilots. Three were naive and easily rolled. Sawyer, Kasten, and Nelson. The rest were Puritan fanatics, like PraiseGod Barebones and his brother, IfJesusHadNotDiedForOurSinsWeWouldNotHaveBeenSavedBarebones. You do remember them, don't you? I'm sure you read about them even in New Haven. They rode into battle with Cromwell's army on Palm Sunday, on donkeys, waving palm fronds, and of course they were killed."

Gieck shifted uneasily.

How much more of this Ivy League shit do I have to put up with? What's he talking about?

"The point is, Wisconsin is the only state that has never managed to pass any federal legislation that benefited that state. They think it would be morally wrong. Deep feelings of unworthiness of anything to benefit them. They have never even managed to oppose any legislation that hurt the state. One of their main industries is dairy farming. But dairy farmers get subsidized by the U.S. government more for every mile they are *away* from Eau Claire, Wisconsin."

Dalton paused to light his pipe.

"Holy Men. Easy enough. There are none."

He glanced at some notes.

"Psychology of the culture. Perfectionistic. Strong undertones of sadism, as you would expect with perfectionists. Leads to good housekeeping, precision ball bearing manufacture, and higher than average police killings. Deep feelings of unworthiness. Wisconsin pioneered stem cell research, worker compensation benefits, unemployment benefits, and gets no credit for any of it. Frank Lloyd Wright did most of his work there, and most people think he's from Arizona."

He looked again at his notes.

"Media. Start with TV. I've really got to play something for you."

He chuckled as he put in a DVD.

"Milwaukee requires the local cable company to provide two free channels for public access. Anybody can go on as often as they want and do whatever they want. No editing. It's the logical extension of Puritan anarchy. We taped quite a bit. This one is my favorite. It was a call-in show, live."

A man and two women appeared on the screen seated behind a desk. Behind them was a scrim of the Milwaukee skyline, and next to them a withered ficus in a pot on the floor. A sign in front of the table said, "Evangelist Preston Johnson."

The man was about 35, handsome, with a wristwatch and several rings. One of the women wore a red dress and hat. The other wore a somber dress, brown, with no hat.

"Praise the Lord. Halleluiah."

"AhHa. Amen."

"And we seek not the riches of this world."

"AhHa."

Whenever the man said anything, the woman in red would nod and say "AhHa" or "Amen."

"And we have our first caller. You on the air."

"Yes. You say you don't seek the riches of this world. But I see you got a fine watch and rings. Where you get them?"

"I didn't get them dealing no dope. Amen. No one say you can't earn things. Amen."

"AhHa. Amen."

"Next caller. You on the air."

"You have been given a big penis to please the ladies."

The man didn't change expression.

"Aha. Next caller. You on the air."

A woman's voice came on, a caricature, like in the cartoons. She trilled her r's, speaking rapid fire and unintelligibly.

The man cut her off.

"Satan have hold of the lines," said the woman in the brown dress.

"Amen. Hallelujah. You on the air."

You know that last girl who talk like Bugs Bunny? She always do that."

"Thank you. Amen."

"And the girl in the red dress can suck my dick."

The man fought back a smile.

"Next caller. You on the air."

"I need help."

It sounded like a middle-aged white man.

"Amen. Hallelujah. You in the right place. What the problem?"

"My father beats me. He won't feed me. He sends me to parochial school. He makes me mow the lawn. Can you hear?"

A lawnmower started up in the background.

"How old are you?"

"Nine."

"You sound older than nine."

"He won't feed me. I'm starving."

"You need food. Amen. Next caller. You on the air."

"I will consult my penis."

"Next caller. You on the air."

"Eat my balls."

The woman in the red dress threw up her hands.

"The lines is open for Jesus. But the Devil have taken the lines."

"Amen. Hallelujah."

"Their mouf be washed in the blood of Christ."

"AhHa. Amen."

Dalton turned off the TV and opened up a large folder of newspaper clippings.

"So much for television. For every culture, the problem is this. The cancer in all its organs must have metastasized from a single site. The question is from where. For Milwaukee, I think I've found it."

He spread out a half a dozen clippings on the table.

"It's their only paper. *The Journal*. Only one. Recently, there were three major events in Milwaukee. The ninety-fifth birthday bash for Harley Davidson, their most famous company. The Greater Milwaukee Open, a PGA Tour event. And the University of Wisconsin basketball team comes out of nowhere to make the Final Four. Two kids on the team are from Milwaukee. National press for all of them. A chance to showcase the city. This is from their paper, their showcase articles."

Gieck rolled his eyes.

"Listen to this: 'Leno Calls Milwaukee Fat.' He called Milwaukee 'fat' last night. In his monologue, Jay Leno, who owns forty Harleys and was in Milwaukee for the birthday party said, 'In L.A., they call me fat. I take it on the chin. But in Milwaukee, I feel skinny. I'm like a supermodel.' Reaction on the street was outraged. 'It came off as a cut', said a razor-thin Oswald Honeyager, perched on his neon blue Harley. 'He has a big enough chin to take it on, too. A lot of those fat bikers weren't even from here.'"

Dalton shifted articles.

"So much for showcasing Harley. And listen to this. Here's how they showcase the GMO:

"'Golfer's Daughter Raped in Dorm.' Jessie Cubb may only be one-hundred-thirty-second on the money list. Jessie Cubb may only have won thirteen thousand, seven hundred twenty dollars this year. But Cubb is a human being. And when he tees off in the GMO next week, he will have more than golf on his mind. Because Jessie's daughter, Leslie, returning alone to her dorm room one night, a room she should have locked but didn't . . ."

Dalton pulled out another article.

"And the best is their article on the Final Four. Most papers describe the fish. *The Journal* reaches in and pulls it out. Brandishes it. Listen to how they treat their first Final Four appearance in fifty years:

"'Methodical Offense Prompts Racial Remarks.' With eight white players out of thirteen, some would say the Badgers don't look like an athletic team. One player feels that they are seen as a bunch of plodders because of their style of play (derisively called white ball), and the color of their skin."

Dalton looked up.

"It's perfect. We found the choriocarcinoma. The obsession with imperfection, unworthiness, correction. With the speck of dust on the Taj Mahal. It's their paper. It poisoned the whole City. Disturbing place. Be careful, Barnes. They'll notice more than you think."

"Do you have a book for him?" said Willis.

"Of course."

Dalton handed Barnes a binder.

"Every local official, police contacts, business and labor leaders, with bios and phone numbers. University contacts, too. History of the city and state. Don't underestimate them, Barnes. And now, let me comment on the pathologies of Azerbaijan. Leaders and Holy Men."

"Excuse me, Dalton."

Willis held up his hand as Barnes stood up to leave.

"Thank you. Good luck in Milwaukee."

He waited for Barnes to leave.

"Dalton, could you do me an enormous favor? Gieck and Hawkin and I have a matter to discuss. Could we reschedule Azerbaijan? Thanks so much."

Dalton gathered his papers and left. The three sat in silence until he was gone.

"So."

Willis got up to pour himself some coffee.

"Your outstanding team handed Barnes the Al Qaeda number, the one we captured in the Congo. Access to that number was restricted. An impaired agent with no expertise in the subject should definitely not have gotten it."

"I agree. You're absolutely right."

Hawkin shifted in his chair.

"It was a serious error. Apparently, Barnes asked for the Ishango number, the sham problem I'd set him, and our man thought he meant the Isangi number, the place in the Congo where they captured it. No excuse, of course."

"The Ishango number?"

Willis ground his lips together.

"What the hell is that?"

"You're not going to like it, but I told Barnes about an ancient number in Uganda called the Ishango number, and come to think of it, it was near the Congo, and may have been the same damned place."

"Yes, you're quite right. I don't like it at all. Doesn't anyone in this place know the difference between the Congo and Uganda? What is this, bad Cole Porter? The Ishango do it, the Isangi do it. I want that number back and out of Barnes' hands!"

"Absolutely right, Willis."

Hawkin scrambled for time.

59

"Here are our options. First, I simply tell him he got the wrong number. Ask for it back."

"No!"

Willis was uncharacteristically harsh.

"Barnes is impaired. I trust him for what he was, and I like him. But I cannot bear even the possibility that he might tell anyone else. We have enemies in Congress. I will not admit a mistake of this magnitude. Barnes has been injudicious in the past. It doesn't go out of this room."

"It won't," said Gieck.

"How about the man who gave him the number. Does he suspect the error?"

Hawkin shook his head.

"It was Mark Bonner. He's a good man. Just followed orders. Wouldn't think it any more unusual than if you and I had asked for it. He simply logged it out to Barnes."

"Why did he give it to him in the first place?"

"I called him to say Barnes was coming out for a number, and he was authorized to receive it. Look, there's a second option. A bit risky. I don't recommend it. But he's only going to show it to a high school kid in Milwaukee. A bit like showing a sheet of Mozart's music to a puppy. Won't mean anything to him. Just a very long string of digits. Shouldn't end up in the wrong hands."

"Absolutely not! I'm not leaving this to chance. It's compromised, and I want it back. Quickly."

"Right", said Hawkin. "I agree entirely. And what means will you authorize to use to get it back?"

"Put a man on it. Someone Barnes doesn't know. Someone discreet who doesn't talk and doesn't need to know all the damn facts. Only that Barnes has a stick, and we want it back. Who do you have?"

"Well, let's see. We're busy. Someone Barnes doesn't know."

"What about that fellow with the blond hair? He worked in Italy and Turkey a couple of years ago. Remember? Seemed competent."

"Yes. Right. Dieter Holz. He might be all right."

"You're not enthusiastic. Why, Hawkin?"

"In the past, he's been overly fond of using force, for one thing."

"He can be told not to do that. Is he peculiar in some respect?"

"He works for us," Gieck said.

Willis ignored the comment.

"Is there any reason we shouldn't use Holz?"

"No."

"Good. Start him on it. Immediately!"

Chapter Eight

Allen Barnes unlocked his office and switched on the light. No janitors or cleaning help were permitted in Agency offices unless the occupants were present. Even then, only on direct request. Barnes had the only keycard. In fact, two keys, for the two locks flanking the knob.

He started to unpack his briefcase. He pulled out the stick with the Europa number, the practice number for the kid in Milwaukee to try to break.

I forgot to take it out of my case when I went home! Suppose I'd been spot-checked on the way out?

It was a grave violation of security to bring classified material home without elaborate checkout procedures. Anyone leaving was subject to random search, from Lathrop Willis on down. Barnes had been lucky.

He opened his desk drawer and looked into it for several minutes. For 30 years, every day he left his office he had followed the same procedure for securing his desk. And he had never told anyone.

Every paper, pen, and object in the desk was pointed in the same direction, always an in-between coordinate—northeast, northwest, southeast, southwest, alternating randomly. This time it was northeast. If it was a pen or pencil, it was the point. If it was a document, the upper right-hand corner. If it was an object, it was the smallest surface.

Now, one document had been inverted. The lower left-hand corner was pointed northeast. Barnes studied the contents further. The base, rather than the point of one of the pens, pointed northeast. Someone had opened his desk. And after they'd gone through it, they'd taken great pains to reconstruct it.

Barnes closed the drawer and looked at the clock on the desk. It was time for the weekly staff meeting with Willis. As he left the office, he slipped the stick back into his pocket.

Willis was on the phone when he arrived. Barnes sat next to David Baker, an analyst known as The Dagger, one of the few colleagues other than Hawkin who didn't avoid him. In spite of his name, Dagger wasn't violent. He had appeared in a performance of *Macbeth* as a high school student at Portsmouth Priory, mentioned it once, and then was christened.

"Dagger. You're not going to believe this," Barnes whispered. "Someone's been in my desk."

He explained his evidence.

"It sounds like a simple mistake."

Baker was patient.

Obsessive compulsive paranoid.

"One pen and one document. It seems to me you could have done it yourself. Inadvertently. We're all busy. Clever idea of yours, though. Must be damned annoying doing it every day."

Willis was off the phone.

"Alright, Gentlemen. I want to tell you something. We are entrusted with protecting our national security. How have we done? As even our friends in Congress have reminded me, we let workmen install a listening device in the woodwork of the State Department and didn't find it until we saw a Russian agent standing in the park across the street, listening in on it. Thank God he wasn't one of their brighter ones."

Willis glared at them.

"Yesterday, on the front page of *The New York Times*, there was an article accusing us of rendition. They named the prisoner, and they named the black site in Macedonia. We had no comment. Now, how the hell did they find the information to print that story?"

He endured a minute of silence. Dagger Baker finally raised his hand.

"Willis, the leak almost certainly came from Europe. Probably from Switzerland. We can't control everything."

"Then, we have to tighten it up over there. Limit the number of people involved. Screen them better."

Willis stopped Barnes in the hallway when the meeting was over.

"How is your Milwaukee project going? Any progress with the boy? Gieck says he may have real ability."

"I'm going out there tomorrow. We've done a full background. I think we have him talked into coming out here so Gieck can give him a real test. And I'm giving him the Europa number when I'm out there."

"Really? I hope the boy turns out to be helpful. So, when are you seeing him?"

"Tomorrow evening."

"Good luck."

Barnes got little done the rest of the day. Phone calls punctuated the silence. He remembered Tracy Manning, an old graduate of Yale and Keys, a contemporary of Lathrop Willis at the Agency. Manning had been friendly and encouraging to Allen Barnes when he started out. Barnes remembered Manning's words at a dinner 40 years ago.

"Barnes, the time's going to come in your career when something breaks the rules. When that happens, break the rules yourself. Do something out of the ordinary."

Barnes stayed put until six. As he left with his briefcase, he touched the stick in his pocket. He hesitated, then turned off the lights and locked the door.

Downstairs, the guard waved him through. It was already dark. As always, he boarded the Metro for three stops. He got off to walk the few blocks to his condo. Few people passed him. On impulse, he stopped to stare at a store window. A man walking just behind him went past. As he did, he seemed to hesitate for an instant.

A moment. A nanosecond. But he hesitated. I saw him. He did.

The man turned right at the next corner onto the street where Barnes lived. A street of handsome townhouses, with brick sidewalks and few streetlights.

Why shouldn't he? He must live there. Or he must have a friend there. Why shouldn't he? Break the rules yourself. Do something out of the ordinary.

As Barnes approached the corner, he reached into his pocket and threw the stick into a bush. The second bush from the corner. Dense, impenetrable. He'd walked by it a thousand times.

He turned the corner and almost made it to his door when he felt a hand on his shoulder and a cylinder stuck in his back.

"Drop your briefcase. Quietly."

Barnes obeyed. The case dropped from his hand. He said nothing. The man's hand swept through his clothing and each pocket. It swept along each arm and leg, back and chest, searching. He took Barnes' wallet, glasses case, and phone. He took seconds to inspect them before dropping them on the ground.

The man picked up Barnes's briefcase.

"You will stand here for five minutes without turning around. Count to three hundred. Make no sound. Pretend to study the building."

Barnes looked up at the windows. He put his hands behind his back and didn't move. He tried to remember what the man looked like, even from behind, but he could not. He waited until morning to return to the bush to retrieve the stick.

Chapter Nine

I stared at the entrance to the Kilbourn Country Club, Milwaukee's most prestigious club. There's no sign announcing what it is, only the initials "KCC" carved in the stone over the doorway. Kilbourn Country Club is not just a tree house for the emotionally impaired, as you might think when you first look into the dining room. It also gives people enough poetry to get them through a life sentence in the supply chain.

Only one famous individual has ever frequented the Kilbourn Country Club. Arthur Bremer, the man who shot George Wallace, worked there as a busboy in the early 1970's.

"You're sure we're all invited, Joe?"

Uncle Frank wore his best sweater under his coat, a grey cardigan with one arm knit several inches longer than the other.

"You're sure we're wanted?"

"We're invited. Let's put it that way."

Bernie's posse was with him. His brother, Frank, Frannie, Sharon, and me.

"It's too bad big Jimmy Sr. can't be here," Frannie said. "He'd be proud of Bernie."

"Joe. Mr. Weber. Congratulations to your family, and of course to you, Bernie."

Stan Stover invaded our conversation with a confident, well-fed smile.

"This is an exciting day for Milwaukee. All the unpleasant publicity about our Math scores. This will show them. The Mayor's even here."

"Thanks. Mr. Stover. I'd like you to meet Bernie's mom and his Uncle Frank. And my friend, Frannie, and Bernie's brother, Jimmy.

After the cordials, Stover inspected Franks's sweater and peeked at his coat and tweed pants. He seemed to particularly admire his slippers. Or at least stare at them.

"Yes. So *nice* to *meet* you. I'll find the mayor and the alderman, and we'll take our seats. So good to meet you."

He walked off.

"Look."

Bernie pointed across the room.

"There's the guy. Remember him?"

It was the man who had thrown the numbers at him at the Math Circus. Sharon glared at him.

"His ears are too low slung."

She pronounced her verdict.

"Ears shouldn't be slung that low on a human head."

The first fairway stretched beyond the window into the distance. The guests, mostly staff from the Milwaukee Public Schools and the Common Council, teachers, and school board members, stood in groups drinking glasses of white wine.

Stan approached our group, guiding a heavy, balding man about 55 years old. The man wore a dark polyester sport jacket and khaki pants, with a wide striped tie that had a knot as big as an apple. He had a classic Sheboygan tumor, his stomach hanging over his belt from years of beer and bratwurst.

"Mrs. Weber, I'd like you to meet Alderman James Fieblewicz. Jim is chairman of the Education and Schools committee of the Common Council.

He's one of our leading alderoids.

Sharon and I shook hands with him. I inspected Fieblewicz.

Alderman. The anus of American democracy. Every poison, every complaint passes through the alderman. Dogs loose, garbage in streets, loud noises—all are filtered through the alderman and violence is avoided. But traces of the poison stay in the alderman. His servile, puffy face is the picture in the attic that absorbs the scorn and contempt of the rabble, cleansing his constituents. Object of universal derision. Less status than a state representative or even a famous criminal.

Alderman Fieblewicz had led a life of small slynesses, finally able to chair the Schools committee. Receptions like this—monkey dinners in fancy places where he mingled with his betters as a constituent got a bizarre award—were the social highlights of his existence.

In recognition of ninety percent attendance at executive committee meetings of the Southeast Chapter of the County Statutory Committee.

"We're proud of you Bernie," said Fiebelwicz to Jimmy, "proud of you, Son. I was busting my buttons, I can tell you that, when I heard that one of our boys, our persons, had won the big award. I hear you can cipher real fine."

"But I'm Jimmy. This is Bernie."

Fieblewicz was a pro. He didn't falter.

"So, it is. So, he is. You boys look so much alike. Are you twins? Anyway, Bernie, congratulations. Congratulations, Son."

A man tugged on Fieblewicz's sleeve and drew him out of our conversation.

"And there's the mayor over there," said Stan.

He waved, and the mayor walked toward us. Fieblewicz and the man were still talking off to the side. I eavesdropped. I always wondered what it would be like to run for politics.

"You remember me, don't you?" said the man.

"Of course, I do. Of course. So good to see you again."

"Then, what's my name?

Irritation crept into Fieblewicz's voice.

"It was on the tip of my tongue. I was about to ask you how you spell it. Your first name has an unusual spelling as I can recall . . ."

"J-O-H-N."

"Right. Of course. Not J-O-N. And your last name, there was an interesting spelling there, too."

"Come on. Come on. The circus parade, remember. You were shaking hands, and I was in the crowd. Remember? Two years ago, I told you my name, and how you could always remember it. What's the first thing you do when you get up in the morning?"

"Your name ain't Piss, is it?"

"What? It's Coffey. John Coffey. Remember?"

"Oh, yes, of course with a 'y', right. Good to see you again. You're a good man."

"And Mayor, I'd like you to meet Mrs. Sharon Weber, Bernie's mother."

"Ladies," said Stan, "let me introduce Mayor Jeff Nuedling."

Like all mayors, Nuedling was a vengeful paranoid, and he was anxious to escape his present position into the governorship at the earliest opportunity. Nuedling had spent a career quarreling over bones. He was an expert at small stakes poker.

"Bernie, you are our future. When I think of our at-risk kids and the problems they have to face, I'm amazed they can even add two and two."

"Bernie's not an at-risk kid," snapped Sharon.

"Of course not. Of course not. He's an *example* to our at-risk kids, who have to go to classrooms where we don't have the dollars to give them what they need."

That's a whip across the ass like they do in Singapore when they catch one of them tagging a building.

69

We were mercifully called to the tables. Sharon, Bernie, and Jimmy were seated at the head table between the mayor and Stan Stover. Frannie and I sat with Frank and the foreign man who'd peppered Bernie with questions. I didn't recognize the rest—a blond man who didn't respond when greeted, and a few women who I assumed from their conversation were administrators with the Milwaukee Public Schools.

The conversation started slowly. The foreign man introduced himself as Amir and avoided any questions about where he was from and what he was doing here.

"I'm foreign graduate student," he said. "Interest in mathematics."

The waitress arrived with their selected dinners, chicken with creamed spinach and potatoes.

"You see that chicken?"

Frank gestured to Amir and pointed to his plate.

"That chicken is descended from a pair of chicks that were released into the jungle in Vietnam by a farmer about fourteen thousand years ago."

This was pure Frank. No one who knows him ever bothers to ask him "How do you know|? Were you there?" because he's always right.

Amir's eyes sparkled, like a biologist observing a new species for the first time.

"All chicken, or just this one?"

"All chickens. Every single one. And in sixty million years, Los Angeles will be near Borneo."

"Are you sure?"

Bernie tugged at my sleeve and squatted down next to me. He was a little stressball.

"They want me to talk," he whispered. "After the mayor. They want me to do primes. What'll I do?"

Amir and Frank were still talking. The blond man stared at Bernie. He turned away when he caught me looking at him.

"I tell you what. Don't do primes right away. Start out with something else. Anything. You got something you can do?"

"The age and address thing. I could do that."

"Okay, do that. Then, see what happens. If they still ask, why not? A trip to Washington would be nice. I'll go with. So will Jerry."

"Okay. And here's the Django Reinhardt you wanted me to burn."

Bernie handed me a CD and slipped away.

The waitresses started to serve dessert. Stan stepped up to a microphone to welcome everyone and do the introductions.

"Good evening, ladies and gentlemen. I am fortunate to have been asked to emcee this great evening. It reminds me of an ad I saw in the paper last week. It said 'Reward for return of my dog. Blind, neutered, lame in one leg. Answers to name 'Lucky'."

Stan had a good chuckle out of that one.

"I'd like to start by introducing the head table and asking several people to say a few words. On my far right, Mr. Allen Barnes of the National Cryptosporidium School." He saw the puzzled looks.

"I mean Cryptologic School. Mr. Barnes is representing the school in sponsoring our own Milwaukee student, Bernie Weber, to a one-week trip to Washington, D.C. in recognition of his mathematical achievements. This is a huge honor for MPS."

Strong applause followed. The man got up and nodded to the crowd but didn't speak.

"Next to him is Bernie's County Supervisor, Chester Turnpaugh. Chester also serves on the Education Committee. Chester?"

Turnpaugh had blond hair and a bushy blond mustache. I recognized the name. He was new on the Board. He'd introduced two bills his first year that got in the paper. One would require the organs of welfare recipients to be sold at their deaths to repay the County for their benefits. Eyes and livers and kidneys and such. The other was to sell advertising space in the holes of the County golf courses. You'd bend over to pick up your ball on the 8th green of the Lincoln Park golf course after you'd putted out, and you'd read "Chew Wrigley Gum" in the hole.

Turnpaugh had panicked at the public ridicule he had suffered over his proposal to sell organs. When TV reporters descended on him, he ran from his office and was actually pursued down several flights of stairs by cameramen. The Channel 12 cameraman stayed on the original landing and held the camera out over the ornate circular stairwell, catching Turnpaugh from above in a scene out of Hitchcock, holding his jacket over his head, swirling down through several levels pursued by cameras and reporters shouting questions.

Turnpaugh had kept a low profile for several months but had recently surfaced with phototropic instincts intact. And unlike moths, statesmen are attracted not only to television lights but also to pads and pencils. He grinned down at *The Journal* reporter with the open pad.

"Friends, a new day is dawning for Milwaukee Public Schools. And we have Bernie Weber to thank. We've all read the horror stories. Fifty two percent of the students don't graduate. Metal detectors in schools. We're almost insolvent. The School Board voted to dissolve MPS and dump our school system on the state legislature. Sure, it's easy to print the bad news."

He shook his finger at the reporter, Roland Cheek.

"Print the good news, Roland. I call on you to print the good news. Print the news of Bernie Weber."

Cheek didn't even bother to look at him. He was about thirty years old, with a round face and almost invisible eyebrows. I stared at his head. The haircut looked self-inflicted. It was unevenly cut. Tufts stuck out here and there. Not large tufts, but noticeable.

Cheek looked like one of Frank's colleagues at Community College, from the hair to the clothes. But the professors have a benign air lacking in journalists. Reporters spend half their time avoiding people who hound them, and the other half chasing people who try to escape them. Because they make no money, they suffer spasms of viciousness, delivering the spastic knee to the groin. They interview wealthy and powerful people, glamorous people. But they're like eunuchs guarding the imperial harem. They never get to harpoon the flounder themselves.

Cheek suffered occasional lapses in the subjunctive mood and the objective case. It was not uncommon to read in his columns phrases such as ". . . if he would have known," or ". . . between you and I." *The Journal* editors never scolded him because they thought he was correct.

"Do you hear me, Roland?"

Turnpaugh was aping for the crowd.

Cheek continued to ignore him. It's true that there are so few famous people in Milwaukee that politicians sometimes have to fill the void. Other than a few criminal supernovas (Jeffrey Dahmer and Laurencia Bembenek), and a few athletes (Bonnie Blair and Brett Favre), the glamour diet of Milwaukee journalists is quite spare. They frequently have to suck the marrow out of the bones of local elected officials for nourishment. But there are limits.

"And next, I would like to introduce Alderman James Fieblewicz. Alderman?"

Fieblewicz rose and adjusted his stomach.

"I only got this to say. I'm not going to try to spell 'potato' and I'm not going to try to do fifth grade math. I'm not as dumb as I look."

He sat down to relieved applause. Stover laughed.

"The Weber family is between me and the mayor. Bernie Weber, our honored guest, and his mom, Mrs. Sharon Weber, and his brother, Jimmy. On my right, our congresswoman, Nettie Love. She serves on the powerful Finance Committee of the Congress that is overseeing the bailout of Wall Street after the subprime meltdown. Congresswoman?"

Nettie Love rose. She was an African American woman, dressed in a blue dress and large beaded necklace.

"Hello, Milwaukee!!"

Love beamed at the applause.

"I am *so* happy to be here tonight with the *great* mayor of Milwaukee, Mayor Nuedling, and the *great* alderman, Mr. Fieblewicz, and the *great* supervisor, Mr. Turnpaugh, and the *great* . . ."

She stopped in mid-sentence as she shuffled some notes looking for her stump speech, her only speech.

"Supreme, where's my speech?"

At a table in front of her sat Love's son, Supreme Star Hussein. Supreme, as he preferred to be called, had been caught slashing the tires of Republican campaign vans in the early morning hours last election day. He pled to a misdemeanor and then appealed. Love and many of her supporters supported Supreme. He occasionally found employment on her staff when times were tight.

Supreme didn't respond. Love gave up on her notes and recited her stump speech.

"My political career began when I was a student at North Division High School. After an historic election, I became Class President. During my administration, it came to pass that a citizen had a refrigerator unjustly repossessed. We got the law changed so you can't do that anymore. After my historic election to Congress, I have served *diligently* on the federal bailout. I do not represent the folk in the limousines. I represent the *community*. I am glad to be at this *great* event."

She beamed and sat down.

Stan had little difficulty quieting the tepid applause.

"And so, Ladies and Gentlemen, it now gives me great pleasure to introduce our great education mayor, Jeffrey Nuedling."

Without warning, Frank seized the basket of rolls and crackers and stuffed them into his coat pocket.

"Jesus, Frank," I muttered. "Not here."

He paid no attention. I saw the basket in front of Sharon was also empty. My arm twitched, like a sleep spasm. I accidentally bumped Frank, who had drawn his chair out into the aisle, right next to me.

The mayor congratulated Bernie, making him sound like a mutant, like an accidentally healthy animal born into a diseased herd.

"Milwaukee is very proud of you, Bernie. You have won the Math Prize. When you can schedule time away from school, you will get to go to Washington for one week as an honorary page in Congress, where you will observe the workings of our government. We are very proud of you, and your wonderful family, who exemplify Middle America. What makes me proud to hold public office is the chance to represent the average American, to meet the average American *the polyester-assed entitlement sows,* the backbone of our nation."

The mayor attacked the state of public education in Milwaukee, with charity toward none and malice toward all. The teachers' union, the Congress, drugs, bad parents: they were all to blame. Eventually, he softened, suddenly remembering the upcoming gubernatorial race.

"And I feel for the less fortunate in our society. I hear the groans of the poor . . ."

I had started to fall asleep but forced my eyes open.

"What did he say?"

"He feels the groins of the poor," Frank whispered.

After the mayor had gotten in touch with all of his inner weasels, he introduced Bernie. I was proud of Bernie as he bowed to the applause. Sharon had dressed him in a sports coat she'd bought for five dollars from St. Vinnie's.

"I want to thank the mayor, and the alderman, and the feds, I mean the Cryptologic School, and my mother Sharon, and my Uncle Joe, and my teachers, and the cook, and the waiters . . ."

Barnes dusted the tabletop with his fingers as he waited for Bernie to finish. He kept glancing at a piece of paper in front of him.

"And now, I'd like to play a game with you," Bernie said. "Everybody write out your age and your address, your house number, on a piece of paper. Go ahead."

People pulled out scraps of paper and pens. Those who had none scrounged from their neighbors or called for the waiters. I wrote down 21 and 2720.

"Okay," said Bernie. "Now take your house number and double it."

I wrote down 5440, double 2720.

"Add five."

I wrote down 5445.

"Okay. Multiply by 50."

The audience laughed and clamored for the few calculators in the crowd. I wrote down 272,250. None of the Webers needed calculators.

"Alright, add your age."

"Just a minute. Hold on."

Most of the audience was still multiplying. Even Fieblewicz and the Mayor were into it. I added 21 to $272,250 = 272,271$.

"Okay? Ready? Now add 365."

I added 365 and wrote down 272,636.

"Now subtract 615."

I subtracted 615. I was left with 272021.

"The last two digits are your age," said Bernie. "The others are your house number."

The applause was warm, and increased as the more challenged in the audience finally saw their actual ages and addresses in the result, no matter what initial numbers they put in.

"Thank you. Thank you."

Bernie took his public very seriously. He nodded in each direction. Barnes raised his hand. Bernie pretended not to notice, and I motioned him to our table.

"Excuse me. Wait a minute."

Barnes was on his feet, almost yelling.

"I was hoping Bernie could answer some questions. We've heard so much about his mathematical ability."

Bernie looked at me and shrugged.

"Okay."

I nodded at the head table.

"Bernie'll give it a try. Bernie?"

Bernie headed back to the head table, like a diva doing an encore, quite pleased by the attention. He solemnly stood before the microphone. The knot of his tie had slipped a few inches, and the jacket almost covered his knuckles.

"Okay, Bernie."

Stover mugged for the audience.

"Mr. Barnes is going to ask you a few questions. Show them what Milwaukee can do. Mr. Barnes?"

Barnes peered down at a sheet of paper.

"Bernie, is the number 12,709,189 a prime number?"

Bernie scrunched his eyes. This was pure showmanship. He never does it when he's showing off at home.

"No."

"Okay. Can it be factored into two prime numbers?"

"Yes."

"Okay. What are they?"

Bernie scrunched his eyes again.

"3571 multiplied by 3559."

Sharon and Frannie applauded loudly. Frank and Jimmy and I joined right in, none of us having the slightest idea if he was right. Everyone else waited for the verdict.

"Yes . . . yes. That's right."

Barnes looked slightly startled.

"Let's try another one. Bernie, is 12,616,679 a prime number?"

Bernie thought for a moment. "No."

"Can it be factored into two prime numbers?"

Bernie thought some more. "Yes. 3557 times 3547."

More applause from the Weber posse. Love and Fieblewicz jumped on the bandwagon, followed by Turnpaugh and the Mayor. It started to ripple through the crowd.

Barnes scratched his neck.

"Right again. Bernie, I'm going to give you one more, a much larger number. Are you ready for it son?"

Bernie held the podium tightly and closed his eyes.

"Go ahead."

Barnes paused as the room quieted.

"Bernie, is 8,330,943,083 a prime number? Take your time."

No one even coughed. More than a hundred people looked with pity on Bernie, most thinking 'thank God they didn't ask me to multiply 9 times 8', much less 'what's a prime number?', much less 'what is a factor?'

Bernie milked it pretty well. He opened his eyes, then closed them again, then peeked out to make sure people were looking.

"No," he finally said.

"That's right." Strong applause burst out across the room.

"Can it be factored into two prime numbers?"

"Give me the number again," Bernie said.

"8,330,943,083."

Bernie hesitated.

"Yes."

"One more question, Bernie."

Barnes looked down at his paper.

"What are its prime factors?"

I was proud of Bernie. He looked out over the crowd, very calm, making sure they were listening. I don't think most of them were breathing.

"81,041 times 95,563," Bernie said.

This time, the applause was muted, as if the crowd was waiting to see if the ball had gone over the fence fair or foul.

Barnes studied his paper longer than he had to before he looked up.

"You're right again, Bernie."

The place erupted. I couldn't hear the rest of what he said to Bernie. Stover came over to shake his hand, and Nuedling, then Love and the rest. In all the commotion, I didn't see Barnes approach me until he was at my side.

"Joe? I'm Allen Barnes. This is important. Do you happen to know a restaurant called Three Brothers?"

"Sure. In Bay View?"

"Right. Meet me there in half an hour. Just you. Nobody else. It's very important. Do you understand?"

"Well, sure, but I was going to . . ."

"I don't care what you were going to do. It's about Bernie. He has a great opportunity, and he could also be in great danger. You must meet me there."

Barnes walked away before I could say anything.

Chapter Ten

Barnes was sitting in Three Brothers when I arrived. It's a small restaurant, maybe twelve tables. Barnes had one along the window at the back wall. I hung up my coat and joined him. Marlene Dietrich sang *Lili Marlene* in German softly from the ancient jukebox in the corner.

Branko Radicevic, the owner, came over to greet me as I sat down. He makes a point of personally greeting anyone he recognizes. Branko's a handsome man in his early eighties. He wears a beret and a combed white moustache. I told him that Barnes was a friend from out of town and sat back for the story I knew by heart.

"You have eaten in a Serbian restaurant before, Mr. Barnes?"

Branko fixed his snappy black eyes on Barnes.

"Yes. In Belgrade."

"Very good. I was a boy in Belgrade during the War. We resisted the Nazis. It was a wonderful day when we could come to America. You will have the chevapchichi?"

He pointed at me, and then at Barnes.

"And you will have the raznichi?"

"Branko, we've eaten. I told Mr. Barnes about your Slivovitz. I thought we'd throw down a glass."

"At once."

Branko hurried into the kitchen and emerged with three glasses and a bottle of clear liquid. He poured three glasses and raised his.

"To America."

He tossed it down.

"To America."

I sipped mine.

I've thrown down some paint thinner in my time, Ouzo and Sake and Limoncello and that, but Slivovitz is the worst. Your liver twitches in fear when it's only halfway down your throat. I can't chug it.

To my amazement, Barnes chugged his and asked for another. Branko grinned and poured. The door opened behind me. I didn't look around. Branko excused himself to seat the new customers.

"What's this all about?" I said.

Barnes leaned across the table.

"Pay attention."

Marlene was singing "Das ist Berlin wie's weint. Das ist Berlin wie's lacht." I wanted to sip a glass of Prokupac and listen to the music, but Barnes was quivering at me across the table. It made me jumpy.

"Okay."

"I work for the government. We believe that your nephew, Bernie, has a special mathematical gift that can greatly help our country. We've intercepted a large number in space, which must be deciphered. I have it on a memory stick. We want Bernie to tell us its prime factors. And it's absolutely essential that this be kept confidential. Only you and Bernie can know."

"Right."

Right. How am I going to escape this nut?

"Look, you said there might be some danger. I don't want that. What were you talking about?"

"There have been attempts made to take the number from me. We don't have much time. At some point, they'll take the number from us."

"Who are they?"

"I don't know. Will you help me?"

"Do you have ID?"

"No."

Barnes was a nut, but I liked him. His eyes reminded me of my brother Jimmy's. He believed what he was saying.

"Look. You've got to look at it from my side. You're a stranger. A number from space. You have no ID. My nephew is sixteen years old. You think there's danger. I don't like any of this. How can a sixteen-year-old kid help you? Really?"

"Galois was killed in a duel when he was nineteen. He was one of the greatest mathematicians of all time. You get too old, you're no good at math."

I started to laugh, but it was only half funny.

"Bernie's not getting killed in any duel. You catch my drift?"

"Of course not. Just help me. They gave me a project. I've got to bring it home. I need this. Just have him look at the number."

He was a pitiful bastard, but I believed him.

What could it hurt? Bernie looks at a number. Probably couldn't figure it out. Math tricks at Milwaukee Community College are one thing. If this is legit, Bernie's probably over his head. If it's not legit, I get a nut job off our backs.

"Okay. I'll have Bernie look at the number."

"And if Bernie can do it, we'd like a program with the algorithm, showing how to do it."

"Okay."

I wanted to get away from him.

"You have it with you?"

"No."

Barnes leaned over until his head was almost in the breadbasket.

"You live on Booth Street?"

He said it so softly that no one at another table could hear. Hell, I could barely hear him.

"Yes."

"Do you know the East Side?"

"Yes."

"Do you know Lake Park? Off Wahl Avenue?"

"Yes."

"Do you know the stone lions that stand guard at the overpass across the ravine?"

"Yes, I do."

"Behind the lions is a statue of a Civil War general on a horse."

"I know the statue."

"The memory stick is buried in a waterproof box an inch below the surface of the grass, exactly in the middle of the statue's base at the rear, right against the base itself. The spot is marked by a tiny Fleur de Lis stamped on the edge of the base."

"A Fleur de Lis?"

"The emblem of Ezra Stiles College."

"What college?"

"My residential college. Don't go there tonight. Go in the afternoon when you're sure you're not being followed. Dig it up and give it to Bernie. Safeguard it. And have him do it quickly."

"Okay. I will."

I'll bring Jerry. He'll bring the Milwaukee Police Department if he has to. The hell with secrecy. I'll deal with these nuts up to a point.

Barnes sat back in his chair. "Durch Berlin fliesst immer noch die Spree" floated softly from the jukebox.

"Another Slivovitz," he said to a passing waiter.

Barnes and I tossed another one down. "

There's an ambiguity about this place I like," he said. "It reminds me of a place I was in a long time ago."

He seemed reluctant to leave when we finally got up. We shook hands.

"Do you have a card?" I said.

"No."

"Do you have a phone number?"

"No."

"How am I supposed to get in touch with you?"

"You're not. I'll call you."

"Do you want my number? It's a cell."

"I know your number."

"Okay."

Barnes left, and I went into the bathroom and stood at the urinal. The door opened behind me before I was finished shaking hands with the mayor. I could see a flash of blond hair in the mirror on the side. I felt a piece of metal jammed into my back.

"If you make a sound, I'll shoot your dick off."

This got my attention. I shook so bad I stopped in midstream. I stared straight ahead, and tried not to move anything while the guy ran his hands over my back and chest. He slipped his hand into my inner pocket and grabbed the Django CD. He felt around some more, and suddenly was gone. I must have stood there for a long five minutes after that to make sure he was really gone.

There was no one on the street outside when I finally left. My car was almost in front of the door. I gave the back seat a good look before I got in and drove away.

Chapter Eleven

The next day, I saw two eyes and a wisp of fur appear and disappear among the parked cars. I pretended not to notice as I walked toward my car. The eyes reappeared under a tuft of grey hair, peeking around a car. As I walked past, a man stood up in my path.

"Hi, Joe."

"Hey, Elmer."

Elmer Dick, the mayor of Booth Street, wore corduroys that couldn't fasten at the waist and a plaid shirt with traces of egg yolk on the collar. His jacket was unbuttoned. Elmer does not ever leave Booth Street. *Ever*. He is my next-door neighbor.

Now, you might say this is hyperbole. He must leave *occasionally*, you will say. To shop for groceries or to go to the doctor. *No*. Elmer retired from his job as a clerk in the city treasurer's office four years ago and has *never* left Booth Street since. Every day, he removes his car from the garage and parks it on the street. Always about five in the morning, in front of his house, so that students from Community College can't park there. Then, he walks Booth Street, our block, one block to the north, and one to the south.

Nothing escapes his attention. *Nothing*. Every visitor to every house, every stranger walking by, every pizza delivery—all noted by Elmer Dick, the mayor of Booth Street.

Elmer's wife shops for groceries and does the errands. They do not go out to eat, or for entertainment. *Ever*. When Imogene Dick goes to the supermarket, she pays cash. They do not have a checking account. Imogene pays the electric bill at the company's office. She pays the phone bills the same way. They vote absentee.

Elmer Dick's father, Ludlow Dick, had been the mayor of Grantville, a small town in the far western part of Wisconsin, near the Minnesota border. During his first election, Ludlow accused his opponent of spending too much time in Madison and Milwaukee, eating in fancy restaurants and shopping for clothes. Ludlow promised that if elected, he would *never* leave Grantville during his term in office. The race was close until the last week when the Dick forces found out that their opponent had not only eaten at a restaurant in Milwaukee, but had attended an opera afterward, *Cosi Fan Tutti*. Ludlow Dick was elected mayor of Grantville.

He served as mayor for eight years and was true to his word. He never left Grantville. When his car could no longer be repaired, he sent Elmer's mother to buy a new one in Prairie du Chien, the closest town with a car dealership. When they ate out, it was at Grantville's only supper club. Ludlow walked the streets of Grantville during the many hours of the day when his phone was silent. He knew every resident, and every resident's business. He died in office.

"I found three cars that hadn't called in last night," said Elmer. "I haven't seen that in a while."

While you may find it hard to believe, Milwaukee has a law that requires everybody without a permit who leaves a car on a city street overnight to call the police department and give the address where it is parked and the license number. The metro population is 1.2 million, and the city proper is 590,000. But every night, most cars on the street have to be called in. And it's not a casual conversation.

Ring, ring.

"Hello, what address? 2720 North Booth Street. Well actually, I live at 2720 North Booth, but it's parked sort of between 2720 and 2722, the Dick residence. The what? The Dick residence. Who are you? Joe. Joe Weber. Just put it down as 2722. License plate number?"

And so it goes, every night, every car. The police patrol neighborhoods in the middle of the night, checking out license plates.

Elmer always calls in every car on the block, this time exposing the
three lawbreakers. He served in the Korean War as an advance scout,
he told me. He likes to take you by surprise, standing silently by a
building or behind a car, until you're right next to him. I usually let him
sneak up and get the drop on me and garrote the sentry, or whatever.
He's always friendly, sometimes touching his cap like a groundskeeper
in an old movie.

"Three, huh? That's amazing. Have a good day, Elmer."

It was Sunday afternoon, with a playoff game between Green Bay
against Dallas. This was roughly the equivalent of the Battle of Kosovo,
the Battle of the Boyne, and Gettysburg, except the feelings were more
intense. I don't get into it that heavily myself, but Frank threw a party.

Most fans in other cities take it or leave it, like in Tampa, New York
or Boston. Some fans in other cities really get into it, but only because
they literally have nothing else to do. Like Denver, for instance. With
Green Bay, it's different. Lombardi and the first two Super Bowls are
like George Washington, Valley Forge and Lexington and Concord.
They did a poll before a playoff game last year and asked 400 people
in Wisconsin if they would be willing to cut off their pinkies if it meant
that Green Bay would win. Twenty-one percent said they would.

I pulled off Booth Street, through the heart of Riverwest, and
headed east on Locust Street toward Oakland Avenue. Riverwest is the
buffer zone between the inner city and the east side. It's 140 square
blocks of aging hippies, students, unemployed, old people, and anyone
whose handicap is his wallet. Riverwest starts to the west at Holton
Street, sometimes referred to as the Mason-Dixon line by the residents
of the inner city who live just beyond it. Riverwest ends east at the
river, where the East side begins.

The East Side is mainly students, but it also holds the only trace of Milwaukee's gold coast, like a vestigial tail or gills. A few members of Milwaukee's old industrial families still live there, on Terrace or Wahl Avenues, Newberry Boulevard or Marietta Street, along with a few newly transferred executives who can't believe they can buy a house for $500,000 that would cost $2 million where they just came from. Everyone else got out a long time ago, to Mequon or Brookfield, north or west, as far away as possible.

I turned south at the corner of Oakland and Locust, Oak and Loke, the best-known intersection in Milwaukee, the heart of the east side. Frank lives in Bay View, the poor man's East Side, a section of the city just south of Downtown, over the Hoan Bridge.

The room was quiet when I got to Frank's duplex. He sat on a stool, drinking a beer. Sharon, Jimmy, and Bernie were already there. Jerry Piano waved at me with his mouth full.

"Where's Frannie?"

"She's correcting exams."

Frank wore a Packers jersey with Ray Nitzschke's number. He had placed autographed pictures of Nitzschke and Vince Lombardi on the TV set, with a candle burning in between. The rest wore Packers caps, or at least green and gold socks.

"Beer, Joe?"

Frank is proud of these football parties. He lays out a few pounds of corn beef from Benjy's, potato salad, pickles, some rye bread, and a couple of cases of beer. I loaded up a sandwich and he handed me a Miller.

Bernie motioned me off to the side.

"I got the invitation. It finally came."

"What invitation?"

"Mr. Schneider told me to go to Washington. You know. They're making it look like I'll be a Congressional page for a week. I get to pick the week. What can I do?"

"Don't go."

I'd told Bernie about Three Brothers, but no one else. Not even Frannie.

"I've got to go, or they'll keep after me. I might be able to do the number. I don't think I can do a program. We've got to do something, Joe."

The rest were watching the game. Dallas had the ball on its first possession. The commentators' chatter was inane, even by football standards.

"Dallas has to control the ball, John. Green Bay has come to play the game of football. Dallas has to take it one game at a time. Take it to a higher level. Got to be opportunistic. The game is a mental game. Got to be mental."

Bernie picked up the phone.

"I want to call my dad."

Bernie explained who he wanted to the guard who answered, and we waited while they went to get Jimmy.

"Hi, Dad? It's me. Sorry to interrupt the game. I need some help."

Bernie spoke for several minutes, then listened. He handed me the phone.

"Dad wants to talk to you."

"Joe, listen to me."

My brother was excited.

"You've got to help Bernie. I don't know prime numbers well enough to do it. But there's a guy you've got to see. Right away. You got a pencil?"

"Go ahead."

89

"Terry Shit Theory Norris. He lives on Weil Street. He's in the phone book, has a roofing business. He was doing a math PhD with me a long time ago, but he dropped out. He can help you. Tell him Bernie's my son. He'll help you."

"What can he do? A roofer on Weil Street?"

"He knows numbers, too. Like me and Bernie, only he's not locked up and he's not a kid. He invented the shit theory at school. We played a lot of seven card stud. Hi Lo. If you went both ways, you had to win both ways. Terry proved that if you have a mediocre hand high and low, like say two middle pair high and a ninety-eight low, you were better off going both ways than trying to pick one. That's how he got his name."

"Jimmy, this is serious. These people are after Berne, and you want me to go to a roofer who plays poker?"

"He's not just a roofer who plays poker. Go see him. Right away. I've got to go now. We only get ten minutes on a call. Let me know what he says. And I told Bernie to delay them. Tell them he can't miss school. Put it off until the summer. Til he gets out. Til I get out."

He hung up.

Jerry was popping another Miller when I went back into the living room.

"Jerry. You got any time tomorrow to help me find something?"

"No problem. I take Jimmy Jr. to the airport at seven to go back to school. Any time after that."

Jerry took a long slug and never took his eyes off the screen.

"I'll call you. We'll ride over to Lake Park. Okay?"

"No problem."

Chapter Twelve

The patrol car sped along North Avenue, with me in the back seat. Jerry Piano was driving, with Officer E.R. "Ernie" Doggs up in front, riding shotgun.

"Hey Jerry, thanks for helping me out."

Jerry waved grandly at the windshield.

"No problem. No problem. Ernie don't mind. Do you, Ernie?"

Ernie shrugged.

"I wouldn't be working here if I was working somewhere else."

"Ernie, is that a new light at Fourteenth? It used to flash only."

"Yup. It's automatic."

"DV in progress, two-two-four-five North Thirty-Fifth Street."

I couldn't make out the rest over the radio. Jerry hit the gas and turned on the siren.

"What's that?"

"Some guy's beating the shit out of his girlfriend. You stay in the squad, Joe. You ain't supposed to be here with us. If we take him in, we'll put him in the back, and ride three up front. Then, we'll go to the park."

We did 60 going down North Avenue. Jerry turned onto 35th and slammed to a stop at 2245.

"Get in the front. We'll be right out."

I watched them trot onto the porch and bang on the door. A child answered, a pretty little girl with long black hair. She looked Indian or Pakistani. Jerry and Ernie went into the house. I got into the front seat.

They came out a short time later, dragging a small man in a turban. He couldn't have been more than 5' 4" or weighed more than 100 pounds. His hands were cuffed behind his back. Jerry opened the back door and pushed the prisoner onto the seat. A metal screen separated the front from the back. I stared back at him.

Why arrest him? These guys were mathematicians and engineers. There must be some mistake. His dignified demeanor. The intelligent, angry black eyes. Angry, of course! Who wouldn't be angry at such treatment! His ancestors invented math! Four generations a century, 28 centuries ago, 112 generations ago, his great grandpa invented math! A classy guy. A Hindu aristocrat, obviously.

As Jerry pulled out into the street, Ernie turned sideways to stare into the backseat.

"What's the matter with you? I thought you guys were into passive resistance. Like Gandhi. What about Gandhi?"

"Fuck Gandhi. He didn't have to live with this bitch."

We turned the prisoner over at the Fifth Precinct. I killed half an hour sitting on a plastic chair while Jerry did his paperwork. He finally came out and motioned toward the door.

"I'm off. Ernie's staying here. Where do you want to go?"

I told Jerry what had happened at Three Brothers as we drove to Lake Park.

"Jesus Christ, Joe! Why didn't you file a complaint with us? Put our detectives on it. You still can."

"I'm going to let it go. Bernie'll do his best. Then we give them the stick back, and never get into it again."

We pulled into Lake Park and parked at Bartolotta's Restaurant. We walked past the nine-hole par three, south of the Indian Burial Mound, toward the statue of General Erastus Wolcott. The General wore a full metal beard as he sat on his horse.

A man was kneeling behind the statue, examining the branches on the bushes just beyond the statute's base. Jerry stepped quickly toward him. He put his hand on the man's shoulder.

"On your feet."

"What?"

Jerry pulled him up.

"Milwaukee Police. Don't raise your hand, sir. Keep your hands at your side at all times. Do you understand?"

"What? I'm just studying the vegetation."

"Sure, you are! Just happening to study what?"

"The vegetation. I'm a member of the Park People. A Park Person."

"Lie down on your stomach and put your hands behind your back. You're not feeding me that line of crap. *Get down*!"

"In the snow?"

"*Down*!"

"I think he's okay," I said. "Take it easy, Jerry."

Jerry totally ignored me.

"If I even see your ears twitch, it will be bad for you. If you so much as sneeze. *Just lie there*!"

"But I'm a Park Person. I belong here. My name's on that bronze plaque near the statute. I gave money to restore it."

"Sir, I will remind you, giving false information to a police officer is a felony. Do you understand that Sir?"

"It's not false!"

While Jerry was harassing the man, I knelt down at the center of the statue's rear base. A tiny fleur de lis was stamped just above the ground. I pulled out a small trowel and dug a few inches. I uncovered a plastic bag holding a small plastic box. I pulled it out and stuck it in my pocket.

"Okay, Jerry. Good to go."

"Okay. And you!"

Jerry barked down at the man on the ground.

"You lie there, and don't move. You want to study vegetation, wipe away the snow and study the goddamn grass. Study it good. Consider this a warning. If I catch you sneaking around again where you don't belong, I'll have your ass."

We walked fast back to the car. As the man receded from view, he stayed perfectly still on the ground. We jumped into the car, and Jerry sped out of the Bartolotta's parking lot.

Chapter Thirteen

Weil Street runs through the middle of Riverwest. Bernie and I drove down Locust Street and turned right onto Weil, past The Poet's Corner. Antler, Milwaukee's most famous poet, used to read there.

Casmir Pampuch, a philosopher of the street, presides over a table in the corner, attended by a shifting band of disciples, sometimes wearing white robes at Easter. No different from Socrates, although with less long-term influence. Patrons with grey ponytails swill tap beer, each working on the same novel or poem or invention that excited his youth. They had not foreseen the empty chairs and empty tables.

2935 North Weil was a frame duplex with a porch that needed repairs. A sign in an upper window said, "Norris Roofing."

"This is the place."

Bernie and I got out of the car. Two young boys walked a pit bull across the street. A Hmong woman called to her daughter from a porch down the block. I rang the bell for the upstairs apartment and waited. I rang again. Finally, I pounded on the glass door. I could hear the door at the top of the stairs open.

"Okay. Okay. The bell doesn't work! Take it easy!"

Terry Shit Theory Norris wore a lumberjack shirt and jeans. He had a black beard so dense it could have nested a family of small birds. He glared at us through rimless glasses.

"What do you want?"

"I'm Joe Weber, Jimmy's brother. This is Bernie, Jimmy's son. We called the other day."

"Oh, yeah. Come on up."

His apartment was cluttered with old newspapers and magazines along the living room wall and the dining room. The leaded windows and oak woodwork remained from the glory days when Milwaukee merchants built these houses. People of substance once lived there. Now, only people who *smoked* substance.

"I'm pleased to meet you, Shit Theory. I've heard a lot about you."

"What? *Pleeze*. There's a kid present. Who are you anyway?"

"I'm sorry. It was a slip of the tongue. Jimmy told me about your skill at poker. How did you get into roofing?"

Norris picked a roach out of an ashtray on a table next to the sofa and lit it.

"It's a sad story. I've been screwed. Me and Jimmy were grad students at Community. I'm a lot older than him. We were good. We really were. But there was a change in the air. You know what I mean? We could do anything. It was all going to change. I wanted to do real work. Be part of it. I didn't know shit about roofing, but you don't have to. You show up with a hammer and a ladder, and some old bag'll put you on the roof. This is the cheapest town in the country. Just don't charge too much. I'll tell you what. I'd rather do work for a Bircher than a leftie. Birchers at least will pay. I swear I've been cheated a hundred times. How's Jimmy doing?"

"Not well.

Norris took a drag.

"Nobody I know's doing well."

"Have you, uh, kept up with your math?"

"What's to keep up? What do you need?"

"There're these guys that keep following Bernie. It started at a Math Circus he and his brother performed in."

I had Bernie explain from the beginning. Norris dragged and listened, showing no surprise at all.

"I'll tell you what," he said. "I'll tell you what. This much I've changed. I fought the chief and the mayor early on. Breier and Maier.

Some guy'd get strangled in the paddy wagon, or get his face rear-ranged by a walky talky, and we'd hit the streets. But I gotta say, the fucking Latin Kings torched my garage last year when I caught them dealing in the alley and called the police. If I catch them again, I'll nuke their ass. But this of course, is different. These federal assholes are a whole different story."

"Right. Anyway, we need help, Shit. I mean Terry. We need to write a program that looks like it factors out prime numbers, like Bernie just made a mistake. Like he doesn't know what he's doing. You know what I mean?"

"Yeah. I know."

Norris sat thinking.

"You know what we could do. There're formulas that can generate primes up to a certain point. Here. Take a look at this one."

Norris took a pen and started to write on the back of the telephone book.

'$n^2-79n+1601$.'

"If you substitute any natural number from one to eighty for n, you'll get a prime number. But it doesn't work for eighty-one. And there are other formulas like it."

"But how can we use it?

"Let me tinker with it. You just want something plausible, right? I mean, you just want them to think that Bernie thinks this works. They'll figure out what we're really doing. But it'll be involved enough that they'll believe a smart kid might be fooled by it."

"That's great. Thanks. But how about a program?"

"It won't be hard to write. I'll string a few formulas together."

"I can help," said Bernie. "I mean that formula you just wrote only produces eighty prime numbers. It's really just a division calculation that we need."

"Yeah, right. By the way, how did you do those tricks at the Math Circus?"

"It's just a thing I do."

Bernie was evasive.

"Thanks a lot for helping me out."

"No problem. Me and Jimmy were running dogs. We'll shake these guys."

Chapter Fourteen

Dieter Holz sat unhappily on the edge of a floral chintz chair in Lathrop Willis' office. Maynard Gieck sat across from him, his right arm folded across his chest, his left hand cupping his chin. Willis and Hawkin ignored them both.

"We had a magnificent weekend in New Haven, Hawkin. Toured the Mellon Museum of British Art. Have you been?"

"I haven't. "

Gieck chuckled.

"British art? Guys on horses in red jackets posing with their dogs and a dead fox?"

"Hardly. It's art you can sink your teeth into. Not a pointillist whip handle up someone's butt."

Willis turned toward Holz.

"So, Holz, you've been unsuccessful in retrieving the stick. Instead, you brought me a disk of music by a gypsy guitarist. Why?"

Holz ground his lips together, showing genuine anguish at being criticized.

"I was misled. They've hidden it well. I searched Barnes's desk. I searched Barnes. I searched the boy's worthless uncle. I have a team searching the uncle's house. And they will also search the house of a family friend, Mr. Shit Theory."

"The origin of the name?"

"A trivial exercise in mathematics he conducted long ago."

"And if the searches are unsuccessful? What then?"

"We may have to interrogate the boy."

"Using what methods?"

"How badly do you want the stick? If you want it badly, it would be a vigorous interrogation."

"Where would it be conducted?"

"At a rendition site."

"Jesus Christ!"

Gieck didn't conceal his contempt for Holz.

"He's a sixteen-year-old kid! He's an American. Forget about it."

"We couldn't use one of the known sites," Willis said.

He paid no attention to Gieck.

"Congress would go berserk. I don't say it will get to that. But we'd need a fundamentalist state with a corrupt ruling family and a culture of extreme violence."

"Texas?"

"Very funny, Gieck. I say again, I don't think it will come to that. But let me stress to all of you that I want that stick back! Do you understand? I will not tolerate failure. I want it back! You may go, Holz."

Dieter Holz rose and stood momentarily at attention.

"I will not fail. I have never failed, and I will never fail."

"Fine. And no extravagant methods. No water boarding Milwaukee teenagers without advance permission. You do understand that Holz?"

Holz nodded to Willis and left. Willis turned to his Japanese table.

"I have an excellent Asiago here, and a fine Madeira. May I interest you?"

"Not me," said Gieck.

Christ, these guys must have cheese and booze for breakfast. Their mothers must have put it in their bottles. They hit it all day long. How can they concentrate?

"Excellent, isn't it Hawkin?"

"Very good."

"By the way, pull that cretin, Nizip. Have him reassigned. Can't have him getting in the way."

"Will do."

"Tell me, what is the report from China on the Uighur killings?"

"Do you want me to stay?" said Gieck.

"I suppose strictly speaking it isn't your assignment."

Willis sipped from a small glass.

"But your work on codes has been quite useful in this. Let me get Dalton in here for background."

Willis pressed a button on his phone.

"Dalton, can you join us? Thank you. We need background on the Uighur issue."

Willis sliced off a generous hunk of cheese and scarfed it down like a gull on a dead fish.

"Historically, our strategic interest has always been this. We must at all costs prevent our enemies from forming alliances against us. A primitive and essential strategy for any great nation."

He sliced off some more cheese and sipped his Madeira.

"But we haven't always been successful. The British allied with the South in the Civil War. The Germans and Italians did the same with the Japanese in the Second World War. Fortunately, neither of those two alliances was insurmountable."

The door opened almost simultaneously with a polite knock. Carroll Dalton walked in with a redwell full of documents under his arm. He sat down and eyed the cheese. Willis ignored him.

"Our major long-term adversary is China. Russia, as we know, is in decline. The Seventh Fleet has the George Washington group stationed permanently in Japan with a full support fleet. Our submarine assets are generations ahead of the Chinese. So, all is well?"

Gieck nodded. Dalton nodded also, still eying the cheese.

When will the bastard offer me some cheese? He'd say he wants to help me lose weight. The truth is he wants it for himself.

"Well, all isn't well!" Willis said. "We have another adversary. The Islamic world. And it goes back to before Islam itself, to the Iliad and even before, to the moment Europe was settled in the first place. Our adversary is the East itself. Under no circumstances, *no circumstances*, can we let the Chinese and the Muslim world ally against us. The East cannot be permitted to unite."

"I thought you wanted me to report on the Uighurs," said Dalton. "I haven't prepared beyond that."

"Quite right. Tell us about the status of the Chinese and the Uighurs. I'm particularly interested in the killings in August."

Dalton consulted documents from his file.

"The Uighurs are an ancient Turkic people. In fact, they look like Turks. They're Caucasians. Some have light colored hair and skin. Their language is Turkic. Their food, their music and their culture are Turkic. But they live in China. Ever since 1949, when the Chinese annexed their territory in Western China and renamed it Xinjiang. The Uighurs call it East Turkistan."

"Their religion?"

"Buddhist until the Tenth Century. Then, they converted to Islam. They're Sunni Muslims, but not quite as nutty about it as some Arabs."

"Tell us about the August killings."

"Unclear. Simple fact? The Chinese have been relocating ethnic Han Chinese into Xinjiang. In the nineteen forties, the Han Chinese population was about five percent. It's now about forty. Starting in the nineteen nineties, Uighur separatist groups began attacking the Chinese government. In August, the Chinese reported two Uighur men attacked a Chinese police unit and killed sixteen men. But some foreign tourists gave eyewitness reports that the attackers themselves wore paramilitary uniforms. We're still investigating."

"One final subject, Dalton. What are the Chinese doing to regulate Uighur religious practices?"

"That's interesting. Reports are, the Chinese select their clerics and interview them on a regular basis, and they remove offending clerics with separatist views. They also screen religious literature for political allusions. They determine what version of the Koran is acceptable. The perception they give is that they view the Uighurs as an ethno-nationalist threat. They smother Islam as a means of eliminating any Uighur nationalist feeling. At least, that is the present perception."

"Do we think they're sincere here? Or are they just giving off that impression?"

"I don't know."

"Very good, Dalton. You may leave."

"I think I'll be going also," said Gieck.

He headed out after Dalton.

"I'm a numbers man. You're the historians."

Willis refilled his glass after they had left. He raised it to Hawkin.

"Pocula elevate, nunc est bibendum."

Hawkin nodded and raised his.

"Bibemus."

"What is the latest intelligence from Xinjiang?"

Hawkin put his glass down.

"I'm not sure we'll ever know. It has the appearance of a frame up. Just days before the Olympics started, too. The Chinese are facing intense criticism over their actions in Tibet and Sudan and Xinjiang. The Chinese government could easily have set it up to turn world opinion in their favor."

"And killed sixteen of their own policemen?"

"Well, really, who cares? You know damned well that we barely protest what they're doing in their own country. Same as our criticism of the Russians in Chechnya. It gives us a good excuse to take shots at both of them. But it's really to our advantage to have them crack down on Muslims. Reduces their influence in the Islamic world."

"I'm not so sure, Hawkin. The rules are changing. There are eight billion people in the world. There are one billion of us, and billions of them. And part of our billion is Russia. They're a basket case, and we don't trust them. It's really just us, Europe, Canada, and Australia."

"You're being a little dramatic, aren't you? Do you really think Africa and South America pose threats?"

"Not now. Africa won't wake up for a thousand years. And then some Z from a collegium in the thirtieth century will have to figure it out. South America is part Indian and part European. We can hold them for now. It's China allying with the Muslims that I'm worried about."

"Alright. Make your case. I'll explain why that isn't possible."

"You, first."

"Alright. They're different races. The great Lathrop Willis himself has always maintained that all alliances are ultimately racial. You said that the Japanese and the Germans only allied because they were so far apart and had little prior interaction. A Russian-Japanese alliance would have been impossible. And the Muslims can't even ally with themselves. They hate each other."

"Anything else?"

"Sure. The crackdown in Xinjiang. If a guard flushes one Koran down a toilet in Guantanamo, a mob burns our flag in Indonesia. The Chinese edit the Koran! They arrest Muslim clerics if one of them even uses a separatist allusion when he preaches. They limit their worship. And no one protests. They're doing a hell of a lot better job containing them than we are."

"Have you ever considered why no one protests?"

"What's your response to that?"

"You know, Hawkin, I once went to a Z session. I recall a fiery young Zanoni, named Wayne Hawkin, giving the address. You know what his thesis was?"

"I was twenty-two years old. And the concept of the Z session is bizarre. You let the current Zanoni, a kid, write a paper on anything he wants and deliver it at a private dinner attended by some leaders of American finance, business, and government."

"Yours was a damned good thesis. You correctly pointed out in nineteen seventy that the future threat was from China, not Russia. That was contrary to every notion we held back then. But you were right."

"I still haven't heard your response."

"It's this. First, the Chinese are showing an understanding of multiracial alliances. They're making inroads in Africa. Fortunately for us, they're a thousand years too early."

"What else?"

"Next, they're allying with Muslims in the Sudan in eradicating Christian and animist tribes. It gives them the chance to do proto-type operations with Islamic governments beyond Africa."

"That's it?"

"No. They've successfully interfered with our efforts to isolate Iran and stop it from producing nuclear weapons. Normally, they shouldn't tolerate nuclear arms in an unstable society so close to theirs and so far from ours. Yet they have."

"But the Taliban in Afghanistan blew up all the ancient statues of Buddha. The Chinese couldn't possibly tolerate a religious culture that blows up the statue of their own prophet."

"Don't kid yourself. We are allied right now with countries that outlaw Christianity. And we don't care. If those countries serve our political and financial interests, they can bark at the moon for all I care."

"Well, what do you propose?"

"We have them contained to the East by our alliance with Japan. My first objective until I leave this agency, and there isn't even a distant second, is to prevent a Chinese-Islamic alliance to the West."

"Willis, do you ever question what we're about? We are making decisions and doing things that get no public review. In some cases, Congress never finds out. Our methods are beyond review. Do you ever think about that?"

Willis reached for the bottle.

"Let's have one last glass. They're quite small."

He poured for both.

"I do think about it. And I'm going to say something that sounds very strange. It's contrary to the Enlightenment and to our Constitution and to every advance we've made in political philosophy since the Eighteenth Century. But it's true. And it's this. There are some things the average person can't be trusted with."

"That's pretty extreme. What do you mean?"

"If you held a truly free election in the Islamic World, the people would vote to outlaw their own right to vote in future elections. They would vote for the imposition of Sharia. It happened in Algeria, and it would happen in Turkey if the elite let it."

"It's a special case, a religious and cultural tradition that has lost all its power and innovation and hates itself. Once they stop projecting their self-hatred outward, and develop a modern culture, that wouldn't happen."

"You think so? If we held a national referendum in the United States right now, with typical campaign advertising, I don't think the Bill of Rights would get a majority of the vote."

"I hope you're not right."

"Really? We don't let people vote on the Fed's discount rate. We don't let them vote on Social Security increases. We don't let them vote for Federal Judges. Why?"

"Those are mechanical things, beyond their expertise."

"Federal judges? Are you kidding? It's because it took a special band of men with the best educations to create the Constitution. And it takes a special band of men, with the best educations of their time, to keep it. That is, you and me, Hawkin. And some others, but not many."

Willis put down his glass.

"Tell me, how is Barnes coming along?"

"He's very eager. Speaking of barking at the moon, I have him barking at Jupiter. Gave him an absurd project, and he won't let go."

"I remember the project. You gave him the wrong number, and he's so impaired that he's thwarted our best efforts to recover it."

"Don't rub it in. It's only a matter of time. Our men are there in Milwaukee right now. I mean, think about it. An average city in an average state. How hard do you think it'll be to get it back?"

"Not very. Shouldn't be. Barnes. He wasn't Z, was he?"

"No. He was Eumenes. The Master of the Feast."

Hawkin hummed from the song for Eumenes and thought the words.

Of all of the Pontiffs in Keys, in Keys, the best is by far Eumenes, Eumenes. The jolly old loafer, he sits on the sofa, his belly hangs down to his knees, to his knees.

"To the jolly old loafer. Just get the damned stick back, Hawkin."

Chapter Fifteen

Bernie kept peeking out of the curtain as Frannie and I pulled on our coats.

"You see anything?"

"No."

"Don't worry. From now on til this is over, somebody'll be with you all the time."

"When's Mom coming home?"

"Later. She's playing Sheepshead with her friends. We'll go with Frannie to her class and get a pizza after."

"I wish Jimmy was here."

"He'll be back for spring break."

A full moon hung over Lake Michigan as we drove to the campus. It was only seven in the evening, but it felt like midnight. When Frannie pulled up in front of Curtin Hall, I pulled a paper bag from under the seat. I reached in and poured out a frayed wire, a small statue of Elvis, and a Pez container. Also, statues of the Beatles, the Stones, Raquel Welch, and what looked like coins.

"Here. Me and Terry bought a bunch of these on Fun Flash Drive, and just burned stuff on them. Stick one in your pocket and your purse, and your knapsack. Put a coin in your shoe."

Frannie put one in her coat pocket, and one in her purse. Bernie took one for his knapsack, and one for his jacket. He put a coin in his shoe.

"You gotta have something for them to steal if they try."

The trout hadn't moved on the ice from last time when we got to the class. Bernie and I took seats in the back. Frannie hung her coat on the side of the blackboard. She beamed at the class.

"Good evening, everyone."

A few muttered in response.

"Before we start, how about some mind-stretchers to warm us up? Let's take two national tragedies. First, who was the man who shot Abraham Lincoln? Anybody?"

There was a considerable pause. Finally, a girl raised her hand.

"Emma?"

"Lee Harvey Oswald?"

"No. That's not quite right. Anyone?"

A boy raised his hand awkwardly.

"Boot."

"Well, yes. That's close. It was Booth. John Wilkes Booth."

She was getting mad.

"Let's turn our attention to *Fuente Ovejuna*, by Lope. Ashleigh, you're writing a paper on the play instead of a final exam. Tell us what happened to Jacinta, and what were the consequences?"

Ashleigh brushed her skirt and sat up.

"Jacinta was, like, ravaged by, like, the Commander?"

"What did that do to her marriage prospects?"

The question was incomprehensible to the trout, but no one blinked.

"Her what?" said Ashleigh.

"Well, in Seventeenth Century Spain, if a woman had intercourse before marriage, her prospects of getting married were very low."

Ashleigh shrugged, as if Frannie had said "If you clipped your toenails in twelfth century China, you couldn't be a lawyer."

"Whatever."

"The Commander was a nobleman," Frannie said. "Jacinta was a peasant. Do we have noblemen and peasants in America today?"

No one seemed to know.

"Well, we don't. The closest thing is rich people and poor people. Or do we? Ashleigh, what is a nobleman? What characterizes someone like that?"

"He wears silks and that?"

"He wears silks and that. Okay, but a lot of people wear silk. Let me ask you this again. Suppose some noblemen came to Milwaukee from out of town, like happened to Fuente Ovejuna, and tried to push us around. Could we beat them? Could we band together to stop them like Fuente Ovejuna did? Brittney?"

"Yeah. We could."

"How would we do it?"

"Well, like Lopez de las Vegas wrote . . ."

"It's 'de Vega,' not 'de las Vegas'. And it's not 'Lopez'. Lope de Vega!"

"Whatever."

"I've got to go to the bathroom," Bernie whispered.

"I'll go with."

The hallway was empty as we walked to the bathroom. I thought I heard footsteps as we went in. I stopped with the door half open. The footsteps stopped, too.

Bernie hung his jacket from a hook.

"I'll wait outside," I said.

I walked to the end of the hall to look out on Downer Avenue and the enormous moon hanging out over Lake Michigan. A few minutes went by. As I walked back to the bathroom, the door opened. A blond man in an overcoat and light brown gloves stopped when he saw me. He started to walk fast the other way.

I've seen him before. Where the hell did I see him? Bernie's dinner!

"Hey! Hey!"

I trotted down the hall after him. He slammed open the double doors at the other end of the hallway and disappeared.

"Joe!"

I turned around. It was Bernie.

"Are you alright?"

"Yeah. But one of the sticks you gave me is gone. It was Elvis."

Bernie tugged at the side of his jacket.

"Go back in with Frannie."

I headed down the hall after the blond man.

Dieter Holz ran out of the building across Downer Avenue and into an alley by the coffee shop. He stood flat in a doorway while a figure came out of Curtin Hall.

The worthless uncle. I'll give him a good tickling when I can. Can't now. Have to make a stop at his worthless friend, Professor Shit Theory. There he goes back inside. Can't figure out where I went.

Holz waited for several minutes, but no one else came out of the building. He walked out the back of the alley over to Hampshire Street and headed east to Marietta, then south.

Just beyond Kenwood, he saw two figures walking toward him. One had a comb stuck in his hair. As Holz approached, one of them walked on the curb. The other hugged the sidewalk's edge against the lawn. When Holz started to walk between them, the man on the sidewalk's edge pulled a gun.

"Check dude pocket."

"What is this?" said Holz.

"What it look like?"

The other man put a hand on Holz's chest and ran his hand in his coat pocket. He stepped for a moment between Holz and the gun. Holz threw him into the gunman, knocking both to the ground. The gun fell to the sidewalk. Holz buried his steel-toed boot between one man's legs. The man fell as if he'd been clubbed with a stone hammer. As the other scrambled from the sidewalk, Holz kicked him in his side.

Holz stood still, scanning the houses. No commotion, no door opened, no lights turned on. He retrieved the gun. One of the men got to his knees, and as soon as Holz saw him he kicked him in the head and the man collapsed.

Still no reaction from the houses. Holz trotted down the street to Linnwood, then east toward Lake Park. He threw the gun down a sewer.

A phone vibrated in his pocket.

"Where are you?"

Holz looked up at a street sign.

"Corner of Lake and Linnwood."

"I'll pick you up in five minutes."

"I can't stand here. There was a small disruption. I will walk south on Lake."

"Okay."

Holz was almost to Bradford when a white Wisconsin Electric van pulled over and he got in.

"Go to the address on Booth Street. Quickly. The uncle will be gone for a little while."

Holz pulled on a jacket that said Wisconsin Electric on the front and back. The driver wore a similar one. He drove carefully through the east side to Riverwest. The truck stopped in front of 2720 North Booth. The two men carefully scanned the front of the house.

"Where should we go in?" said the driver.

Holz eyed the door on the side of the house.

"Piece of cake. We'll go in the side. Put some cones in the driveway. Make it look legit."

Holz and the man got out of the truck. Each carried a box of tools. They passed between parked cars and stepped onto the curb. A head of hair appeared instantly from behind one of the cars. Holz almost dropped his tools.

"Good evening!"

Elmer Dick stood less than a foot away, smiling as his radioactive eyes took in every detail of the two men.

"Evening."

Holz started to step around him, but Elmer didn't move.

"Where's Stan Hagelbarger?"

"He's sick."

Elmer bored into him like a boot camp instructor breaking down a trainee.

"Do you know who Stan Hagelbarger is?"

This isn't possible! I've done jobs in New York, Cairo, Vienna and Paris. I even worked in Moscow before *things opened up. Never even been challenged. Sending me to Milwaukee's like sending Babe Ruth to bat in a T-Ball game. This can't be happening.*

"I don't know him well. I know of him."

"Stan Hagelbarger is the one they usually send for service around here. What's the problem?"

"Power out just north of here. We think it's a short in this area. We're spot-checking houses."

"That sounds strange. Why don't you spot check my house? I'm right next door. Joe's gone right now."

I'll spot check you. I'll take you up in a helicopter and throw you out over Lake Michigan.

"That's okay. We have our protocols."

"Can I help you? What's your name?"

A man who'd committed a hundred contract murders could not have stared more coldly at Elmer, who didn't blink.

113

"Hugo Jarvis. And this is my partner, Larry Grimmer. We're fine. We have a lot to do tonight. We've got to get going."

Elmer watched them as they walked around the side of the house.

"Call home immediately," Holz whispered. "They'd better make sure it's covered if he calls in."

"We could monitor all his calls from outside, you know. Maybe we should abort."

"No! I want to hear a cat walk on velvet. I want to hear every breath when he bangs his girlfriend. He's stolen something. We may not have it all back. I want to hear every drawer that opens. This is the only way to get that detail."

The other man went back to the truck and unhooked a ladder from the roof. Holz took out a key and slipped in the side door. The man left the ladder propped against the side while he opened the back. Out of Elmer's sight, he opened a plastic box and dialed.

Elmer watched him emerge a few minutes later, carrying the ladder into the alley between the houses. Elmer walked slowly around the rear of the house. He peeked around the corner and saw the man named Grimmer on the ladder, pretending to work on a wire. Grimmer dropped a tool, and Elmer retreated.

"He's watching us," said the man on the ladder. "Are you almost done?"

"Almost," Holz said.

He was in the bedroom on the second floor.

"Did you call in?"

"Yes. How much longer is it going to take?"

"A few minutes."

The man went back up the ladder. Elmer scurried to the rear of the truck and opened the back. Instead of equipment, there were a half dozen computers bolted into the floor. Elmer pulled a pad from his jacket and wrote down some numbers from the frames. He wrote down the license plate. When they left, Elmer hurried into his kitchen and dialed 611.

"WE Energies service department. How can I help you?"

"Did you send a repair crew to Twenty-seven-twenty North Booth Street? I want to check on two men who came here."

"Just a minute. I'll transfer you."

Elmer waited.

"Hello. Can I help you?"

"Yes. Two men came to Twenty-seven-twenty North Booth Street and said they were from the electric company, spot checking houses because of a short. They were named Hugo Jarvis and Larry Grimmer. Is that true?"

"Just a minute, Sir. Do you have reason to believe there's anything wrong?"

"Maybe. Just checking."

"Just a minute."

Elmer was put on hold for several minutes.

"Sir? Yes. Our men were sent to that location."

"Jarvis and Grimmer?"

"I don't know, Sir. But men were sent. If there's a further problem, call me back."

"Can I speak to Stan Hagelbarger? He's one of your repairmen."

"I'm sorry, Sir. Our employees are not permitted to receive calls at work. Do you have a repair request?"

"No. Thank you. Listen, I'm going to read you some numbers. Can you tell me if it was your truck?"

"Not really. I told you . . ."

"License Plate CSP 322. And there were computers in the truck. No equipment. I saw Q6X on two of the frames . . ."

"Sir, I really have no authority to verify that sort of thing. Please call back during normal business hours and ask to speak to a supervisor. Okay? Bye."

Elmer checked, but were no entries at all for Stan Hagelbarger, Hugo Jarvis, or Larry Grimmer. He called information. Hagelbarger's number was unlisted at the customer's request. There was no record for Jarvis or Grimmer with those first names.

When I got home that night, Elmer was standing in plain view on the sidewalk by the driveway. It took a lot for him not to garrote me in the garage and that. He was obviously excited.

"Joe, they bugged your place. They did it today."

"What happened?

"I don't know," I said, after Elmer told me the whole story. "It is kind of strange." We walked around to look at the wires, but you couldn't see anything. Suddenly, I heard the phone ring inside.

"Thanks, Elmer. I'll take care of it."

I ran in and caught it on the fourth ring.

"Joe? This is Terry. Listen, I'll tell you what I've come up with . . ."

"Shit Theory!" I shouted. It's so good to hear from you! Can you hear me?"

"Jesus Christ, Joe. You're calling me names again. Goddamn it, I try to help you, and this is . . ."

"The Poet's Corner!" I said. "Meet me at The Poet's Corner in half an hour."

I hung up. The phone rang again, but I didn't answer it.

A half an hour later, I was sitting at a table in The Poet's Corner, drinking a beer. Casmir Pampuch sat at a table nearby with four of his disciples. One of them was a girl about 18 with a chest that strained the buttons of her blue work shirt.

"What is justice after Bush?" said Pampuch.

He stared at her chest.

"What is buttons, I mean beauty? What is beauty?"

I saw Terry enter and waved him over. He was not happy.

"What the hell are you doing? You yell at me over the phone. What kind of thanks is that?"

I explained what Elmer had told me, and Terry got very quiet.

"I've got a stash in my dresser. I better get rid of it. I gotta go."

"What did you come up with?"

He handed me a disk.

"I've talked to Bernie about it a few times."

Norris took a napkin and started to write.

"Here's what I strung together. Basically, I used all the prime formulas, like $n^2-79n+1601$, that only work for some numbers. Then I used Fermat's false theorem, that 2^{2n+1} is a prime number."

"Wait a minute. I thought Fermat's theorem was true."

"His last theorem is true. Plenty of his others weren't. This one isn't. It doesn't always generate a prime number. Okay? Then I threw in one of the false proofs of the Goldbach conjecture."

"What's that?"

"That every even number greater than two is the sum of two prime numbers. Like six is three plus three, and eight is five plus three. And so on."

"But six is also four plus two, and four isn't a prime number."

"I *know* that."

Norris took a sip of my beer.

"I didn't say it was *only* the sum of two primes. But every known even number greater than two *can* be shown as the sum of two primes. No one's proven it, and no one's disproven it. Look, what do you want? I don't know how to write a program that'll factor out primes. No one does. I don't know how Bernie pulled his shit. But this program will tie them up for a while, make them think that a smart punk jerked their chain."

He gulped down the rest of my beer.

"I gotta go. If you need me, leave a message to meet me here."

Chapter Sixteen

Dieter Holz once again sat unhappily in Lathrop Willis' office. Hawkin looked elsewhere when Holz glanced at him. Willis leisurely finished a phone call without the slightest regard for the convenience of the others until he finally hung up.

"So, Holz, you've been having adventures in Milwaukee? You were kind enough to bring us the disguised stick you retrieved. Let me play it for you."

Willis pressed a button.

"You ain't nothin but a hound dog . . ."

He stopped it.

"Last time you brought us jazz. One would think you were burgling music stores. Why, Holz?"

"I have no excuse. They obviously know we're interested in them. They're planting distractions."

"You did manage to seed the home of the uncle. Let me play some of the results for you."

Willis pressed another button.

"Bite me! I know you're listening. You stole my Reinhart. Bathroom thief!"

"We ran it through voice recognition software. That's the uncle, Joe Weber."

"I heard why they threw you out of the orphanage, Blondie! They caught you fucking the cat!"

"That's the friend, Shit Theory, as you refer to him."

"You prollly beat up the two guys on Marietta who were walking to the library! We'll have your dead ass if you come out here again! Hey, give me another brewski!'

"That's the police officer, Jerry Piano."

The room was profoundly silent. Willis let Holz squirm.

"But the most disturbing thing," he finally said, "is that a neighbor called in the license plate of your truck and casing numbers on the gear inside. How the hell did that happen?"

"The neighbor is quite difficult. He has nothing better to do than hide among the cars all day. There is no problem. The license and casing numbers are contrived."

"I will decide if there is a problem."

The coldness in Willis' voice made Holz look down.

"Of course, they were shams. But this has caused us difficulty. A fake truck from the Energy Company with fake plates is detected. Every municipal hack in the country is concerned about the security of his electrical grid. We're having difficulty diffusing this."

"This is a more challenging assignment than you might think. I will reconsider my methods."

"Holz."

Willis took a sip of water.

"You did splendid work in Lahore. You blended right in. They believed you were an Austrian convert. You found your man, we snatched him out for questioning, and you left no footprints. What did you call yourself, Hussein something?"

"Tarek Hussein Farid."

"Right. He was the fugitive Austrian war criminal who died in Egypt in 1992. Changed his name from Aribert Heim. You said you were his son. They believed you in Pakistan. Yet you can't impersonate a repairman from the Electric Company in Milwaukee. Why?"

"Milwaukee is quite unusual. They notice more. I will be more careful next time."

"I will decide the next time. For now, you will cease your operations in this matter. We are bringing the boy to Washington for an examination. If we are successful, no further action is warranted. If we are not, I will ask you to return to Milwaukee."

"Yes Sir!"

Holz stood stiffly and nodded. Willis did not offer him his hand as he left.

"Hawkin, I took the liberty of making dinner reservations at Zaffiro's. Will you join me? I want to talk about next steps."

"Of course."

The bar at Zaffiro's was crowded when they arrived. Willis ordered two kirs while they waited for their table. They drank them standing in a corner.

"You know, Willis, there is only one other man in history I know about who could drink continuously and show no effects whatsoever. That was Socrates. Are you related?"

"Don't know. My grandmother did vacation in Greece. To your health, Z."

"To yours."

"Table's ready, gentlemen."

"So, what's your plan?" said Hawkin.

"It's in progress. We're bringing the boy out. Perfect backdrop. It's Wisconsin night in the Capitol. The local pols pressured him to come. We'll give him a full battery of tests. I've told Barnes to tell the boy to bring the stick."

"Ready to order, gentlemen?"

"I think so," Willis said. "You ready?"

"Sure. Go ahead while I look at this."

"Alright. I'd like the paparadelle with rabbit ragu, and a Caesar with a side dish of chopped raw onions and Gorgonzola."

"To drink?"

"A bottle of your worst Chianti."

"What?"

"The kind that people in sleeveless undershirts drink on stoops in the Bronx."

"Ah hah."

"He's kidding," Hawkin said. "A bottle of the Classico. Serve it in jelly glasses to make him happy. And, I'll have the lobster ravioli, with the pomodoro, shaved onion, and Gorgonzola salad."

"Thank you, Sir."

She took their menus and left for the kitchen as Hawkin buttered a slice of bread. "So, what do we expect to accomplish with our examination of the boy?"

"For one thing, we should get the stick back."

"What if he made copies?"

"It should be uncopiable. Was it not?"

"Bonner told me Barnes wanted it manipulable. I assume it could be copied."

"We'll find out."

"What sort of examination do you have in mind?"

"Deep math ability and prime number theory. My own belief? The boy is a fraud. A high school kid from Milwaukee. But in the off chance he's an idiot savant, there may be some trivial assistance he can provide for us. His main claim about factoring out prime numbers is of course absurd."

"Right."

They ate slowly when the meal arrived.

"Dagger Baker had an intriguing idea," Willis said. "First, he posed the problem. A billion of us and billions of them. Eventually, we'll all die, and we must trust that a new team of Keys men can keep a lid on

122

things. Defuse the shifting coalitions of Wogs who could rise up to overwhelm us. Is there a better way to ensure America's perpetual ascendancy?"

"Good question. What's his answer?"

"It's intriguing, really. Let other countries gradually become states of the United States, with strict guidelines."

"You're joking. Do you want sixty-million Mexicans swarming our Social Security system?"

"Of course not. There would have to be strict protocols. For the first hundred years, no voting rights or entry to other states, and no benefits. Gradually, we introduce our education system. Give them a few sweeteners at the start. Manage their resources for them. Second hundred years, if they make good progress, limited citizenship. And so on."

"Do you really want Somalia and Zimbabwe as states?"

"Have to clean them up. Might take longer. Perhaps a lot longer. Look, you can't just airdrop copies of Plato's dialogues and the New Testament into the jungle, tell them to read them, and expect them to clean up immediately. It would take time."

"Britain and China wouldn't do it."

"Someday, Britain won't have a choice. They're just like a ruined aristocrat roaming around a burned plantation after history's march to the sea. But China *is* a problem. They kill their girls at birth. They'll have fifty million men who want a woman. Can't have that."

"You could send them to Africa. Or Thailand, for that matter."

"There you go. I think you're getting into this, Hawkin."

"I'm kidding you. I think it's ridiculous."

"I don't know. Even our own ancestors were a bit on the gnarly side a thousand years ago. Plenty of time to get the toxins out of the cultural groundwater. We need to incubate their few pleasant local customs. The good will remain. We like Asian food, for instance. Let me pose this challenge. If we cleaned them all up, what cultural habit of any of them can you truly not stand?"

"Only one. The hats on Bolivian women. I really can't stand them."

"I'm with you. They'll have to go. For me, I can't stand to see a street full of men chanting 'Death to America!' May take some time to make them post-religious. But you know, Dagger had another idea that intrigued me."

"What was that?"

"The problem of incompetence. Take Africa. After colonial rule ended, they all fell apart. Their kings take a hundred wives. They starve. Kill each other. Vicious bastards. Life expectancy cut in half. But they also can't knuckle under to us. Pride, and that sort of thing. So, Dagger came up with his plan."

"And that was?"

"Keep a hold on the illusion of political self-control to soothe their narcissism. They sign hundred-year contracts with us to run them for a percentage of their resources. Binding arbitration in Stockholm or New York to resolve any disputes. It would keep them from each other's throats. Plump them up a bit. Educate them. But they keep their pride. Just contracting out management. In this case, of course, management of their government, courts, military, and economy."

"Dagger's a man of unexpected talents. Most operations men focus on what's in front of their noses. Dagger's is by no means a small nose. That must explain it." Hawkin reached across the table.

"Here, give me your glass for the last few drops of Jove's nectar."

Chapter Seventeen

It was Wisconsin Night at the Mayflower Hotel in Washington, a chance to showcase Wisconsin products and politicians. Miller Beer, Monroe Cheese, Usinger's, Bratwurst, Harley, Kohler, and at least a hundred other products were on display. Sliding around them were a hundred lobbyists, each sniffing for advantage on his issue, each sniffing like a dog on a log.

The politicians were there. Aldermen from out of state, Alders from Madison, Alderoids from Milwaukee, County Board supervisors, Mayors, and Congressmen. Fieblewicz was there, representing his fellow Milwaukee Roids. So was County Supervisor Turnpaugh, stroking his moustache as a lobbyist licked his face.

Hundreds of constituents also attended. Lawyers with Wisconsin roots, now in the Washington bureaucracy. Students. Many Wisconsin residents visiting Washington. Party activists. Anyone in Washington with a Wisconsin tie.

Most states have Nights. Oklahoma Night. Virginia Night. Oregon Night. But Wisconsin Night is special. You see political fauna there unknown in the rest of the country, like a Doctor Seuss petting zoo.

Congresswoman Love sat on a chair in a corner of the ballroom, attended by Supreme Star Hussein. He stood erect by his mother's side, holding a box of Kleenex. Recently returned from an historic fact-finding trip to Austria to benefit the assholes she represented, Love sat with her eyes half-closed, planning her next historic trip to Paris for the further benefit of their nasty asses.

Journalists prowled around the crowd like hyenas around a dying antelope, each looking for his chance to snatch a steak. Among them,

Roland Cheek commanded the highest status as the representative of the largest newspaper.

Senator Russ Feingold was there with troubled eyes, assessing how to get a headline, what 99 to 1 vote to get in on to compare himself once again to the Senators who voted not to impeach Andrew Johnson.

Of course, no economic benefit to Wisconsin ever resulted from any of these events. *The Hill* got a good laugh from this muscle flexing by Eddie the Eagle politicos. The lobbyists picked off their targets one by one, rolled them, and left them standing naked in barrels they made them pay for.

Lathrop Willis and Wayne Hawkin stood at the edge of the crowd, each sipping a tolerable, but not excellent cab.

"You're taking a real interest in this case, Willis. We could leave it to normal channels, you know."

"In due course. I want the number back. The longer it's out, the greater the likelihood of damage."

Willis grimaced as Supreme handed Love a tissue.

"This is quite unpleasant. All the disquieting aspects of a foreign culture with no suggestion of exotic pleasure."

Congressman Paul Ryan stood with a lobbyist along the wall. Ryan had a hangdog face, large eyes, and no visible trace of a sociopath, character assassin, or thief. He didn't look like a man who wanted to torch a lingerie factory. For this reason, his party desperately described Ryan as a future Republican "leader," a "moderate" who might some-day surface "to do something."

Ryan looked at Peever Henry, a lobbyist on agricultural issues who went back and forth representing an agricultural conglomerate and then the State of California.

"Peever, you've got to help me. I have dairy farms in Rock County. They say to me, 'Congressman, why is Eau Claire ground zero? Why do milk prices go up the farther you get from Eau Claire? From Wisconsin? That ain't right.' What do I tell them, Peever?"

Peever Henry was a belly on two short stilts, holding a head with two filmy black eyes. A mass of boiling pathologies that occasionally sloshed out of his pores. Ryan shivered as Henry started to smile.

"Paul, you're a valuable man. A scholar. I think we can do something. Tell them we'll move it from Eau Claire to Rice Lake. That gives Rock County another forty miles. It's a start."

"Thank you, Peever! Thank you!"

Ryan emptied one nostril into a cocktail napkin.

"It's a start. But I'll be back, Peever. I won't rest until we have true reform. This is just a start."

"Of course, it is. Of course, it is."

"Can I have your attention please? Attention please?"

Two unpleasant looking young men stood near a podium along the wall farthest from the door. They surveyed the room with cold eyes as it quieted down.

"Thank you," said one.

He looked like a highly evolved rodent.

"I am Morden Snearly. I have been asked by the Speaker and the Majority Leader to co-host this wonderful event. Wisconsin commands enormous respect and influence with the Democratic Leadership. This is a wonderful night. We're here to welcome an exceptional young man, a young math genius from Milwaukee, to serve as an honorary page for a week, and to become acquainted with some government agencies. He and his outstanding family will be here shortly. But before we begin, there are several distinguished diplomats from two of our close allies whom I'd like to acknowledge, as well as representatives of Wisconsin's Alderpersons, County Supervisors, and Congressional delegation.

Snearly combined the least attractive qualities of Iago and Rasputin. His close-set eyes and thinning hair were not a welcome sight in an empty corridor of the Capitol.

"I am Cody Rains. I have also been asked by the Minority Leader to co-host this marvelous, historic event. I assure you that Wisconsin also has the greatest influence with the Republican Leadership. After all, the Party was founded in Ripon, Wisconsin."

Rains had a saintly, almost angelic face, with a thick head of tawny hair and unusually pale blue eyes. He wore a bow tie with a white shirt and a sports jacket. Unknown to the audience, he also wore the words 'I'm Cody Ride Me' tattooed between his shoulders.

For Snearly and Rains, this was a welcome break in the battle, much like the holiday lull during World War One, when German and Allied troops would mingle between the trenches, sing Christmas carols, and then return at dawn to bayonet one another. Snearly and Rains would have a bit of fun, whip the tethered Wisconsin pols, then resume mortal combat in the morning.

For the moment, each ignored the fatal paradoxes that were destroying their respective parties. Rains could ignore the terrible Republican paradox: job killers, who hated to see anyone working for more than the minimum wage, whose core belief was securities fraud. The paradox: how to kill jobs while leaving victims with fat wallets to defraud.

Snearly could ignore the terrible Democratic paradox: quota addicts in a loose federation of race and gender caucuses who pandered to any hack, any victim with a posse, no matter how small. The paradox: how to quota all caucuses and posses yet *prevent* the majority from finding anything out.

"First," said Snearly, "I want to introduce Congressperson Nettie Love. The incomparable Congressperson will make a few remarks and will take questions from the media. Congressperson?"

Nettie Love walked to the microphone and looked at the audience. Slowly, she started to dance in place.

"This is unpleasant," Willis whispered to Hawkin. "Grotesque. I truly regret having come here. I don't mind saying it. Where the hell is the boy?"

"We're tracking him," Hawkin said. "Plane was late. He'll be here."

"Hello Wisconsin!"

Love continued to dance slowly.

"I do *not* represent the folk in the limousines. I represent the folk on the street. In the neighborhoods. I represent the community."

She stopped dancing.

"I will take questions."

Roland Cheek raised his hand.

"Congresswoman, a prominent non-partisan policy group voted you the seventh worst member of our current Congress. Four-hundred-twenty-nine out of four-hundred-thirty-five. Several of those voted worse than you are now under indictment. Discounting the indicted Members, you are second from the bottom. How do you respond?"

Love was a pro. She didn't move a muscle.

"If I'm so bad, how come you endorsed me? I say, if I'm so bad, how come you endorsed me?"

Because we suck, that's why. We're a joke. About to be a blog. You were the only game in town. The Green running against you gave idiots a bad name.

"You were unopposed."

"Exactly! *Why* was I unopposed? Because the Community honors me with their support."

She had him. Light applause swept the room. Very light.

"Very good. Thank you, Congressperson Love."

Rains looked at his notes.

"We will now hear from representatives of two of America's allies: the United Kingdom, and Ecuador. First, to introduce Mr. Pantaleon Flores of the diplomatic delegation from Ecuador, please welcome the distinguished Alderman from Milwaukee, the Honorable James Fieblewicz. Alderman Fieblewicz?"

Fieblewicz walked to the podium. As he made a show of adjusting the microphone, Rains handed him a sheet of paper.

"Here are your remarks," Rains whispered. "We included some greetings in Spanish. We understand you aspire to be in the Senate. Bit of international exposure. You have many well-wishers out here."

Rains pointed to the sheet.

"When you introduce Señor Flores, the 'j's' are pronounced like 'h's'. Every 'j' is an 'h'. And the words that end in 'n' have the accent at the end of the word. Okay?"

"Sure."

Fieblewica tapped a water glass on the lectern and waited for the room to quiet down.

"If I may have your attention."

He nodded gravely. A short man with large black eyes and black hair stood uneasily at his side. Fieblewicz beamed at him, then looked out over the crowd.

"It is a great honor to recognize Señor Pantaleon Flores, from the Ecuadorian Embassy. We are happy to have you here with us, Señor Flores."

Led by the lobbyists, the crowd clapped. Fieblewicz waved like Evita Peron from a balcony at what he assumed was applause for him.

"Señor Flores is new to the embassy, so I'd like to tell you something about him."

He glanced down at the sheet on the lectern that Rains had given him.

"In the first place, he is a man of unequalled Carajo, great courage."

Fieblewicz paused to let his audience grasp his point. Flores put a handkerchief to his forehead but said nothing.

"I can also tell you that he is a man of large Pendejo, great weight of intellect."

Fieblewicz paused again.

"He was tested as an athlete on the football field, soccer to us norteamericanos."

The Roid winked.

"He played Ladron, the forward position. His proud nickname was . . ."

Flores was dying a slow death.

"El Cabron, the Cobra!"

Flores waved at the crowd, in spite of having been introduced as a pubic hair, a cuckold and a thief. He made short remarks, then sat down.

Morden Snearly stepped to the microphone.

"Now, introducing another great friend of America, Sir Peregrine Throgmorton, from the Embassy of the United Kingdom, will be the distinguished Milwaukee County Board Supervisor, the Honorable Chester Turnpaugh. Supervisor Turnpaugh?"

Turnpaugh walked grandly to the podium. Like a Clydesdale, he carefully planted his feet as he walked. Snearly handed him a sheet of paper.

"Here are your remarks, Supervisor. We understand you aspire to be in the Senate. Bit of international exposure for you. You have many well-wishers out here."

A skinny man in an absurdly thick woolen sports coat looked warily at Turnpaugh. His eyes sat deep in the sockets, and wisps of hair were combed down over his forehead.

"It is a great honor for me to introduce Sir Peregrine Throgmorton."

He studied the sheet of paper Snearly had given him.

"By the looks of this now, Sir Peregrine is undoubtedly the most distinguished individual I have ever had the honor of introducing. Let me tell you something about his background. First, when he was in the Sixth Form at Eton, he was elected the head of the Society of Catamites Minor. This is an honor that had also been bestowed on Disraeli and Churchill in their Sixth Form years."

Turnpaugh paused to look solemnly at the audience. Throgmorton closed his eyes.

"After graduating from Borstal College, Oxford, he served as the Silver Stick in Waiting to the Mayor of Liverpool. He then served as Maltravers Herald Extraordinary to the Housing Council of Wales, and most recently served as . . . let me see if I get this right . . . Rouge Dragon Percy? Pursivant? Rouge Dragon Pursivant to the Earl of Pegoshire."

The lobbyists again led a lusty round of applause.

"And it is a well-known secret . . ."

Turnpaugh winked at the audience.

"That Sir Peregrine is being prominently mentioned to be the Cap of Maintenance of all municipal services for the City of London!"

More applause.

Not a muscle moved in Throgmorton's face as he waved languidly at the crowd.

I will personally fry the balls of Morden Snearly. I will then nail them to the bottom of the Hyatt elevator and spend an afternoon watching him go up and down screaming, while I enjoy a glass of sherry.

Throgmorton smiled at Snearly and Rains, and they smiled back.

"Thank you. Thank you. Of all the introductions I have ever had, that was certainly the most recent. So pleased. So pleased to be here."

Throgmorton waved at the audience. Like Flores, he too made brief remarks. He sat down.

"This is intolerable," Willis whispered. "I've got to leave. What's the status of the boy and his uncle? I just want to get a look at them."

Hawkin took a phone from his pocket and dialed. He covered one ear as Snearly lavished praise on an assortment of politicians.

"They'll be here any minute," Hawking said. "They've checked in. We'll have their room searched while they're gone. Already searched their luggage. Nothing. If our men can't find it in their room, we'll have to hope he brings it tomorrow."

"I'm losing patience, Hawkin. The boy had better bring it tomorrow. Or I'll send Holz back to Milwaukee. With much greater latitude in operations protocol."

He surveyed the room again.

"It'll be a piece of cake with these people."

"Attention!"

Cody Rains banged on the podium.

"Attention. We'd ask all elected Wisconsin officials to come to the podium for a group picture. Thank you."

People stopped in mid-sentence to hurry to the podium. Several brushed by Willis and Hawkin without excusing themselves.

As Fieblewicz shoved his way up to the podium, he passed within a few feet of Lollie Peters, who was a vice chair of the Milwaukee County Democratic Party. A tired looking woman with stringy hair and a wan face. The Party was her life. She went to all conventions, and all Wisconsin nights.

"My father died," she called out as Fieblewicz went by.

He froze.

The bitch! The attention- starved bitch! Relentless! The ultimate I-gotcha. The one thing that couldn't be ignored. He'd almost made it past her. Now he was screwed. The picture was about to be taken. Have to get away.

"That's great. Great. You're great."

"What?"

He could see the water forming in her eyes.

Too late for the front row. Still time to get in on the side.

"Great God. Great God! I'm so sorry. I pray that he didn't suffer."

Peters sniffled and wiped her nose on her sleeve.

"He had Alzheimer's. He was ninety-five. He was a veteran. He was always very proud of that. He worked for many years at Allis Chalmers. His father was Wendell Peters. Wendell once greeted President Taft when he came to town."

An historian! And Wendell begot Mr. Peters. This was too much! Some things you don't hear when they're called out from the crowd. He'd made a rookie mistake. Thirty seconds.

"I'll pray to God for Wendell's soul," said Fieblewicz.

"Wendell was his father," Peters shouted.

Fieblewicz took his position on the side.

"My father's name was Elwin!"

"I will pray for Elwin's soul too," Fieblewicz said.

The photographer snapped the picture, and then a small group walked into the Mayflower ballroom as the picture broke up.

"There they are."

Hawkin touched Willis' arm.

"There's the boy. His uncle. The policeman, and a few others."

Someone passed a note to Cody Rains, who looked over at Bernie and the rest.

"It is my pleasure to welcome and recognize Master Bernie Weber, and his wonderful family," said Rains. "I understand that Bernie, and his whole family, are mathematically gifted. It is my honor to call on the Honorable James Fieblewicz, Bernie's alderman in Milwaukee, to present Bernie with an official proclamation. Alderman?"

Fieblewicz lumbered once again to the podium. Bernie stood erect next to him, the jacket from St. Vinnie's covering his knuckles.

"Bernie," Fieblewicz said. "I myself am not good at figures. No, Sir. None of this business of 'A train leaves from Philadelphia for New York, and one leaves from New York for Philadelphia, and a bumble bee flies in between' for me. No, Sir. I'm a country boy. But people like me have to be represented, and I represent 'em."

The applause was thin as many checked their watches. Fieblewicz reached under the podium to produce a framed certificate.

"Bernie, it gives me great pleasure to present you now with this Resolution of the Common Council of the City of Milwaukee, and we are designating today as 'Bernie Weber Day' throughout the City. You show them, Bernie. Show them you can cipher with the best of them. Congratulations, Son."

The applause picked up as Bernie accepted the certificate. Hawkin's phone vibrated. He picked it up and turned toward the wall.

"Yes? Okay. We're leaving now. We still have tomorrow."

Hawkin put the phone back in his pocket.

"They searched the rooms. All of them. No stick anywhere."

"I'm leaving. I've seen enough."

Willis walked out into the hallway. A flat screen TV on the wall of a conference room across the hall was turned to CNN. The door was open, the room empty.

"Let's check the Dow."

A reporter was doing a standup in front of the Capitol.

"Campbell, I must tell you that the Chairman of the House Foreign Relations Committee blasted the CIA for sloppy intelligence in Iraq, and in his words, 'material security compromises.' He's proposed an investigation by the House Oversight Committee into the Agency at all management levels."

Willis stalked out of the room.

"I'm tired of these bastards. Hawkin, it's very simple. We get the stick from the boy tomorrow, or Holz takes a team to Milwaukee and does everything necessary to retrieve it. Do you understand?"

"Yes, Sir."

Chapter Eighteen

Bernie and I met in Frank's room at the Mayflower with Jerry and Shit Theory to go to breakfast. Our rooms were courtesy of the government. Bernie stayed with me.

I noticed the shelf in Frank's bathroom was bare. The shoeshine kit, shampoo, conditioner, lotion, needle and thread were all secure inside Frank's duffel bag. So were the stationery, envelopes, and magazine describing the sights in Washington. No towels or hangers, of course. Milwaukeeans are frugal, but very honest.

"Okay," I said. "Let's go over the game plan. At no time is Bernie ever alone. You got it? If he goes to the bathroom, somebody goes with."

They all nodded.

"Bernie, how long do you think it'll take you to crack this thing? The sooner the better."

Bernie squinted.

"I think about two weeks. I got a paper to do on *Merchant of Venice,* and I got a chemistry test coming up. It's taking longer than I thought. With shorter numbers, I just do it. With one this long, I have to come up with an algorithm."

"Can you do it?"

"Yeah. I think so. I'll spend the whole weekend on it."

The phone rang.

"Hello?"

"Can I speak to Joe?"

"Speaking."

"This is Allen Barnes. I need to talk with you. Immediately."

"What?"

"I'm at a corner table in the coffee shop. Meet me immediately."
He hung up.

"It's Barnes. He wants to talk with me in the coffee shop. Here's the plan. All of you take Bernie in there for breakfast. I'll see Barnes, and then join you. Then, we take a cab to the meeting."

"Roland Cheek might try to join us," said Jerry. "He's been bugging me."

"Fine. He can ride with us."

There was a short line at the coffee shop. I left them there while I went in to look for Barnes. I saw him sitting in a corner.

"What do you want," I said.

"You want some food?"

"No. I'm eating with the others. What's up?"

"Is Bernie making progress?"

"Absolutely."

"When will he be done?"

"I don't know. Could be tomorrow, could be next year. You know? It's hard."

"Joe, listen to me. There's something wrong."

"What?"

"All is uncertain. Life is changed. Be careful."

Barnes leaned into the table.

"I didn't tell you this in Milwaukee. Somebody held me up at gunpoint and tried to steal the number. I don't know who. I don't know who to trust."

"Bullshit. You know when we met at Three Brothers? Somebody stuck a gun in my back and stole a CD. They stole another stick from Bernie's jacket. You telling me you don't know about that?"

"Right. I don't. Listen carefully. Did someone ask you to bring the stick today?"

"No," I said.

I fingered it in my pocket.

"I don't think you're telling me the truth. On the off chance you brought it, do *not* give it to anybody. You understand. Nobody. Until I figure this out."

Barnes put a twenty-dollar bill on the check and got up to leave.

"Nobody."

I walked out into the lobby and up a flight of stairs to the business center.

"Can I help you?"

"I'd like to mail something home. Do you have a padded envelope?"

"Sure."

The woman handed me a padded CD mailer. I put the stick in it and addressed it to Frannie. I also put her address for the return and handed it to the woman.

"Could you please add the right postage and mail it?"

"Certainly. Do you want to put it on your room?"

"Sure"

She handed me a slip to fill out.

"No, on second thought, I'll pay cash."

"With the mailer, five dollars."

I gave her the money.

"Thanks."

In a room several miles away, Lathrop Willis tapped impatiently to get everyone's attention.

"Let's start, Gentlemen. They'll be here in an hour."

He looked at Hawkin, Gieck, and Dalton.

"Gieck, explain our objective and your plan. They tried to postpone this. It took a lot of effort to get them out here. Now, I want results."

Matthew J. Flynn

"Right. I'm going to pose some preliminary problems to see if the boy has exceptional mathematical ability outside of prime number theory. I personally believe the boy is quite talented. The few problems I posed to him on my trip to Milwaukee showed me that."

"I know your opinion. I want it confirmed, in much greater detail."

"Well, I thought I'd use a problem that was given to Gauss when he was young, and a quite interesting probability problem involving the Money and the Rattlesnakes. Then, I'm to propose some problems based on factoring out prime numbers. Some are relatively simple. Some we devised after a little work on the computer."

"Okay, Gieck, but how about the program? Have you analyzed it?"

"Program?" Hawkin said. "Has he given us a program?"

"There was a program in his luggage on the plane. It wasn't the number we gave him. We took the liberty of copying it. We've been working on it since yesterday afternoon. Gieck?"

"It's not very helpful. A lot of gobbledy gook. Basically, what they did is run together a couple of prime formulas that are known to be false, for instance this one."   Gieck walked over to a board and wrote in black magic marker.

$n^2-79n+1601$

"This formula produces a prime number for some numbers n, but not all."

He wrote again.

2^{2n+1}

"This is one of Fermat's theorems, in this case a false theorem. It produces a prime number for some n's, but not all. He also put in one of the false proofs of the Goldbach conjecture, which is that every even integer greater than two can be written as the sum of two primes. It's never been proven nor disproven, but it's not terribly helpful. It certainly doesn't provide a basis for arriving at a number's prime factors."

140

"You know what I think?"

Willis looked at each of the men.

"They did this on purpose. It doesn't tell us anything about his unique ability to factor out prime numbers. They want to throw us off the trail. The boy sent his uncle an E-mail referring to 'Norris's program.' And his uncle got a call from Norris wanting to tell him what he'd come up with."

"Who is Norris?" said Dalton.

"Here he is."

Hawkin touched a button, and a picture of Norris shone onto the wall across the table.

"Has a small roofing business in Milwaukee. Did graduate work in Mathematics. Friend of Bernie Weber's father. We're searching his house now. The point is, no matter how the program was prepared, it's worthless and it was intended to be worthless. We just don't know how good the kid really is. They're just trying to stall."

At a quarter to ten we were heading off in two cabs to the address they had given me. Roland Cheek came shining around just as we were finishing breakfast and asked to come along. I put him in the first cab. Bernie rode with me, and we rehearsed the plan.

"So, if they throw math problems at you that aren't prime numbers, what do you do?"

"I deal with them. Solve them."

"Right. And if they throw primes at you?"

"I deal with them."

"Right. And if they ask for the stick? What about that?"

"I don't know where it is."

"Right. And if they ask you how you can work on it if you don't know where it is?"

"When I need it to work on, I call you."

"Right."

"But what if they ask you where it is, Joe?"

"I'll handle it."

The cabs pulled up in front of what looked like a private home on a pretty Georgetown street. I paid the drivers, getting receipts for reimbursement. We rang the bell. A stylish looking older woman with a large birthmark on one cheek answered. The place gave me the shivers.

"You are the Webers."

Frau Blucher. NNNGGGHHH! A horse whinnies in the distance.

Her smile could have cracked a block of ice.

"Yes we are. I think we had an appointment at ten?"

"Come in."

We all stood around staring at the furnishings. Most government offices have metal desks, with calendars on the wall. This place had the largest Oriental rug I'd ever seen, with a guy's head in the middle surrounded by peacocks and pistachio trees. The drapes looked as if they'd been lifted from an opera house.

"And would you please identify yourselves?"

"I'm Joe Weber. And this is Bernie Weber, my nephew."

"I'm Frank Weber, Bernie's great uncle."

"The professor?"

"Yes."

"And I'm Terry Norris."

"The mathematician?"

She snickered.

"Mathematician and roofer."

"I'm Jerry Piano."

The woman looked hard at Jerry.

"What are you doing here?"

"Security, Ma'am. I'm a police officer. Milwaukee. I provide security for Bernie."

This greatly amused the woman.

"I'm sure that's very helpful."

"I'm Roland Cheek, with *The Milwaukee Journal*."

"Bernie is fortunate to have so many uncles and relatives."

You could almost hear screams from the basement when she spoke.

"In any event, I wonder if I could ask the rest of you to remain here while I escort Bernie upstairs to meet some people from our agency?"

"Well, I'll tell you," I said. "We all came out to be with Bernie. We're real proud of him. I think we'd like to all come upstairs to be with him."

"As you wish. Just a moment please."

We watched her walk up the stairs and disappear from view. The woman knocked on the door of the conference room and entered.

"They're here. But there's a reporter with them from *The Milwaukee Journal*. And the boy has something taped to his shoe."

"Send them up," said Willis.

He turned to Dalton when the woman left.

"Distract the reporter. His name is Cheek."

We followed the woman upstairs to the second floor. A very fat man was talking on a phone in the hallway, with his back turned to us.

"Eighty column inches?" he shouted into the phone. "*The Post* is doing eighty column inches this Sunday? I can't believe it!"

Cheek pretended to nose around the hallway while the woman showed us into a conference room. Four men sat on one side of a conference table. Bernie, Frank, Jerry, Shit Theory and I sat across from them. Cheek stayed in the hallway pretending to admire a picture of a man in a wig and red knee breeches.

"They're blowing the lid off of parking! No kidding! But what's the focus?"

Dalton was still almost yelling into the phone. He seemed to listen for a while.

"So that's it! The 'fixing broken windows' angle. Little crimes lead to big crimes! Parking violations lead to drugs! Does anybody know?"

He seemed to listen again.

"Okay. Okay. I won't tell anybody. Keep it quiet. Eighty column inches on Sunday. My God!"

He hung up and hurried into the conference room, paying no attention to Cheek. *The big rat leads the little rat to the cheese.*

Cheek pulled out his phone. The call failed. He slipped down the stairs.

"I can't get a signal," he told the woman. "Can I make a credit card call from your phone?"

"I'm afraid it's against policy. And signals are blocked in this location. People who make calls frequently go to the corner."

Cheek hurried to the corner and dialed. He kicked the pavement as the phone rang.

"Hello, Augie? This is Cheek. Roland. I've got something big. It's really big. Listen. *The Washington Post* is doing eighty column inches on Sunday."

He spoke in a reverential tone.

"*The Post*! Eighty column inches! On parking! What? Yes. Parking. The fixing broken windows angle! Little crimes lead to big crimes. We'll scoop them! Put ours out on Friday. We should do eighty, too. Here's my concept. You know the jaywalking piece? Let's move it up! Put some interns on parking. The call-ins aren't working! Gang activity is up! We'll do a wraparound! And a sidebar! I smell Pulitzer, Augie!

Local coverage. I'll do a few streets here. I'll get license numbers! Have Sandler do the same in Milwaukee. We'll get them by two days!"

Cheek listened.

"Okay. Okay!"

He hung up and walked to the first car. The sign read "No Parking from 8 AM to 6 PM." Cheek peered at the license number and started to write in his pad.

As we sat down at the table without Cheek, I didn't recognize any of the men. One of them came around the table to shake our hands.

"As a preliminary matter, Gentlemen, I wonder if you could accommodate me by taking off your shoes for inspection."

"What?"

"It's a routine matter. Everyone who enters this building is scanned."

"We didn't go through a scanner."

"You mean you didn't see the scanner you went through. We check shoes separately."

We each took off our shoes and put them on the table. Frank handed over his slippers. The older man who seemed to run the meeting pressed a button. A woman responded almost immediately.

"Please do a routine scan of these shoes and return them quickly. Thanks."

"So, Gentlemen, let me introduce the members of the Cryptologic School who are here. I am Mr. Willis. This is Mr. Hawkin. This is Mr. Gieck, and this is Mr. Dalton."

As people greeted one another, Uncle Frank made sure to he shake every hand, telling each man how honored we were to be there.

"Do you like the football?" Frank asked Willis.

"I beg your pardon. What football?"

"Football. I'm a Packers fan."

"Oh, yes. Of course."

"I'm sure you root for the Redskins."

"Of course. I'm quite a fan."

"They play hard," Frank said, "but they claim to never go for the groin."

"Do they? I suppose that's right. Why do you wear slippers? Do you have issues with your feet?"

"I like them. They're very comfortable."

"So, you're Professor Weber," said Hawkin. "I've read your paper. 'How Did Chemicals Manage to Combine Themselves Into A Chemistry Professor?' Ingenious. Strong metaphysical overtones."

"You liked it? You may be interested in my next one, 'Neutering Schrödinger's Kittens.' The title, of course, is intended to be humorous. A little joke I permitted myself. The thesis is a fusion between quantum mechanics and chemistry. That is, how chemistry in some respects may be seen as non-local . . ."

He was well into the subject of his next article before Hawkin interrupted him.

"Fascinating. I'll be sure to read it. Now, if we can be seated."

"And you are Professor Theory," said Willis to Norris.

"Norris, actually. Terry Norris. And I'm not a professor."

"I've heard a great deal about you. Your High-Low Conjecture is known to us. Had enormous influence here. Tell me, in five draw, when I'm dealt two jacks and an ace, do I keep the ace kicker, or draw three?"

He was pimping Shit Theory. I didn't like it.

"Well, you know," Norris said, "It depends on how many people are in the hand. Can two pair win it?"

He pulled out a pen and a napkin.

"There are fifty-two cards in the deck. Here are the factorials."

He started to jot down numbers.

"That won't be necessary. Thank you."

"Now that we've been introduced," said Willis, "I thought that we might suggest a few questions to Bernie. We've heard quite a bit about his abilities, and the abilities of the entire family. It may be that we will be in a position to open up opportunities to Bernie that are not normally available to students. Gieck, perhaps you can begin."

"Certainly. Bernie, I thought I'd pose you a few problems that interest me. First, can you add up all the numbers from one through one hundred? Without a calculator or pencil? How long would it take you to do that?"

Bernie stared at him for about a minute, without speaking. There wasn't a sound in the room.

"I just did," he said. "5,050."

The silence was so intense I could hear people breathing. The men on the other side of the table all looked at Gieck.

"That's *very* good. Very *very* good. How did you do that?"

"Well, it's easiest to look on it as a series of fifty numbers. 100 + 1. 99 + 2. 98 + 3. And that down to 51 + 50. Each one is 101. 101 x 50 = 5,050."

"Wonderful. Amazing."

Gieck nodded approvingly at Willis.

Frank patted Bernie's shoulder. Jerry gave him a thumbs up. Willis frowned and gestured to Gieck.

"And now, Bernie, let me give you another problem. The Money and the Rattlesnakes. Suppose Mr. Willis is a very wicked man and puts you in front of three doors. Number One, Number Two, and Number Three. There is a million dollars behind one of the doors. There are rattlesnakes behind the other two doors. Mr. Willis says you have to open one of the three doors, but you don't know which one the money's behind. Okay? And if you pick a door with a rattlesnake, it'll bite you. Understand?"

"Yup."

"You pick door Number Two. Mr. Willis opens door Number One, and there's a rattlesnake inside. You can hear it hissing. He slams it before it can get out. Okay?"

"Yup."

"So, the money's got to be behind either door Number Two or door Number Three. Mr. Willis says you can stay with your pick of door Number Two, or you can switch to pick door Number Three. The question is this. Are the odds of your escaping from the remaining rattlesnake, and getting the money, better if you switch to door Number Three, or are the odds worse if you switch, or are the odds the same whether you stay with Number Two or switch to Number Three?"

"This isn't that difficult," said Hawkin to Willis. "It's 50/50 either door you pick."

Willis nodded.

Bernie thought hard for several minutes.

"I'm much better off switching to door Number Three."

Hawkin and Willis exchanged smiles.

The kid was just a kid after all. Didn't understand that 50/50 odds don't change just because of an external event. Too bad!

Gieck looked dumbfounded.

"That's very *very* good," he said softly. "Very *very* good! Half the mathematicians in the country wouldn't get that right! How did you do that? Can you explain?"

"Wait a minute," said Hawkin. "That's the wrong answer, isn't it? I mean there was a fifty/fifty chance of the snake's being behind door Number Two or Three. It doesn't make any difference to the odds if you switch!"

"You're wrong," said Gieck.

Willis waved at Hawkin impatiently.

"You majored in History of the Arts and Letters, Hawkin. So, did I. Let's leave the math to the experts."

"How did you figure that out?" said Gieck again. "Can you show me on the board?"

"Sure."

Bernie walked up to the board and picked up the magic marker.

"When I picked door Number Two, there was a one-third chance the money was behind it. That didn't change when he opened door Number One. If there are only two doors left, and only a one-third chance the money's behind door Number Two, there's got to be a two-thirds chance the money's behind door Number Three. So, I should definitely switch to Three."

"Absurd!"

Hawkin couldn't contain himself.

"Simply absurd. What is this? Probability changes because a door opens? There are only two doors left. The money is behind one or the other, which makes the odds 50/50!"

"That's not right," said Gieck. "Actually, Bernie's right."

The woman who had greeted us knocked and walked in.

"Here are your shoes."

She handed me a plastic shopping bag with eight shoes and left. We put them on.

"Alright, alright," Willis said. "You have more questions, Gieck?"

"Right. Bernie, is 11,630,747 a prime number? Do you know?"

Bernie thought about it a little.

"No."

"Does it have prime factors?"

"Yup."

"Do you know what they are?"

"3,571 and 3,257."

"Excellent."

Gieck looked at a pad on the table.

"How about 1,707,776,311? Is that a prime number?"

"Jesus Christ," said Jerry. "Give me a break. The kid don't have a computer here."

Bernie thought about it.

"No."

"Does it have prime factors?"

"Yes."

"What are they?"

"42,589 and 40,099."

"That's really excellent, Bernie. Incredible. All right. Let me ask you a few more questions."

Gieck got up and wrote with a magic marker on a long whiteboard: 3,093,215,881,333,057

"Is that a prime number?"

Bernie studied the board.

"Yes."

"I'll be damned."

Gieck stared at him.

"It is. It's a Padovan Prime."

"What's that?" Bernie said.

"I'll tell you sometime. Let me ask you one final question."

Gieck wrote again on the whiteboard: 68,480,406,462,161,287,469

"Is that a prime number, Bernie?"

Jerry glared at Gieck. He fidgeted around, darting looks at Bernie. Bernie stared at it for a really long time.

"Yes."

"Yes it is."

Gieck said it almost reverentially.

"It's a Pell Prime. A *very* large prime."

The men on the other side of the table sat silent.

"You know," said Gieck. "I could go on, but there's no point. Bernie, you're a very talented young man. Very, *very* talented."

"And we're very glad to have your help," said Willis. "We're interested in your work on the number Mr. Barnes gave you. For now, though, we appreciate your giving it back to us. Could I have it please?"

"I don't have it," Bernie said.

"What?"

Willis' pleasant expression hardened.

"Why not? I thought you were working on it."

"My Uncle Joe keeps it. When I need it, I ask him."

"Where is it, Joe?"

"It's not here. It's back in Milwaukee."

"Where in Milwaukee?"

"I'm not saying. I don't want guys sneaking around my house. We've had trouble with a guy."

"Well, we'd appreciate getting it back.":

"Okay. Sure. We'll give it to Mr. Barnes."

"That would be fine."

"Would you like a copy of a program Bernie's been working on?"

I pulled a stick out of my pocket.

"Bernie's been working on it. Here."

Willis accepted it as if it were a dead animal on a stick.

"Thank you. Good-bye."

Gieck and Dalton excused themselves. The other two turned to whisper to each other. Roland Cheek had still not reappeared. We left without him.

"I've had it, Hawkin."

Willis walked over to the window to watch their Wisconsin visitors walk toward the Avenue to catch cabs.

"That's it. I want Holz back in Milwaukee. With all assets necessary to question the boy. Now!"

The phone rang. Willis listened and hung up.

"The coin in the boy's shoe. It held a Beatles song. 'I Want to Hold Your Hand.' They know we're after them."

"One piece of good news. I spoke with Bonner again. The stick he gave Barnes could be manipulated, but not copied. At least not with any technology they'll find. When we do find it, our job is done."

"Excellent. The only good news I've heard in this entire matter. And now, I want it back. Are we clear on that?"

"Yes. I suppose we could see if they give it to Barnes. Have him work on it."

"The hell with Barnes. He's been acting oddly. Retrieve it!"

"Sure. But there's an issue we have to address. They've been clever at hiding it. If we can't locate it through ordinary methods, what then?"

"We question the boy until he discloses its location."

"Willis, come on. He's sixteen years old!"

"You apparently have forgotten our work in Afghanistan. Look, Hawkin. Do you think I like this? To preserve what we have created, there are some things that can't be left to the people for whom we've created it."

"He's an American, for God' sake! This is Milwaukee we're talking about."

"Jose Padilla was an American. Technically. Look, I admit 'Weber' is a little more troublesome than 'Padilla'. But our security has been compromised, Hawkin. The boy's holding an Al Qaeda number. He has no business doing that. I'm sure he won't have to be questioned too far before he'll disclose."

"Where were you thinking Holz would do this?"

"That's a very difficult decision."

Willis poured a cup of coffee and offered it to Hawkin. He poured himself a cup and added a generous splash of cream.

"My instinct is that we shouldn't do it out of the U.S. We lose too much control. This is far too sensitive. But if we do it here, we add another issue that the press hasn't tumbled to. They've never suspected domestic renditions. And we'd need a venue that was absolutely secure. Absolutely trustworthy."

"Such as?"

"There are only two known venues in the United States that are such profound pathologies, run by strongmen with Potemkin legislatures, that I would trust an interrogation like this to remain secure."

"And they are?"

"Alabama and Texas."

"Well, Texas is bigger. Might blend in. A scream here or there might seem local."

"I'm not interested in sarcasm, Hawkin. It's not going to get that far. The boy will probably confess on the plane ride. I have concerns about Texas."

"What are they?"

"It may be starting to change. The University in Austin has some able men. They're all starting to fancy themselves important in some respect. They might notice something."

"And Alabama?"

"Still a feudal pathology. I'd be surprised if they didn't still have ius primae noctis in some areas. I think we go with Alabama. Look, here's the paradox. We're doing this precisely because we don't ever want to become like Alabama. We want Alabama to become like us. But they won't become like us if Al Qaeda blows up the country. Do you see?"

"No, I don't. We'll become like Al Qaeda if we use their methods."

"We already use their methods, precisely to stop them. Look, if you were a Tutsi, would you rather walk past a crowd of Hutus, or a crowd of white Alabamians? If you were a Shiite, past Sunnis or Mississippians? If you were a black Sudanese, past Arabs or South Carolinians? The cruelest dictators in the world are in Zimbabwe. Sudan. Myanmar. North Korea. Eritrea. Iran. I'm damned tired of our taking the rap. We *are* civilization, and we will preserve it. Send Holz in a rendition jet to Milwaukee. Send him now.

"And his orders?"

"If necessary, waterboard Bernie!"

Chapter Nineteen

A white jet landed at General Mitchell Field in Milwaukee. The late January thaw had brought the temperature back into the teens. Holz shivered as he descended from the plane, carrying a duffel bag. He called up to the pilots.

"You'll need to be ready on thirty minutes notice."

"We'll be there when you need us."

"Shouldn't take long. Do you have your instructions for the flight?"

"All set."

A car was waiting at the bottom of the stairs. Holz got in.

"Where to?" said the driver.

"Passengers Arriving."

The driver started to drive on the side of the runway toward the main terminal.

"Better to exit and approach from the public road."

The driver did a U-turn and left the private jet area. He drove onto the road, turned left on Howell, and looped around to the main terminal.

Holz got out.

"We'll be back as soon as his flight comes in. Circle around if they make you move. But be back here."

"Right."

Holz rode the escalator to the departure area and stood with a small group by the baggage screeners, waiting for arriving passengers. He looked at the electronic board. The flight was 20 minutes late. He found an empty seat.

A man stood nearby, approaching people, asking questions. He sometimes wrote down the answers.

"Hello," the man said to a middle-aged woman. "I'm Roland Cheek of *The Milwaukee Journal*. Mind if I ask you some questions?"

Holz listened without looking at him.

"No. That's fine."

"First, Ma'am, is the recession affecting your travel plans? Are you flying less often?"

"No. I don't really fly anyway. I'm here to meet my daughter."

"Okay. Next question. Airport security. Is it too tight?"

"Not really. Why are you asking?"

"We're doing a story on the airport."

A megaturd. And I'm banished to the airport because Augie over-reacted, that miserable bastard.

Cheek closed his eyes briefly to remember the painful facts. He was sitting in the office of Augie Krupp. Augie had a *Washington Post* and a *Milwaukee Journal* lying on his desk side by side. He had looked from the papers to Cheek and back to the papers. Cheek remembered the conversation.

"What are you trying to pull, Roland? Eighty column inches we did on parking on Friday. You were bylined on the sidebar. 'No Parking leads to No Gangs,' we headlined. Cute. We even had license plate numbers. We scooped the Sunday Washington Post. Not! Read our headline! Then read their headline!"

"No Parking Leads To No Gangs" Cheek had read dully. Then The Post. *"President Blasts AIG Bonuses From Bailout Money."*

"Not a word on parking in their whole paper! Not a column inch. And we led with it. Because of you. So, what's your excuse Roland? Who was your source?"

"I didn't catch his name, Augie. Big ugly son of a bitch. But I swear Augie, this town loves this shit. They love the weather better than the

news. They love parking. They love jaywalking. They're fucked up! This won't hurt us!"

He remembered Augie's quick response.

"Your ass is going to the airport, Roland. At the first blizzard, you're on loan to WTMJ, and your ass does standups for the ten o'clock along the highway in Waukesha. You're transportation, Roland."

Cheek lasered onto Holz as the woman walked away.

"Sir, may I ask you some questions?"

"No."

"Thank you. Are you here on business?"

"Yes."

"What kind?"

"Transportation."

"Me, too. What do you transport?"

"People. Look, I must go."

Holz walked away from Cheek to the roped area where a handful of people were greeting passengers. He spotted Hawkin carrying a bag.

"Do you have more luggage?"

"No. Do we have a car?"

"Yes. Let's go."

Holz and Hawkin stepped onto the escalator. They looked at the crowd around them. Invading generals, surveying the village before the capture. Holz grimaced as he rode down behind a large woman who wore white stretch pants and floral underwear.

When they got to the first level, Hawkin walked next to a tall, thin man with enormous eyebrows, wearing a Brewers baseball cap. The man looked at Hawkin. He had a wan, passive look. He suddenly raised his eyebrows. The cap rose three inches on his head. He looked away. He looked at Hawkin again. The eyebrows rose. The cap lifted three inches again. He looked away.

How does he do that? This is quite unsettling. Why does he do that? He must have muscles on top of his head.

The car was waiting for them. Hawkin threw his bag in the trunk, and they sped away. Hawkin dialed a number while they drove east on Layton to the freeway crossing over the Hoan Bridge. Willis answered the phone.

"Hello? Willis? Holz is with me. Is Dalton there?"

"Yes. The two of us. You're in Milwaukee?"

"Right. You wanted Dalton to give us a further briefing."

"That's right. I don't want any mistakes this time. I want to dig into the psyche of these people. Really understand them. Not the usual 'this is the medicine man; this is the strongman' like those more primitive operation venues. Do you understand, Dalton?"

"Right."

"Go ahead."

"Right. First, be very careful at the Pfister. Can't you stay some-place else?"

"Why?"

"It's their most famous hotel. Some might think it's their only hotel. Everybody stays there. If someone thinks you're coming, they'll expect you to stay there. They notice everything. When The Rolling Stones stayed, the paper published what they ordered from room service."

"We're hardly The Stones."

"You don't have to be. A Milwaukee judge assaulted an opera singer in a room at the Pfister. It appeared in the paper. Not because she pressed charges. She didn't. She left town. It's impossible to stay undetected at the Pfister."

"You're joking. What was the judge's name?"

"Christ Seraphim"

"Are you sure it wasn't Jesus Cherubim? Are you making this up?"

"No. Be very careful."

"Alright. Alright."

Willis was getting impatient.

"Proceed, Dalton."

"Right. It comes from the strong German tradition of the city. The Germans accomplished more than most in math, physics, music, and philosophy. But they don't get credit for it. Milwaukee is defensive, notices everything, and believes it has no status in anyone's eyes. But they're also more accomplished than other cities, and don't realize it."

The car drove over the Hoan Bridge into downtown. Hawkin rolled his eyes at Holz.

"Give me examples. I don't have time for amateur sociology."

"If you were at a cocktail party, and said you liked the wine, they would lecture you on wines. If you praised a musical that had gotten a bad review, they would scold you. If you said you liked their zoo, they would lecture you on the difference between zebras and horses. Right down to their goddamn hooves."

"Where are you going with this, Dalton? What's the point?"

"They are larger than most people. Smarter than most people. More insecure than most people. And if you whispered to your girlfriend in a park at night that you loved her, someone would ask you the next day if you were going to marry her."

"Alright. We're pulling up to the Pfister now."

"My last word of advice," Dalton said. "There are actually people in the Milwaukee phone book with names like Hitler and Auschwitz. These particular people are perfectly fine. But the point is they don't feel the need to change their names in Milwaukee. I don't care what you get away with in Karachi or St. Petersburg. You'll have a much more difficult time pushing these people around. We've given this some study. Stay somewhere else."

"Dalton. Holz has worked out of the Europa in St. Petersburg. The National Hotel in Moscow. I've worked out of hotels in Berlin, Cairo, Mexico City, London, and Paris. *We've never been detected*. Willis, you saw these people at Wisconsin Night. I'm not going to stay at a Budgetel next to a McDonalds just because they've got horny judges. Holz and I will be fine at the Pfister. I assure you."

"We're done for now," Willis said. "You may leave, Dalton."

There was a pause while Dalton left the room.

"Good luck, Gentlemen. I want you down in Alabama with your passenger in forty-eight hours."

Chapter Twenty

They sat at a corner table in the lobby bar of the Pfister after they had checked in. Jeffrey, the piano player, played softly in the background. The waitress walked up to their table. She was pretty, in her early twenties, with long brown hair down to her shoulders.

"Are you gentlemen ready to order?"

"I'll have a Perrier with a lime," Holz said.

"And I'll have an Arnold Palmer."

"Here's the plan," Hawkin said. "Barnes reported last time that he met with Joe Weber in a restaurant called Three Brothers. I had a call made to him asking him to meet Barnes there tomorrow evening. I'll tell him Barnes couldn't make it. I'll ask him for the number. I'll expect him to refuse. Or say he doesn't have it. You will be there, but at another table."

Hawkin handed Holz some keys.

"Here are your keys to the rental. It's in the parking ramp. I have a set, too. If you need help, call your pilots. They're trained in more than flying, aren't they?"

"Yes. They're my team."

"They're in a motel?"

"Yes. Near the airport. Waiting."

"Joe Weber won't recognize you, will he?" said Hawkin.

"I don't know. I was at the dinner where Bernie performed his tricks. I sat at the uncle's table. I saw him in the hall at the College. Why take the chance? Why don't I stay here? You can call me when he gets there so I know that Bernie is unguarded."

"You look like everybody out here. Keep your head turned. You will sit at another table. Do you understand?"

"Yes."

"I need you there. If he has the stick, and won't give it to me, you will take it from him when he goes to his car."

"Alright."

"But I expect Joe will be suspicious. Won't bring the number. May show up with friends. The inept policeman, or that Norris fellow. I will keep them busy. If I put my jacket on the back of my chair, leave. You will go to get Bernie. You have all the addresses?"

"Yes. Bernie's mother. Shit Theory. The girlfriend. The cop. I will locate him and call the team. That's our procedure."

"He should be at one of them. Take him to the plane. Find out where the number is. He must know if he's working on it. And if he really doesn't, we'll come back to take the uncle."

"If I leave you with them, how will you get back to the hotel?"

"Cab."

"The boy will only be gone for a day, or maybe two. How is that explained?"

"Kids run away for a while. They stay over at friends' houses. He'll be back, and no one will believe him. Little green men flew him to Mars?"

"Alright. But you'll have to detain the uncle at the restaurant. I'll need a few hours."

"Here are your drinks, Gentlemen."

The waitress bent low over the table as she served them. Holz stared at her breasts.

"Have you seen the piano player, Jeffrey?"

She put her hand gently on Holz's shoulder as she pointed to the piano. Briefly, they turned their heads.

"A few years ago, a man was having a drink here, and he went up to play the piano when Jeffrey took a break. It was Paul McCartney! Oh, look, that looks like Ringo Starr over there! Isn't it?"

She touched Holz's arm. Again, they turned briefly to look.

"I guess not. Well, here's your check. Will you be charging it to your room?"

"Yes."

"Okay. Let me know if you'd like anything else."

"Where shall we have dinner?" Holz said.

"There's a place called Karl Ratzsch's. I'm hungry for German food. Are you ready for some liver dumpling soup and goose and red cabbage? And a boot of beer with a lemon in it?"

"Let's go."

As they got up to leave, they didn't notice their waitress walk from the bar into the ladies room across the hall.

She dialed.

"Hello, Frannie? This is Natalie. I think I saw someone like them."

Natalie took several photographs from her apron.

"You know those pictures you gave me? It's one of those guys. Plus, with a blond guy, like you said, maybe."

She pulled out their bill.

"One's named Henry Jensen. The older guy. Not the blond guy."

"Did you take a picture?"

"Yeah. Two. I'll send them to you right now."

Natalie hung up. She punched on her Blackberry.

Frannie sat at her screen as an email came in. I walked in as she opened it.

"What's that?" I said. "Who called?"

"Natalie. A student. Spanish Comp. You know the pictures Jerry took in Washington on his phone? At the test they gave Bernie? I had

Natalie give them to all the girls who work in the bar. She thinks one of them came in."

The first picture appeared on the screen.

"That's the guy named Hawkin," I said. "I'm not sure about the other guy."

Frannie scrolled to the second picture. The second man's profile was more distinct.

"I think that's him. The blond guy in the hall. And at the dinner. What's his name?"

"Natalie said one of them's named Henry Jensen. The first one."

"That's not right. His name is Hawkin."

I dialed Jerry's number.

"Hello?"

"Jerry? It's me. It's the moment of truth. Two of the assholes are at the Pfister. With a fake name. Henry Jensen. Hawkin, and the blond guy who ripped me off."

"I'll arrest them."

"You can't just arrest them. I can't prove the blond guy robbed me. Look, I got a phone call from a woman. She said she was calling from Allen Barnes' office. They want me to meet them at Three Brothers tomorrow night at six. I'm supposed to bring the stick."

"I'll go with. How close is Bernie to getting it done?"

"Close. I'll get Terry too. Bernie's staying at a safe house, right?"

I looked over at Frannie. She nodded.

"You going to bring it with you?"

"I'm not bringing them jack. They'll keep after Bernie until he solves it. So, he'll solve it. And we'll keep these guys away from him til he does. But hey Jerry, what if they show up with a bunch of guys? What do we do?"

"It's hard to get more officers without a reason. This is a little skimpy. I tell you what. We'll have other people there. They won't be able to pull anything."

"What other people? How are you going to get them there?"

"Leave it to me."

Chapter Twenty-One

I stood outside Three Brothers with Jerry and Shit Theory. The wind chill on the cold February evening was five degrees. It was six on the nose. There was a car parked in the loading zone right in front of the restaurant.

"You guys ready?"

"No problem."

Terry shivered and threw his shoulders back.

"I did a little wrestling in high school. Boys Tech. I was pinned a fair amount. But I smoked. We'll take these guys."

"Jerry. You got other people coming?"

"Soon."

"Okay. Let's go."

I pushed open the doors to Three Brothers. The place was about half empty when we walked in. Branko sat at the bar sipping coffee. The jukebox was playing *Mack the Knife* in German:

'Und der Haifisch, der hat Zahne . . .'

I saw Hawkin sitting at a table by himself along the wall near the kitchen. A blond man was sitting by himself at a table alongside the bar, with his back to the door. The same one at the dinner and in the hallway. The three of us walked across the restaurant and stood in front of Hawkin.

"Were you the one who called?"

"Yes. My office did!"

He was cheery as hell for a cold night on the south side. He gestured at some chairs, but I didn't sit down.

"What do you want?"

"Will you join me? This Serbian wine is quite good."

"That's okay. How can I help you?"

"Well, I'll tell you. Allen Barnes couldn't make it. We appreciate all the work Bernie has put in trying to factor the number Allen gave him. But we need it back. Bernie's assignment is over. Did you bring it with you?"

"No."

All is uncertain. Life is changed. Be careful.

"I didn't tell you this in Milwaukee. Somebody held me up at gunpoint and tried to steal the number. I don't know who. I don't know whom to trust. Bernie's pretty close to cracking it. Kind of got excited about it. We should have it back to you soon.

"Okay. Fine. But I really wish you would join me for a drink and some of this excellent Serbian cheese."

"Righteous," said Terry.

He sat down and poured some wine into a water glass. Jerry and I joined him.

Hawkin smiled.

"Let's toast Bernie's success. And his future accomplishments."

He poured for Jerry and me.

Branko suddenly got up and stepped to the door.

"Can I help you?"

Two men with TV cameras had walked in. They turned to shoot Congresswomen Nettie Love as she made her entrance into Three Brothers. Supreme Star Hussein marched in behind her, followed by a dozen African American men, women, and teenagers.

"The Secretary of Education's representative desired my presence for a confidential dinner to discuss federal aid to Milwaukee public schools."

She said it loudly toward the directional mikes.

"I will permit a brief photo opportunity before the business at hand."

Branko was smooth with his shit and took her hand in a very warm greeting.

"So good to see you, Congresswoman Love. And so unexpected."

He fixed his large black eyes on her, his beret tilted to the left.

"Forgive me, but is this not your first historic visit to see us? To the south side?"

The cameras were rolling. They panned the restaurant. Hawkin turned around in his chair. The man at the bar had his chin almost on the wood, and his hands on his head.

"The right wing says that."

She over enunciated, more out of pride than to accuse.

"They say I never come to the ethnic south side. That I stay in the community on the north side. They are wrong!"

She pulled out a piece of paper with a few words on it.

"I have come to savor your *raznichi*! And your *chevapchichi*!"

She spat the words out the way Branko might have called for boiled ostrich penis in an Aboriginal village in the Outback.

"And then I will consult with the Secretary's emissary."

She lasered in on Hawkin. The truth was, he was the only one in Three Brothers, in fact on the whole south side who looked fancy enough to be anyone's emissary. I saw Jerry grinning.

"You represent the Secretary? You are Mr. Henry Jensen?"

Hawkin was stunned.

"I . . . how did you come to that conclusion? Who are these people? And could we turn the cameras off, please? Thank you."

"We got a call inviting us to dinner. In the Community, when one is invited to dinner, it is customary for the family to attend. These are my nieces and nephews."

"There are a lot of them. I think there has been a mistake, Congress-woman."

"It's legal for you to pay for them, isn't it?"

"It's legal. The question is whether I want . . . all right. They may be seated."

Love's relatives occupied two tables before Branko could bring them menus. The blond guy at the bar would dart quick looks at Hawkin, and then peer away. The cameras finally left.

"I am known as an Education Congressperson," Love said.

She started to drone. The bartender interrupted her. He had briefly gone outside and was standing at the door.

"Excuse me. Whose license plate is CCJ 288? You'll have to move your car, please. It's blocking the unloading zone for our guests."

Hawkin pulled out his keys.

"It is I. Excuse me, I have to attend to it."

Nettie Love snatched the keys from his hand. He didn't have a chance. He didn't see it coming.

"My son will park the car. The Emissary should not have to park his own car." She handed the keys to Supreme.

"No."

Hawkin looked agitated.

"Please, Congresswoman. It is a magnificent gesture. Magnificent. And very kind. But I must attend to my car."

Love ignored him.

"Supreme, can you park the man's car?"

"Yes, I can."

"I say, Supreme, can you park the man's car?"

"Yes, I can!"

Hawkin sat down reluctantly. I walked with Supreme to the inner door and stopped him before the storm door.

"Supreme, that man is an enemy of your mother."

He looked at me warily.

"Supreme. He does not respect the Community. He will use the car to injure the Community. He must not do that. "

Supreme's eyes narrowed.

"Supreme, the man is a Republican."

Supreme's ears seemed to flatten against his head.

"I will park the man's car!"

His smile gave me the willies.

"I will park the man's car!"

Branko was sitting at our table next to Jerry when I went back in. Nettie Love sat next to Terry. I joined them. Branko and Love were hitting it off. Hawkin was dying.

"In Europe," Branko said, "we went to school six days a week. We were expected to work. And to obey our fathers."

Love nodded.

"We must have that here," she said. "And we must help working families realize 'The American Dream.' And those who make more than two hundred thousand dollars a year must pay more taxes."

Love's posse was deep into the goulash and burek. She turned to wave to them occasionally as she spoke.

Branko chugged a glass of slivovitz.

"And we must contain the Turks, I mean, the Russians. We must contain the Russians."

"The Russians," Love said. "Yes, and we must quell the peace."

Branko nodded and poured himself another glass.

Supreme Star Hussein finally rejoined us. He handed the keys to his mother.

"It's down around the block," he said.

Love gave them to Hawkin.

"And so, Emissary Jensen, what plans does the Secretary have to bail out Milwaukee's public schools?"

Hawkin looked drained. He took off his jacket and put it on the back of his chair.

"That's an important question," he said. "Local control is important. So is money."

The blond guy at the bar stood up to leave. He didn't acknowledge Hawkin as he walked out.

"Money is important," said Branko. "But it is not everything. A loaf of bread. A piece of cheese. A walking stick. Hiking on Koritnik, under a bright sun and a blue sky, with a skin of wine."

"We must have that here," Love said.

"If you don't mind, Madam Congresswoman, I wonder if I may take my leave. I feel suddenly ill."

Hawkin actually did look bad.

"Perhaps we could reschedule this? Branko, would you be so kind as to call me a cab?"

"With pleasure. May I offer you an aspirin?"

"No, thank you."

The door burst open. The blond man stalked into the restaurant. He stopped when he saw everyone staring at him. He beckoned to Branko, who hurried over to him. You could hear what they were saying. The man was angry, even as he tried to keep his voice down.

"My car! It's been vandalized! It can't be moved! You should see the tires!"

"I'm so sorry. I'll call you a cab. You must file a report with the police."

"No! No reports. I will take care of it. I just wanted you to know. To protect future customers. Post a guard."

He glared at Supreme. But Supreme chilled peacefully, studying the mountain mural over the bar as if he were memorizing every blade of grass.

"But I can use a cab."

"At once. Perhaps you can ride with this gentleman. He is ill."

Branko picked up a phone on the bar and dialed.

"Three Brothers. St. Clair Street. Right away, please."

"They will be here soon. May I get you some water?"

"No. No," Hawkin said. "I'll be alright."

Jerry pulled out his phone. He stepped to the corner and dialed. I stood next to him.

"Suleyman. This is Jerry Piano. Officer Piano. Yes. There was a call for a cab on St. Clair Street. Three Brothers."

"Yes."

I could hear the voice on the other end.

"This is a crime scene. Do not send a cab."

"Have to respond to all calls."

"Suleyman. Let me be more specific. If I see a turban or a black moustache on St. Clair Street tonight, his ass is going straight to the Chicago immigration office."

"Could be Anglo driver."

"If any cab shows up, it will be bad for you. And your cousins."

"Call could have gone to competitor."

"You have one competitor. Your brother. If one of his cabs shows up, I will consider them your cabs."

"Okay. Okay. St. Clair is sometimes a bad street."

"Especially tonight."

Jerry snapped his phone shut.

"Let's get out of here."

We got Terry. I stepped outside to call Frannie as he was putting on his coat.

"It's me. How's Bernie?"

"Fine. Are you alright?"

"Yeah. Listen, I'm worried about this. I don't think it's safe for him to be with you. Or me. Where's a safe place we can put him?"

"Maybe Frank? Or one of my girlfriends. I'll set it up."

"Okay. For tonight, we might go to Jimmy's old apartment. Don't tell anyone else. Tell Sharon he's staying with us for a few days. Have him skip school. These guys are stranger than I thought."

I looked back through the door as Jerry and Terry joined me. Love's relatives were digging into the dessert. Hawkin was slumped back in his chair while Branko and Nettie Love were deep in discussion. The blond guy sat with his elbows on the bar and his head in his hands.

Chapter Twenty-Two

"Where are you now, Hawkin?"

"Hotel. Holz and I are in my room. We waited half an hour for a goddamned cab. Holz finally called the pilots. We have another car."

"The team should have remained immobile until the actual pickup." Willis didn't disguise his irritation.

"Using them for transportation was a breach of operation protocol. Why did it occur?"

"There was no other way. Cabs don't cruise here. One never came. There was no alternative."

"Holz. You walked in Nairobi. Recall? Through the worst neighborhoods in the world. You can't walk in Milwaukee?"

"It's five degrees! We have thin coats and no hats."

"You have thin coats and no hats! What did you have in Nairobi?"

"I had a gun."

"So, as I understand it, Hawkin, the Congresswoman appeared at the restaurant. She called you by your operation name. Her son slashed your tires after you gave him the keys. And you appeared on television. Well done! Congratulations! Bravo Zulu!"

"I'm sorry," Holz said.

His chin was down on his lapel.

"It won't happen again. We have a plan to end this. Starting right now."

"And it is what?"

"Our men monitoring the transmissions from the uncle's phone now report that the boy and his uncle have just left. They may return. I am going there now. There was a reference to the father's apartment.

They may be hiding the boy there. If they don't return, I will proceed to the apartment and seize him there."

"Very well. Hawkin, I assume you will distance yourself from this?"

"Of course. I'll stay here."

"Very well. And Holz. No more songs! No more excuses! No more bungling! At some point, it will be too dangerous to proceed. You are a man who succeeded with difficult renditions in Mumbai. Mogadishu. Macao. Rio. And Khartoum. It's beyond belief that you can't do the same in Milwaukee."

"Yes, Sir!"

"Willis. Holz will brief me as he proceeds. But one thing. You don't fully understand Milwaukee. I'm beginning to. They're different from the rest of Middle America. They're cagier than you think. Intolerant of imperfection, and no respect for the inevitable. We'll be careful."

"Carry on, Gentlemen. Good luck."

Holz left for the parking ramp. He pulled slowly out onto Mason Street. He headed east to Prospect, then north. As he drove, he hummed to the radio.

"Hello darkness, my old friend. I've come to talk with you again."

Holz was suddenly in a good mood. The hunt. The snatch. The escape. The surprise and terror on the quarry's face.

He bent onto Maryland Avenue and turned west on Locust Street. At Booth, he turned north. He pulled over a half block away. The neighborhood was quiet. Holz locked the doors. He checked his vest. Garrote. Weapon. Chloroform. Gag. Rope. None would be needed, of course. Not likely. The team was on standby. They'd be there quickly to execute.

Holz walked by a few houses.

WHAP! WHAP! WHAP!

What the hell is that?

Holz saw Elmer Dick on Joe's lawn, beating out rugs. Elmer had rugs on the two small swatches of lawn by the walkway to the door. He was beating the hell out of them with an old wooden tennis racket.

What is this? A guy beats out his rugs on his neighbor's lawn to spare his own grass at 10 p.m. in the winter? This can't be!

It was too late to turn away. Holz hunched his shoulders and tried to walk past.

"You look familiar. Can I help you?"

The Mayor of Booth Street was on the job.

"No."

Holz hurried past.

The worthless uncle has him at the father's apartment. I've got him!

Elmer hurried into his house to telephone.

"Joe!"

"Yeah. Elmer?"

"Joe, the electric company guy just walked by. He walked away when I talked to him."

"What were you doing out there? It's cold as hell out."

"Beating out my rugs. Snow isn't too deep."

"Right. Okay, thanks, Elmer. I really appreciate it."

Elmer usually waits until April to beat his rugs out on my lawn, when he thinks I'm gone for spring break.

Bernie and I had just pulled in front of Jimmy's old apartment on Michigan when Elmer called. Bernie was sitting next to me, working a Rubik's Cube.

"Who was it, Joe?"

He didn't look up as he worked.

"Elmer. The guy went by my house. When do you think you'll be done?"

"A few more days. Frannie's getting me some time in the computer lab. I think I know how to do it."

"Okay. You can stay out of school a few more days. The sooner the better."

"Why don't we just give it back to them now?"

"They'll think you broke it, and they'll really be after us. When we give it to them, it's done. You got your stuff?"

Bernie threw his knapsack over his shoulder.

"Where we going?"

"Your dad's old place. It might still be empty. I kept a key."

There was no lock on the front door of the apartment building. On the ground floor, there were extension cords coming out from under Rosa Martinez's and James' doors, plugged into the landlord's sockets in the hallway. We went up the stairs. More cords were run out into the hallway sockets.

I knocked on Jimmy's old door, and immediately tried the lock.

"Bullet through the door, muthufucka!"

A man shouted at us through the door.

"That's what you gets! I don't wants none! Get out! Bullet through the door!"

We scampered quickly down the stairs. Rosa's door opened, and a large brown eye appeared.

"What's the matter?"

"Rosa, I thought Jimmy's apartment might be vacant. There's a gentleman in there who seems to want his privacy. We need a place to stay for a few days. Are there any vacancies?"

"No. Go someplace else."

The door opened wider, and all of Rosa appeared in front of us.

"There's a new tenant in there. All the stuff is gone."

"Right. But how about the paintings?"

177

I could see past her into the living room. A picture of the Last Supper hung on a side wall. But on the large wall over the sofa hung Jimmy's No. 2 Pencils.

"They're all gone."

"Rosa!"

I pointed to the painting.

"That's Jimmy's most important painting. *Untitled*! Do you know how much it's worth?"

"No."

Her voice was strained. She couldn't look me in the eye.

"Yes you do! It's worth ten thousand dollars!"

"Jesus Mary! He gave it to me! I swear!"

She seemed certain that I was debating whether to call the police. She shook slightly, darting glances at Bernie and me.

"Alright," I said. "But you've got to promise me two things."

"Sure! Of course!"

"You have to get a good frame for it. Okay? And keep it in your family. Leave it to your children. Don't sell it."

"Sure! Of course! I try!"

She was almost giddy at having been spared.

"Michael sold one, though."

In her euphoria she ratted out Michael.

"Michael sold one?"

She nodded vigorously.

"How much?"

"Two hundred dollars. For drugs."

"He sold a five-thousand-dollar painting for two hundred dollars?"

I almost shouted. She looked pleased at my feigned anger, pleased to direct it against Michael.

"How many paintings does Michael have?" I said.

"I don't know. A lot."

"How many do you have?"

"A few. "

She shrugged. "Jimmy give them to me. I keep them."

"You'd better. Don't go selling them for a few hundred dollars. Even a thousand dollars. You understand?"

She nodded quickly, her eyes gleaming as she counted the money.

"Alright. Second thing is this. We need a place to stay tonight, maybe for a few days. We're going upstairs to see Michael. But if he can't put us up tonight, we're coming back down here to sleep on your floor. Understand?"

"Yes. Yes."

She was anxious to close the door.

"What apartment is he in?"

"209."

"Okay. Goodbye."

"Goodbye."

She slammed the door. I knocked on 209. Rap music pounded through the door. I knocked again. The door opened. Michael looked at us and grinned. He had a bottle of malt liquor in his hand.

"Mickey mouf in the houf, And Donald Duck don't give a fuck!"

"Michael! Remember me? Jimmy's brother, Joe? And this is his son, Bernie?

"Whassup?"

We hit palms.

"Whassup?"

I could see two of Jimmy's paintings on the walls.

"Come on in."

Michael waved the bottle toward the sofa and closed the door just behind us.

"Glad you caught me. I been in Chicago."

"Chicago? What were you doing there?"

"Doin tha bitches."

"You've got some of Jimmy's paintings here."

"Yeah. Rosa give em to me."

"Yeah, right. Do you know how much they're worth?"

"No, man. How much?"

"Five thousand dollars. Each."

"No shit?"

Michael's shoulders spasmed. He pretended to be surprised. He took a drink.

"Yeah. Listen."

I sat next to him on the sofa.

"We've gotten reports of some people selling them for two hundred dollars. Five hundred. Even a thousand. That's a big mistake."

"Big mistake! Yeah!"

"Just because someone can make that kind of money on art doesn't mean they should sell it around. You know? It'll keep going up."

"Right. Right."

Michael drew out the words, anxious to agree, to get me out of there.

"How many of them do you have?"

"A few. Can't exactly remember. Keep em at my cousin's, you know. I let him have one. Yes, I did."

"Who else has them."

"Few my friend. They down on they luck. They pay me back. And Rosa. That bitch steal a whole lotta art. You know."

"Okay. I just want to make sure nobody's making money off them."

"Never! Won't happen!"

"Michael. You have one of the most valuable art collections in the city. Get a job. What if you get evicted?"

"You right! Right!"

"One more thing. Bernie and I are temporarily out of our apartment. We need a place to stay tonight. I'll sleep on your sofa. Bernie can sleep on your floor. Just for tonight."

"No problem! No problem!"

Bernie had been looking out from behind a shade as we spoke.

"Joe, there's a guy out there. He's been sitting in a car across the street for a while."

We looked out the window. A man sat with a newspaper on the steering wheel.

"Must be the po-leece," said Michael. "They always here."

"No, it's not the police."

I took Michael's arm.

"Remember last time we talked you said you'd help Jimmy?"

"Yo!"

"The guy's a sociologist."

"Muthafucka!"

"That's right. From Washington. He's after Bernie. We don't want to talk to him. Bernie, I think we're getting out of here. I've changed my mind. We'll stay somewhere else tonight."

"Okay."

"Michael, we've got to delay him. Bernie and I'll sneak out the back. We'll come around to our car. You go out the front and stand up to the guy. Whatever it takes. Just so we leave, and he can't follow."

"We handle the muthafucka."

Bernie and I hurried down the hallway to the rear door. We crept around the building. My car was maybe 60 feet in front of his. We stood behind the corner of the building, watching Michael in action. Michael rolled across the street, shoulders back, arms swinging at his side.

"Yo! My man!"

He beat on the man's window.

"I needs a job!"

The blond man got out of the car and pushed Michael.

"Get the fuck out of here."

He started to get back into the car.

"You sorry ass muthafucka!"

Michael was screaming.

"Bitch be havin my shortie! You know I gots a right to ask the man fo Benjamins muthafucka! Who you pushin?"

Suddenly, he fell to the ground and slid under the man's car.

"You gots to kill me, muthafucka!"

"Okay, Bernie, *now*!"

We trotted across the street toward my car. The blond guy didn't see us until we were getting in. He started in our direction, then turned to get in his car. I leaned on my horn until people opened their windows to watch. The blond man was frantic. He started his engine too, but he couldn't move. He jumped out and grabbed Michael by the ankles.

"Get out of there, you cocksucker!"

Michael kicked and drew his legs back under the car.

"That Chinese muthafucka represent in front of the tank."

Michael shouted from under the car.

"I represents unda the tank, you playa-hatin muthafucka!"

As I sped around the corner, the last thing I could see was the man crawling under the car after Michael, while more windows opened. A few men with silk bandanas knotted on their heads did a saunteroll over toward the car, to see why the blond man was pulling on the brother's legs. Why he was disrespecting the brother.

Chapter Twenty-Three

"How long do we have at the lab?"

Frannie shrugged as she pulled the car into the parking ramp under the student union.

"I got three hours. It's all I could get this time."

"Bernie? Is that enough?"

I looked into the back seat. Bernie was working a sudoku. He shrugged.

"For now. I think I got it. I want to test the algorithm. I'll need a few more hours later."

"There's a wrinkle," Frannie said. "The governor's announcing his education budget on campus. They're giving him a tour of the computer lab. But I think Bernie can keep working if he comes through. They're not shutting it down."

"No problem. Those guys won't go near a TV camera again. Might be the safest place to be."

"Where's Bernie staying tonight?"

"By Frank. He'll pick him up by Terry. Can you give Bernie a ride?"

"Where are you going?"

"By Jerry. I've got to put a stop to this. We're talking about some options."

Frannie parked. We left and walked the short path to the lab. I prowled around while Bernie was setting up. The place was full, mostly with grad students. Each on his own island, oblivious to everything, consumed with his research.

Bernie paid no attention to anyone. He was dressed in jeans, sneakers, and a Green Bay Packers sweatshirt. He looked like somebody's kid, playing on a computer while his father graded papers.

We sat there for a couple of hours while Bernie worked. I sat at a desk in the reading room across the hall, filling out applications for teaching assistant jobs in Poli Sci at colleges around Wisconsin.

I finally went back in and whispered to Frannie.

"I'm going. You okay with Bernie?"

"Sure. He has a little more time, and then I'll take him to Terry's."

"Okay. You take the car. I'm meeting Jerry by the bookstore."

As I started to leave, a door opened. A throng of people entered, along with three TV cameras. A man at the front held up his hand.

"Excuse me. Don't mean to disturb you. The chancellor is giving the governor a tour of our campus. The governor expressed an interest in seeing our computer facilities. Please continue working. Thank you."

The man stepped aside, and Chancellor Carlos Santiago entered alongside Governor Jim Doyle. Their staffs and the media followed. The governor walked slowly down the aisles, admiring the equipment. He would occasionally shake hands when he caught someone's eye.

A man in an elaborate Indian headdress walked directly behind him.

"That's Praisesong Brideprice," Frannie said. "He's a friend of mine."

I had heard of Professor Praisesong Brideprice. He was the Chair of the Department of Victimology, an interdisciplinary department that served as an umbrella for all Victimology studies. Brideprice was one of twelve Regents professors in the entire state college system. He did not publish. Twice a year he submitted to the Regents a video of himself performing a traditional dance, choreographed by him after much study of hundreds of Westerns.

No one had ever asked him his given name, believing it irrelevant and almost certainly a colonial imposition. In fact, he was born Tom Larsen, and went to work for a taxidermist after high school. But the wages were low and the work scarce. On reflecting that his maternal grandmother had been half Chippewa, he took a PhD on the Internet in Indigenous and Aboriginal Rights. He made a good living in academic victimology.

Governor Doyle and Chancellor Santiago stopped behind Bernie. Praisesong stopped, too, winking at Frannie. Bernie kept working.

"Your grad students look very young," the Governor said.

The Chancellor smiled down at Bernie.

"We allow a number of MPS students to use our lab. Some of their facilities are quite impoverished. We're very grateful for your support, Governor. Your budget will make a big difference to a number of students who are struggling to learn."

Bernie turned his chair around and looked at them shyly. The Governor stuck out his hand. Bernie shook it.

"What's your name, Son?"

"Bernie."

The TV cameras zoomed in on the exchange. Kathy Mykleby of Channel 12 wrote a few notes.

"Struggling with math, Bernie?"

"Not really."

"Attaboy!"

The Governor pinched Bernie's cheek.

"Have you gotten to square roots yet, Bernie?"

The Governor mugged for the cameras.

"Yeah."

"What's the square root of eighty-one, Bernie?"

Bernie frowned, looking for the trick. It was as if the Surgeon General had asked him, 'Bernie, do you have ten toes?' or 'Bernie, is your name Bernie, Bernie?'

The Governor smiled gently at the pause.

"It's nine, Bernie. You'll get to it next semester."

"Thanks."

Bernie turned back to the computer, and the governor went on to the next station.

Kathy Mykleby got set for a stand up right behind Bernie's chair. Her cameraman got a good shot of her standing with her microphone, Praisesong's magnificent feathers receding in the background.

"Toya, the governor announced his education budget today on the campus of Community College. He's touring the computer lab with the chancellor leading the way. We'll bring you the full details of his budget live at five. This is Kathy Mykleby reporting live at *12 on 12* for WISN."

She stared straight into the camera as it faded to a commercial. In a motel room near the airport, two men sat watching her fade from the screen. One picked up his phone and dialed.

"Hello?"

"Can you talk, Holz?"

"Yes."

"The boy was just on television. He is in the computer lab at the college. The governor is there, but he will leave shortly. Shall we meet you there to pick him up?"

"Yes. I'm going there now."

Holz hung up. He paid his bill at the Pfister Coffee Shop. His phone rang again as he drove out of the parking ramp.

"Please stand by for Mr. Willis. I have Mr. Hawkin on the line."

"Well, Gentlemen."

Willis was barely courteous.

"More adventures, Holz?"

"It was an unfortunate coincidence."

Holz was almost mumbling.

"A black man was looking for a job. He was drunk. He jumped under my car. By the time I pulled him out, they were gone."

"Why are idiots always attracted to your car, Holz? I understand you pulled your gun on a crowd. We are close to removing you."

"I had no choice. Some gang members attacked me, but I defended myself without firing my weapon."

"In Nairobi, you fired with impunity. In similar neighborhoods in Milwaukee, even displaying your weapon can compromise us. You know your assignment. Devise a strategy to take an unguarded sixteen-year-old boy in a small American city without inciting a mob. Is this too much for you?"

"No, Sir! One more chance. It's all I ask. The boy is at the College computer lab. I'm on my way there now. The team will join me there. We should be at the airport within the hour."

"Carry on, Holz. And exercise more discretion in carrying arms. Hawkin, you'll return this evening then?"

"As soon as the boy is on the plane."

"Very well."

Holz went north on Prospect Avenue, angled onto Maryland and parked a half block away from the Community College computer lab. He spread a map on the steering wheel and pretended to read it. A van finally pulled up behind him with two men in the front. Its rear windows were darkened. The driver got out to approach Holz's car.

"Is he still there?"

"I assume so," Holz said. I'll go in now. You sit in my car. Move it if the parking patrol comes by. Then, circle the block and come back."

Holz walked up to the lab's front door. He pulled on his gloves as he followed a few students in. They paid no attention to him. Holz looked briefly in each doorway on the hall. The large room at the end had a window in the door. He could see Frannie through the window putting on her scarf. Bernie stood next to her with his knapsack, ready to leave. Holz hurried out of the building. Both cars were still there.

"They're leaving."

The man got out of his car. Holz jumped behind the wheel.

"The two of you follow me. Stay in telephone contact. I will tell by the route where they're going."

He saw Frannie and Bernie emerge from the building. She dangled her car keys in one hand. They walked toward the student union.

"They're walking toward the union," Holz said. "The entrance to the garage underneath the union is on Kenwood. Follow me around the block. If they don't come out soon, I will go in to look for them."

Holz drove around the block, with the van behind him. He pulled over on Kenwood, 50 feet from the entrance to the parking garage. He didn't have long to wait. He saw Frannie pull slowly out onto Kenwood, with Bernie in the passenger seat. They turned on Maryland to head south. Holz pulled out into traffic several cars behind her. The van followed immediately behind him.

"They're turning right on Locust Street," Holz said. "Heading to Riverwest. That means the house of Professor Shit Theory, or the house of Joe Weber. You remember the configurations of each."

"Yes."

Frannie drove over the river, past the billboard for Ma Bensch's Herring, with its picture of a slightly deranged elderly woman peering out at the world. She turned left on Weil Street.

"They turned on Weil Street. The target is Shit Theory, 2815 Weil Street. You remember the door in the back from briefing?"

"Yes."

"One of you remain with the van. Park it on Weil Street a half block away. The other secure the door in the back off the alley. I will go in the front."

"It'll be difficult with the woman. And if Shit Theory's there, it will be three of them."

Holz turned the corner and pulled over, and the van came in behind him.

"She's standing at the door with the boy, but her car is still running. Perhaps she'll leave him there. The door is opening. Shit Theory lets the boy in. She's leaving!"

"Good."

Holz turned off his engine.

"Let's coordinate. I'm going in the front ten minutes from now. One of you secure the back. When I call for it, bring the van around back in the alley."

"Right, Holz. But are we taking one or two? Just the boy, or both?"

"I'm beginning to think they'll never leave the boy alone. We must take them both. We'll keep them apart on the flight. Perhaps we'll lose Shit Theory over Kentucky. He irritates me."

The passenger in the van got out. He was about five feet ten inches and 180 pounds. He looked like an accountant. He wore a khaki jacket with large pockets. The man walked to the end of the block, and around to the alley. The alley was flanked by garages for the houses on the two adjacent streets, Weil and Bremen. Between the garages were narrow alleyways for trash bins and recycling bins, perpendicular to the main alley. He stopped at the garage for 2815.

Two men in their early twenties walked down the alley toward him. They had baseball caps tilted to the right. Both their jackets were open.

One of them had a thick gold necklace down to his waist. The other had rings on all ten fingers.

The man in the khaki jacket paid them no attention. He stepped into the narrow alley between the garages and stood with his waist leaning against a garbage bin.

The two young men stopped to look at him.

"Ay, man. What you doin here?"

"I'm inspecting garbage cans."

"Ay, man, you ain't the police, are you?"

"No."

"You got a cigarette?"

'No."

"You got any money?"

"No."

"You got any drugs, man?"

"No."

"I think you lyin, man."

The two walked toward him. The man in the khaki jacket backed up until they were all in the bin alley, out of view from the garages.

"I forgot," he said. "I do have some drugs. Something for your nose. But first, the anesthesia."

He pulled a gun, and tasered the man with the chain. As he fell, he tasered the other man with the rings. He tasered them again while they writhed on the ground. The man with the rings started to hyperventilate.

The man in the khaki jacket put away his gun. With his gloved hand, he pulled out a handkerchief and a small bottle. He poured liquid onto the handkerchief and forced in on the first man's nose. After a minute, he went limp.

The man with the chain tried to roll over. The man in the khaki jacket took his hair in his fist and slammed his head into the ground. He forced a wet handkerchief on his nose. He, too, went limp.

The man in the khaki jacket replaced the handkerchief and bottle in his pocket. He looked around. No one walked by, and no one could see him. He rolled two garbage bins to block the view of the prostrate men from the main alley. When he was done, he walked out into the alley and around to the back door of 2815 Weil. He took out his phone.

"Back door secure. Are you going in the front?"

"I'm getting out of the car right now. Anybody see you?"

"Two banditos. They are now asleep. Electric and chemical massage. No one else."

"Will they wake up?"

"I think so. If they don't go ventricular."

"Okay. Stand by. I'm going in now. Move the van around to the alley."

Holz got out of his car and walked toward 2815. Terry Norris opened his front door. Holz stood still for a moment, then walked slowly. Norris didn't look up. He checked his mailbox and went inside.

"So how do you like the house, Frank? This is the first time you're here, right?"

Frank Weber sat on the sofa, admiring a bronze knock-off of a Remington rider on a rearing horse that filled the coffee table.

"Very impressive, Terry. Very impressive. Bernie, you should see what Terry has in his basement. He gave me a tour before you came."

"What is it?"

"Come on down. I'll show you."

The three of them went down the basement stairs. Frank opened a large metal chest on the workbench. It had hundreds of bottles and glass containers filled with chemicals.

"What is it, Frank?"

"It's a chemistry set. Just like I had when I was a kid. You don't see them very much anymore. This one's really great."

"I played around with it all the time through high school," Terry said. "Still do a little bit. I still restock it. It's kind of a hobby."

"Remember before the College expanded?" Frank said. "When it was just a big field on Kenwood, and no buildings? I was in high school. We'd fill lead cylinders with sulfur and charcoal and potassium nitrate."

He and Terry chuckled.

"Then we'd light a fuse to them, and throw a stone at the night watchman's door, and run. He'd poke his head out, and BOOM! It was like mortars hitting out in the field."

"You a bad boy, Frank! You take your bad self down to detention!"

The two of them chuckled until Frank remembered himself.

"Don't you do it, Bernie."

"I won't."

"I was younger than you. It was an experiment. No one got hurt."

"I won't. Hey Frank?"

"Yeah?"

"There's a man in the alley. I watched him walk by a few times."

Terry peeked through the blinds on the window.

"I don't see anybody. I'll tell you what. Frank, you and Bernie stay down here. I'll go upstairs and look around outside."

Terry went up the basement stairs. He went through the kitchen. As he stepped into the living room, a man in a black hood slammed him against the wall and held a gun to his head.

"What are you doing?"

Frank and Bernie could hear the fear in his voice. Bernie started toward the stairs. Frank took his arm.

"You stay here, Bernie," he whispered. "Go into the little storeroom there. Get behind those big boxes."

Bernie scurried into the adjacent room. Frank walked up a few steps and listened.

"What the fuck you doing? This is my house."

"You have something I want."

"I don't have any money. Take whatever you want."

"Where's the boy?"

"What boy?"

"Quit struggling. If you so much as move a muscle, I'll blow your fucking brains out! The boy. Bernie."

"I don't know. He's at school."

"You're lying. I saw him come in here. Is he upstairs or downstairs?"

Frank ran over to the chemistry set. He grabbed a small empty tin can from the paint shelf overhead. He opened the top and rummaged through the bottles.

"I don't know. He left."

"Take me to him. Or I'll have to shoot you and find him myself."

Frank set aside three bottles. He started to pour them into the can.

"Look. I know what you want. It's the stick. I have it upstairs. In my dresser."

"You will walk me up. Show me."

Frank measured the contents of the last bottle. He packed the mixture tightly into the can. He jammed in lead sinkers from Norris' tackle box to cap it. As he finished, he heard them enter the living room.

"So, Shit Theory, you asshole. This is what you give me. A statue of Ringo?"

"Yeah. It's on there."

Frank tiptoed up the back stairs into the kitchen on his long, skinny legs. He put the can on the stove and turned the gas on high. He tiptoed down again and held his ears.

"You're lying. He has no numbers in him. Let me guess. It's either 'Hey, Jude' or 'Yesterday.' Which is it, Shit Theory?"

"Take it and play it. You'll see what's on there."

"Alright, we're going down into the basement."

"I'm not moving."

"Get off that chair."

"No."

"I'm going to make this very simple, Shit Theory. The boy is in the basement. I can't leave you here alone while I go to the basement. So, you will come with me, or you will lie on the rug here with a bullet in your head. Which is it?"

"I'm not going."

KABOOM!

The top of the stove exploded around the kitchen. Holz and Norris hit the ground. Frank hurried up the back stairs into the pantry, grabbed the phone and dialed 911.

"Your location?"

Frank went looney into the phone.

"2815 North Weil! Bomb! Al Qaeda! *Bomb*! 2815 North Weil!"

"What?"

"*Bomb*! Al Qaeda!"

Holz ripped the phone from his hand.

"Goddamn you, get in the living room!"

He shoved Frank into the living room. Frank pulled his car keys out of his pocket as he stumbled in and pressed the red button toward the window. The car alarm in front of the house went off.

"I am very tired of you two assholes," Holz said.

He raised his gun.

People were coming out of their houses, looking for the explosion. A woman came out of her house across the street and started shouting, pointing at Frank's car, then holding her ears. Then in the distance, Holz heard a siren.

His hand trembled as he held the gun on them. He grabbed his phone.

"Abort! *Abort*! Coming to van now."

He started to trot toward the back stairs. Terry Norris jumped up to chase him. He grabbed some cans from the counter. As Holz ran down the stairs, a can of peaches hit him in the back. He stumbled and headed toward the back door. A can of string beans hit his right shoulder. Holz ripped open the back door and ran into the alley. As he jumped in the van, the siren was much closer. They sped away down the alley.

Chapter Twenty-Four

"Can you hold for Mr. Willis?"

Hawkin looked glumly out the window as he listened.

"Hawkin, what the hell is going on out there?"

"There have been complications. That's all."

"Complications? They tasered two drug dealers. Stirred up the neighborhood. They blew up Shit Theory's stove. And the police came? That's all?"

"There's some indication that Shit Theory blew up his own stove. Or Schrödinger's kitten blew it up. Remember him? The slippers? The chemist?"

"I'm trying not to. And am I to understand that someone threw canned vegetables at Holz, and sprained his shoulder?"

"The good news is that there was no ID. Holz was hooded. And the two drug dealers refuse to talk."

"So far. What do you recommend?"

"Holz is resting. He's depressed. And he's entirely unrealistic. He thinks that if this were Mogadishu, he could shoot a few people, throw them in the river, and take what he wanted."

"So, our man's depressed, is he? Well, this isn't Mogadishu. It's Milwaukee. And he can't shoot anyone and throw them in the river or anywhere else. Does he understand that?"

"Yes. I think he's been remarkably restrained given his history. And the assignment."

"Well, what's your answer? What do you recommend?"

"There is no change of objective. Holz has not been compromised. I would give him one more chance."

"And if he fails?"

"If he fails, we have two choices. Resign ourselves to the fact. Let the kid keep the number. The odds of its falling into the wrong hands are very low."

"That's unacceptable. Word will get out. And when it does, we're gone. We'll be disgraced. And what's worse, we'll lose a generation of support in Congress just when we need it the most."

"The second choice is to send in a larger team, with a new leader. Isolate all these characters at once. Search them all simultaneously, and all their houses and offices."

"I don't like that. They could easily hide it in a thousand places we'd never find. Barnes gave it to them in a box in the ground, you know."

Hawkin massaged his forehead.

"We know two things. They can't copy it, so there's only one stick. And when the kid goes to the College lab to work on it, he has to have it with him. The next time he goes there, we do a full sweep of the lab, the computers, the kid, who's with him, that whole part of the campus. Half-hour in and out should do it."

"Alright. We'll decide that later. Holz can try one more time."

"Can we withdraw the plane?"

"You've never been comfortable with that, have you Hawkin?"

"Frankly, no."

"Don't withdraw anything. Leave all assets in place. The easiest solution would be just to find out where it is. May have to question the uncle too."

"Okay. Goodbye."

Hawkin dialed again.

"Holz. Willis will give us another chance. What is your plan?"

"We've seeded the kid's mother's house. He hasn't been home in five days. Been with the uncle. She's worried. She let something slip."

"What?"

"He'll be with her tonight. She's taking him to church bingo. At St. Hedwig's on Brady Street. I'll have my team there. We'll separate them and take him."

"It must be a trap, Holz. The uncle knows a man with a hood drew a gun on two men and demanded the boy. You think he'll let his nephew go unescorted to a Bingo game with his mother?"

"Not unescorted. She said the uncle will pick him up after bingo. I'm assuming he'll have the policeman, Piano, with him. And some friends and relatives. But the boy must see his mother. She demands it. This is their time together."

"How will you take him? If you can't take him from a man's house, how will you take him from a bingo hall with a crowd around him? On the street as he leaves?"

"Too dangerous. The others will join him by then. We'll take him in the middle of the game."

"How the hell will you do that?"

"The lights will go out. People will scream and steal each other's money and boards. They're a rabble. Remember Puerto Rico?"

"I remember the fire. The lights in the casino went out, and the hotel automatically locked the doors to prevent thieves from getting away. People were trapped. Fifty people died. You aren't planning something like that?"

"Unnecessary. That was an accident. But lights out in a casino is a beautiful thing. Human nature asserts itself. There is stealing, assaults, and screaming. It will be easy to snatch the boy."

"You think a church bingo game in Milwaukee is like a casino in Puerto Rico? I don't like this. It's obviously a setup."

"You may be right. But we have limited opportunities to see the boy. We have to take advantage of all of them. My team is unrecognized. I'll stay outside. If I have the slightest doubt, we will abort and try later."

"I think it's too dangerous."

"What can possibly go wrong? If he is unguarded in the bingo hall, the lights will go out. He probably will not be unguarded. I understand that. I will probably not do anything tonight. I almost certainly will not. So how can it go wrong if I do nothing?"

"Holz. I've done this longer than you. I've learned certain things. An arsonist should never go to watch the fire. Bad things can happen when you do nothing. Even in Milwaukee. *Especially* in Milwaukee."

"I'll be careful. Your advice is good."

Holz hung up. As he resumed listening to the sounds from Sharon Weber's house, he heard Sharon's voice.

"When is Bernie coming home, Joe? Why is he by you so much?"

'He's got a big project. Could get a prize for this one. He says he can concentrate better. You'll see him tonight."

"What time are you getting there?"

"About ten. Jerry's coming with. I might get there early and play a few boards."

Holz heard the sound of a door closing. Then silence. He dialed.

"You will meet me at St. Hedwig's on Brady Street at six forty-five tonight. You remember the address? And the layout of the bingo hall?"

"Yes."

"Secure your gear. We may go directly to the airport."

"It is secured."

The afternoon went slowly for Holz. He arrived on Brady Street early and parked a few blocks away from St. Hedwig's. He walked East to Farwell, past the Italian restaurant Mimma's, an old drugstore with a lunch counter, and shops that sold turquoise jewelry and tie-dyed dresses. Then, back slowly from Farwell to the bingo hall, weaving his way through a throng of young bohemians and elderly couples. Past Glorioso's, an Italian grocery store that hadn't changed in eighty years, past Scortino's, advertising the best hot rolls and ham in Milwaukee.

He finally stood at the entrance to St. Hedwig's bingo hall. It was 6:45 p.m. Across the street, he saw the van. Two men got out to approach him. One wore a black nylon parka, the other a blue cashmere overcoat. They stood at the edge of the crowd that had begun to file in.

"What's the plan, Holz? Is he here yet?"

"Not yet. I want you two to go inside like everyone else. I will stay outside on the street. If you see the boy inside, call me. I will do the same if I see him out here. You know where the lights are controlled."

"Yes. We did reconnaissance this afternoon."

"If I give the word, one of you leave to move the van into the alley behind the church. When it has been moved, I may give the go-ahead. If I do, you have five minutes."

"For everything?"

"For everything. The lights, secure the boy, transport him to the van, and leave."

"And you?"

"Hawkin will pick up the car later and return it. I will ride with you to the airport. The flight plan is in order? Fuel?"

"All set. We can leave immediately."

"Attack, gentlemen."

Holz walked back across Brady Street. The two men stood in line to get inside, unprepared for the medieval circus that is parish bingo in Milwaukee.

An assortment of political candidates shook hands along the captive line.

A man and a woman stood apart at the door, handing out leaflets. The woman was attractive, about 50, wearing a sandwich board. "Capra for Mayor" they read, in large block print. She wore a straw hat.

"Capra for Mayor" she said.

She sounded sullen, desperate as she shoved leaflets at the people entering ahead of the two men.

Mark Capra, her husband, barely smiled as he extended his hand. Until two months before, he had been the frontrunner. An MA from Harvard in Public Policy. Long experience in state government. He was the most intelligent, most articulate mayoral candidate Milwaukee had ever known.

Then *The Journal* published an article, pointing out that he liked to read Dickens, that he had a "wine collection," and that he was always "fastidious" about his appearance. He had several bottles of Merlot and Cabernet in his basement, and he wore ties that went with his shirts. He was denounced as an "Anglophile" by a professor at the County Technical College. It spelled death for his campaign. *The Journal* gave the charge prominence and pronounced its opinion. Insufficient evidence.

He sank like a stone in the polls. Half the city thought he must be a coprophile, although they didn't know what that was either. Just being a "phile" was enough to indict.

He has too high an opinion of himself. A blueblood.

Although his father had never gone to high school, in fact he worked in a grocery store, the damage was done. His volunteers left. Contributions stopped. Mrs. Capra had to strap on the sandwich boards.

"I never met anyone in person before," a woman said.

She gushed as Mrs. Capra thrust a piece of campaign lit at her. Mrs. Capra grimaced. The two men also took the leaflets.

Inside was a sign-in table, with three ladies seated behind it, chitting and chatting among themselves. The man in the black parka waved them away when they offered to sell them bingo boards for the evening.

"No, thanks. Not just now. Thank you, anyway."

An old man and woman sat at a cardboard table just inside the door. A handwritten cardboard sign said BET ME $5 FOR THE MISSIONS.

The men in the parka and the overcoat stood off to the side. They watched a young couple approach the table.

""What's this all about?" said the young man.

"I'll bet you five dollars you can't guess the year my grandfather was born, within fifty years."

The young man laughed.

"We've got to play this. How old are you, old man?"

"Very old."

"What's your name?"

"Itchy."

"Itchy what?"

"Itchy Itchkowski."

"We can't lose this," said the young man to his girlfriend. "Let's say his grandfather was very young when his father was born. Let's say fifteen. The latest the grandfather could have been born is 1900. So, we go back fifty years, to 1850. That covers us from 1800 to 1900."

"I don't like it," the girl said. "It's crazy. Let's go in."

"No. This is great. I can't believe his grandfather was younger than fifteen when his father was born. If his grandfather was born before 1800, what'd he do, fight under George Washington? We have the whole nineteenth century covered. Okay, old man, here's five dollars. I guess 1850."

"Wrong century."

Itchy snatched up the five-dollar bill.

"What?"

"My grandfather was born in 1798."

"What?"

"He was," the woman said.

"He was forty-seven when my father was born. My father got a purple heart at Bull Run."

"What?"

"My father was seventy when I was born. I don't remember him."

"Come on. Let's go inside."

The man in the black parka whispered to the man in the overcoat. The two sat at a table in the corner, looking over the crowd.

Three very large men sat at a card table next to them playing three-handed Sheepshead. Gervase Hephner, Waldemar Schultz, and Gordon Werner were regulars on bingo night at St. Hedwig's. They'd come in second at the last Sheepshead tournament at German Fest and planned to win next time.

"You mauered, Gordon."

"No, I didn't. You want me to go in on the red death? And you need aces in three handed."

"Right. And you only had three. Mauer."

"Bull. You got schnitz?"

Gervase Hephner leaned over to the man in the black parka.

"Your weapon is showing, Officer," he said. "You may want to conceal it."

The man looked down at his jacket.

What the hell is this? I don't even see a bulge. Everybody here have x-ray eyes?

"Thank you."

The sooner we get out of here the better. I don't have a good feeling about this.

More than 100 people were already sitting at long tables throughout the bingo hall. Vendors in straw boaters wandered among the tables selling boards. The caller sat up in front, on the dais, waiting to call the first numbers.

Many players had small statutes and artifacts around their boards. Statutes of saints, of animals, of celebrities. Unicorns. Pictures. Glass. Most had several boards. Some had four or five. They had DayGlo magic markers to mark the numbers when they were called, to keep track of the boards. Many sipped from drinks. Coffee, beer, soda. The crowd was largely middle-aged or older, mostly women.

Waldemar Schulz sat down by the man in the overcoat.

"You new here?"

"Not really."

"Do you know the history of St. Hedwig's?"

"No."

"Hedwig was married to Henry the Bearded in 1186 when she was twelve years old."

"Hedwig was a woman, then?"

Schulz took offense. He fixed his extremely pale blue eyes on the two men, his head almost as big as both of theirs.

"Is that a joke?"

"No. No! Of course not. My error."

"Her son was Henry the Pious. He was killed by the Mongrels."

"The Mongols, was it? A damned shame."

"Frederick the Great built St. Hedwig's Cathedral in Berlin in 1773."

"Fascinating. Absolutely."

We better get the hell out of here. These people will smother us. Have to get to Holz.

The man in the black parka nudged the other. Bernie and his mother had just come into the bingo hall from across the room.

"Excuse me, I have to make a call."

He stepped to the back of the room.

"Holz. They're here. Did you see them outside? Anybody else with them?"

"I didn't see them. Must have come in through the main building. No one else out here that looks like police."

"What do you want to do?"

"Stand by. Not too long. Let the bingo start. I'll give the sign."

"Got it."

The man walked over to sit near the prize table. The other got up. He walked over to sit near the exit that led to the bathrooms and down into the basement.

Bernie and his mother walked up to the prize table.

"If you win? What prize do you want, Mom?"

Bernie peered at the table.

"How about that picture?"

He pointed to a large print of the Mona Lisa propped up against the table. Sharon squinted at it and shook her head.

"Nope. I don't like to hang pictures of people I don't know."

"I thought you liked the bingo at St. Robert's, Mom?"

"I like the popcorn at St. Bob's. But the prizes are better at Hedwig's."

Bernie's phone rang.

"Yeah? Hey, Joe."

"How you doing? I'm here with Jerry. We're down the block."

"Okay."

Bernie's voice was a little flat. I knew he was scared.

"Don't worry, Bernie. Some of Jerry's friends in the police union are around outside. They're off duty. I'll be there in a few minutes."

I hung up. Jerry stood next to me down in front of Glorioso's.

"What's the plan?" I said. "Bernie's scared."

"I called in the Dog Lady. It's her night off. She's doing it for me. She'll be here any minute."

"Who?"

"Karen. She's an officer on the Vice."

"Doing what for you?"

"She goes up to the guy . . ."

Jerry's phone rang.

"Yeah? Hey Karen. We're in front of Glorioso's. Come by here."

He turned back.

"Anyway, we've got to take this guy off the street. How much more time does Bernie need?"

"Can we give him ten days?"

"Ten days. Okay."

"But how you going to do it? Terry thinks it was the guy, but he didn't see him. Do we press charges with Michael?"

Jerry shrugged.

"Michael's done time. We can't go in just with him. And the other guys belong to the Two-Seven crew. No one'll believe them. The Two-Seven wouldn't talk anyway."

"So, what do we do?"

"Joe, there's only one crime that the D.A. cares about. That this town cares about."

Jerry can get condescending when he talks from experience.

"You want a guy locked up for ten days, there's one way to do it."

Karen Dudek walked toward them in a leather miniskirt with a foot of leash hanging from the dog collar around her neck. She was slim and quite attractive.

"Karen!" said Jerry. "Karen! Jesus Christ! Where's your teats?"

"I forgot them in my locker at the bowling alley. Don't start in on me, Jerry. It's my night off. I'm doing you a favor. Hi, I'm Officer Dudek."

She shook my hand.

"Well, there's nothing we can do about it," Jerry said. "Tonight, they're not essential anyway. You're going up to him."

"What do you mean?" I said.

"Here's the plan. The blond guy will find you sooner or later. Probably tonight. Karen trolls the street. She goes up to him and asks him if he wants a blowjob. It doesn't matter what he says. We arrest him. Ask him his name. He lies, right? We know he's using a fake name. We arrest him for obstruction. We got him."

"Is that, like, constitutional?"

"It is in Milwaukee."

Jerry put his arm around my shoulder in a fatherly way.

"Look, Joe. You know all the tourism everybody in this town is always talking about? New basketball arena, new convention center? Right? It's all bullshit. You know why Milwaukee gets the sorry ass conventions? The prison chaplains, and that? It's because you'd have an easier time getting laid in Cincinnati. That's why."

"I don't have all night, Jerry," said Karen. "I'm hitting it now."

"You remember the description."

"Yeah."

Karen Dudek walked up the block to St. Hedwig's. She leaned against the door of the bingo hall, smoking a cigarette.

Holz walked slowly down the other side of the street, speaking into his phone.

"Bingo started?"

"Going strong."

"Anybody in there? Relatives? Police?"

"No. Just his mother. Could be some undercover. Doesn't look like it in here, though."

"There were no orders given in the department. We checked. If there's a couple of off duty playing by accident, we'll have to take the chance. Give it five minutes. I'll call you back to say go."

"The kid keeps going over to check the prize table. It's near the exit. When you give the word, we'll execute next time he walks over."

"Okay. Time to move the van into the alley. One of you come out."

When Karen saw Holz, she stepped inside the hall to call.

"This could be him. Fits the description."

"I'm walking up the block now," Jerry said.

He had his collar up, and wore a Navy watch cap. He stopped at a meter and pretended to insert some coins. Then he walked back toward me, still talking on the phone.

"That's him," he said. "The guy in Three Brothers. Get him."

"Backup ready?"

"Backup ready."

Karen lit a cigarette. She walked outside. A man walked out of the hall after her and headed toward a van. The blond man stood across the street, pretending to read an advertisement in a store window. Karen strolled over to him. The leash dangled over her chest.

"Hi, Honey. You want some company?"

"Get lost."

The man kept reading.

"I'll suck your dick for fifty bucks."

Understatement is rare in Milwaukee, non-existent on the Vice Squad.

"I said beat it."

Karen pulled on her right earlobe. Officers instantly converged from all directions. Two men ran out of the alley next to St. Hedwig's, guns drawn. Another man who seemed to be delivering flour to Scortino's rushed down to help. Jerry Piano ran up the street to put a gun to the blond man's head.

"Put your hands on your head. Don't move."

The man complied. One of the other officers patted him down and pulled out the garrote.

"What is this?"

The man was silent.

"A jump rope for a midget?"

"What's going on?" the man said. "I'm looking in the window. She comes up. I tell her to get lost, and I get this?"

"Shut up. You were talking to who you thought was a prostitute. What's your name?"

"Herman Jones."

"You don't look like a Herman Jones. I think you're lying. You got any ID?"

"What the hell are you talking about? I left it at the hotel. You have no right to hold me. I want to talk with my employer. This can all be cleared up."

"Who is your employer?"

"You'll find out."

"Take him in," said Jerry.

The other officers handcuffed the blond man and walked him to an unmarked van.

"What's the charge?"

The man shouted over his shoulder.

"Talking with a hooker," Jerry said. "And if it turns out you aren't Herman Jones, we'll add obstruction."

They drove off. The man in the van sped away in another direction, talking urgently on the phone.

Chapter Twenty-Five

Wayne Hawkin sat looking out over downtown Milwaukee from his hotel room. His cell phone rang. He picked it up slowly.

"Mr. Hawkin?"

"Speaking."

"Hold for Mr. Willis."

"Hawkin?"

Lathrop Willis was angry.

"Look, before we get the others on the phone, what the hell are you doing out there? Goddamn it! The bungler solicited a prostitute in the middle of an operation?"

"It was a vice squad sting. He was set up. One of our men was walking toward his van. He said she approached Holz."

"Who cares? He's compromised. How did the others get away?"

"The man in the van drove back to his motel. He called the other. He walked downtown and caught a cab."

"What went wrong? Holz has been successful elsewhere. Here in Milwaukee, he's vandalized, assaulted, and arrested."

"It's an unusual culture. We may have underestimated it."

"I want Holz released, and the charges dropped. Immediately. We'll discuss whether and how the project continues later."

"Who's going to be on the call?"

"Dalton. And two experts on criminal law. Professor Norman Abrams of Yale Law School, and Paul Nilsson, a senior partner in Hunt and Bundy, the best law firm in Wisconsin."

"Wasn't Abrams in Keys?"

"Right. Collegium of 1989. He's the leading authority on Criminal Procedure. Wrote the textbook everybody uses."

"He wasn't Z, was he?"

"No. He was Periander."

The song for Periander popped into Hawkin's head.

And unless our Periander, gobbling like an ancient gander, should come over from the happy land of Canaan . . .

"And what is Nilsson's background?"

"He heads the white-collar crime defense team at Hunt. Best lawyer in Wisconsin. He and Abrams should get this right."

"How much have you told them?"

"Only that we have a Homeland Security agent who was wrongly arrested doing a security assessment in Milwaukee. Their fees will be paid by the Justice Department."

"What if they want to get more details for his defense?"

"It's classified. Unnecessary anyway. The arrest was bogus. I'll have them added now."

Hawkin stared glumly to the west, toward the county jail 12 blocks away where Holz was being held.

"Let me take roll call. Hawkin?"

"Yes."

"Dalton?"

"Present."

"Professor Norman Abrams?"

"I'm here."

"Attorney Paul Nilsson."

"Here."

"Alright. Gentlemen, I'm Lathrop Willis. We've already spoken. We also have Carroll Dalton on the line. Carroll's an analyst with Homeland Security. And Wayne Hawkin. He's a senior advisor in Homeland Security. I want to start out by asking Paul Nilsson to outline the legal issues. I'd like to discuss them one at a time and get the advice of both Paul and Norman. Paul?"

"Yes, thank you. Here are the issues. First, do we keep the present judge on the case? Frawley Watkins. Next, who should represent Mr., is it Jones? Third, what do we do with the obstruction charge? And how do we assert an entrapment defense at the motion to dismiss stage?"

"Right, "said Willis. "Give us your recommendation. And then let's hear from Dalton about your research on the judge."

"Alright," Nilsson said. "Under Wisconsin law, unlike in most states, you can demand a new judge. You can do it once. You don't have to give a reason. Here, we don't recommend substituting against Frawley."

"Why is that?

"There are forty-five judges in Milwaukee County. Ten of them are assigned to misdemeanors like this. If we bounce Frawley, we'll get one of the other nine. Several of them are excellent. But a few of them are unusual. One assigns shaming sentences. Makes people stand in a Square with signs around their neck saying they're criminals. It gets a lot of press."

"That's unconstitutional," Abrams said.

"Is it?"

Nilsson's voice showed some traces of the contempt that high level practitioners have for academics.

"If it keeps you out of jail on a plea bargain, who appeals?"

"We need to see this case dismissed," Willis said. "Would Watkins dismiss it, Paul?"

"I think so. Look. I'm no fan of Frawley. He's no scholar. But he's in the middle of the pack. *Anybody* should dismiss this case. So, why take a chance we might get one of the peculiar ones who might do something aberrational?"

"Professor Abrams?"

"It's a very interesting procedure. Gives you the right, no questions asked, to one substitution of judge. It's a legacy of the old LaFolette Progressive tradition. My own view is that this arrest is so obviously unconstitutional that it doesn't matter who the judge is. Anybody would dismiss it."

"Are we at least agreed that Hawkin will be released on bail at the hearing this afternoon," Willis said. "So, we can get him out of there?"

"Without question," said Nilsson. "I have never made a guarantee in thirty years of practice, but I will guarantee you one hundred percent that for this kind of charge, he will be released immediately pending trial. Almost certainly on his own recognizance. And at worst, for under five thousand dollars in bail."

"I agree," said Abrams. "It would be unconstitutional to deny him bail."

"Dalton?"

"I'm not so sure. Let me outline our research. First of all, the words most often used about Judge Frawley Watkins are strange and stranger. He's politically wired. He's very afraid of the unions and any interest group who can hurt him at the polls."

"Why would he care about that?" Hawkin said.

Abrams butted in before Nilsson could respond.

"Wisconsin elects its judges. The trial judges run every six years. It's another legacy of LaFollette."

"Well," said Dalton. "If he had a single good quality, many people out there think he'd be on the court of appeals. He's that connected."

Willis was becoming irritated.

"So, what do we do? Opinions, please. Paul?"

"Don't substitute."

"Norman?"

"Don't substitute."

"Dalton?"

"Get a new judge. I have an uneasy feeling about him. He may have very little respect for the law. There are always some forces at work that you can't predict analytically."

"We keep him," Willis said. "I think that the experts are right. Next issue, Paul?"

"Next? Who should appear in court with Mr. Jones. Our advice is that Hunt and Bundy not appear. It will elevate the profile of the case, which is exactly what we don't want. We refer many criminal cases to a lawyer named Steve Schaefer. He'll do an outstanding job. I'll advise in the background."

"Done," said Willis. "Next issue?"

"What to do with the obstruction charge. This is a little trickier. It's a felony to give a police officer a false name. It's frequently dropped in a plea bargain, but of course we don't want a plea bargain. We want a dismissal. What is the man's name anyway?"

"His real name is Dieter Holz. His operational name is Herman Jones. That's how I ordered him to represent himself in Milwaukee."

"Then we have an obvious defense," Abrams said. "He wasn't trying to mislead. He was required as part of his job to assume that identity. That *was* his correct identity for purposes of his work in Milwaukee."

"That's awkward," Willis said. "We'd prefer that his true identity not be put on the public record. But I agree with you otherwise."

"Here's what we should do," Nilsson said. "We'll get him released on bail today. Steve Schaefer and I will meet with the D.A. and explain the issue. There are certainly good arguments on reasonable doubt if it went to trial."

"Okay. Last issue."

"How do we get the case dismissed immediately on an entrapment defense? The challenge is that at the early stage of a prosecution, the facts in the charge are assumed to be true. I don't want to see Mr. Jones take the stand to explain anything."

"We should brief the constitutional issues," Abrams said. "From my research, the Milwaukee police only set up sting operations in high traffic areas for prostitutes. As I understand it, Brady Street is not known for that. Why were they there? Is this a sting targeted at one man? Shouldn't they be required to tape these encounters to document who said what?"

"That's fine as an academic matter," Nilsson said. "But it would drag things out. We'd be in the paper a lot. Look, my advice is we get him out on bail today, and I raise all this with the D.A. privately. He may agree to kick it. We'll bring motions as a last resort."

"I agree."

Willis sounded relieved.

"Alright, Gentlemen, proceed as planned. You're absolutely sure that our man will be out on bail this afternoon?"

"You can count on at least that," said Nilsson. "It's inconceivable he won't be."

"I don't know," Dalton said. "You're looking at this in two dimensions, in black and white. You're looking at the law. But if you look at it in three dimensions, in technicolor, a lot can go wrong. A lot has gone wrong. Don't be too sure."

"Thank you, gentlemen."

Willis sounded irritated.

"That will be all. Hawkin, I will call you later."

At precisely 1:30 p.m. in the Milwaukee County Courthouse, a thin judge with a bird-like head entered the courtroom.

"All rise," said the Bailiff.

The courtroom stood until the judge was seated.

Judge Frawley Watkins glared down at the courtroom. He turned his head like an ostrich at the slightest sound. In front, the prosecutor, Tim McGuckin, sloops of hair hanging over his ears, shuffled through his files. Dieter Holz sat in an orange jumpsuit, the uniform of the jail, at the table behind the prosecutor. His counsel, Steve Schaefer, sat at his side.

Frawley brightened when he saw Karen Dudek in a black leather miniskirt and a dog collar sitting in one of the witness chairs behind the lawyers. The judge clenched his fist in his lap.

The leash! She was wearing the leash! Damn!

He glared at the blond man in the orange jumpsuit.

"The Bailiff will call the first case."

"State vs. Herman Jones. Case No. 09 Crim 0913. Appearances of counsel, please."

"Here's what's going to happen . . ."

Jerry whispered to me as the lawyers introduced themselves on the record.

"Frawley has a serious jones for the Dog Lady. But he's strange. He couldn't get laid if he went to the women's prison with a fistful of pardons. I had Karen wear the get-up. He will have a diamond-cutter under his robe. Anyone comes on to her, he gives them an awesome fucking."

"Did we get him assigned by accident?"

"Let's just say he's assigned."

"But can Frawley hold him for ten days? For something like this?"

"Not usually. But I've got the room full of guys from the union watching. One of them will make a statement. And the prosecutor's on board."

I saw that most of the pews were filled with officers, in uniform and plainclothes.

A lawyer waiting for his case to be called later rustled some papers as he rummaged through his briefcase. Watkins cocked his head in that direction, staring like a bird without movement or expression. The rustling stopped.

"Your Honor," said McGuckin, "we are here for a plea and bail on two disorderlies and an obstruction. This is certainly an unusual case. The defendant identifies himself as Herman Jones, but he has produced no identification. You've already read the affidavit of Officer Dudek. Before your honor takes the plea and sets bail, we would like to put on a witness to one of the disorderlies."

"Alright. Mr. Schaefer?"

Attorney Schaefer rose.

"Your Honor, my client, Mr. Jones, pleads not guilty. This case is absolutely ridiculous. The undercover officer approached him. He told her to leave. He gave his name. As to the other disorderly, the man crawled under Mr. Jones's car. What was Mr. Jones supposed to do? Mr. Jones pleads not guilty. We ask for personal recognizance and we will file a motion to dismiss."

Frawley cocked his head at the people sitting in the back of the courtroom.

"I see my friends from the police union. Do you have a position on this?"

A plainclothes officer stood up.

"Your Honor, I am Sergeant David Click. I think I speak for all of us in saying we believe Mr. Jones, if that is his real name, is a potentially dangerous individual. The man has a fetish. God knows what he was planning to do to Karen when he got his hands on the dog leash."

Frawley turned red. He looked longingly at the Dog Lady. Karen crossed her legs slowly, giving him a quick Sharon Stone shot. She smiled at him. Watkins trembled and crossed his legs.

"We can't be sure of his identity," Click said. "We'd like to see him held until that is verified. And until we can be sure he will stay in this jurisdiction. Ten days should be enough."

"McGuckin, call your witness on the bail issue."

"We call Michael Parsons."

Michael rolled through the low wooden gate that separated the bench from the spectator section and walked up to the witness chair. He raised his hand to take the oath. He gave his name and address.

"Tell the judge what happened," McGuckin said.

Parsons sat down.

"I be unda the man car, that blond man. He pull my legs. Call me a name."

"What did he call you?"

Michael drew his shoulders back proudly.

"I don swear."

"That's okay," said Frawley. You have to tell what he called you."

"He call me a cocksucka."

"And then what happened?"

"Then the muthafucka grab my ankle."

"Silence! Enough!"

Frawley waved at him.

"We don't want that kind of language in here, Sir!"

"Your Honor, I wonder if I could ask Officer Dudek to approach the witness so he can demonstrate the actions of the defendant?"

Frawley nodded vigorously.

"Objection, your Honor!"

Schaefer was on his feet.

"This is absurd. It's simple. No need for a demonstration."

"Overruled," said Frawley.

Karen Dudek walked slowly up to the witness, her leash swinging over her breasts, which she had not left in her locker at the bowling alley.

"Alright," said McGuckin. "Mr. Parsons, lie down and demonstrate what happened."

Parsons left the witness stand and got down on the floor.

"The man grab my ankles."

Karen bent over and grabbed his ankles. I must say she looked quite fine as her leather mini–skirt rose higher.

Frawley could see the leash dangling between her legs as her head came near Parsons's ankles. He turned red as a tomato. His robe moved slightly in his lap. Unfortunately for Frawley, the only beneficiary that night of his mounting appetite would be Mrs. Frawley Watkins.

After a few more questions, Schaefer started his cross.

"You were under the car, right?"

"Yo."

"Why were you under the car?"

"Get away from him."

"You approached him, right?"

"I axe him fo a job. He call me a cocksucka and chase me unda the car."

"Alright, I've heard enough," said Frawley.

He took one more look at Karen. Then, he cocked his full ostrich head at an angle and glared at Dieter Holz sideways.

"But I haven't finished."

"You'll get a chance. I've reached a decision. T-T-T-Ten years."

"What?"

Holz's sphincter tightened. He leaped to his feet. "

"*What?*"

Schaefer leaped up with him.

"D-D days. I mean ten days. The not guilty plea is accepted. I'm taking it under advisement. Defendant to remain in the County Jail and return in ten days for another appearance. I'll decide on bail in ten days."

Frawley rose and started to walk to his chambers.

"Your Honor, you can't do that," said Schaefer. "With all respect, this is a typical entrapment disorderly. That's all. It's a clear personal recog. You can't just think about it for ten days."

"Go away," said Frawley. "Come back in ten days."

He disappeared into his chambers.

Chapter Twenty-Six

Hawkin's phone rang. He couldn't bring himself to answer. When it rang again a few minutes later, he finally picked up.

"Hold for Mr. Willis."

There was a pause.

"Hawkin, *what in God's name happened*? How could he possibly not have been released?"

"I don't know. Everyone agrees it was aberrant. Irrational."

"There's a lot of that going on. Look, we'll have the lawyers on now. They're counseling an appeal. But you should know this. I am sending more assets to Milwaukee to finish this once and for all. They will be there tomorrow. They will fan out through all locations where this family lives, and they will recover the stick! Do you understand me? I will not have a highly classified piece of property taken in this manner and not recovered."

"Yes, Sir."

"Alright. Join the others."

Hawkin heard the connections.

"Paul Nilsson, are you on?"

"Yes."

"Professor Abrams?"

"I'm here."

"Dalton?"

"Present."

"I have two questions," Willis said. "First, why was the man not released? And second, how do we get him released?"

No one jumped in.

"Paul?"

"Well, it was surprising. Shocking, really."

"You guaranteed his release on bail 100% "

"That was probably imprudent. I will say that what the judge did was against the constitution and all precedent."

"Clearly unconstitutional," said Abrams. "No judge can just hold a man for ten days while he thinks about it."

"And that brings up your second question," Nilsson said. "We've gone ahead and filed an appeal. The court of appeals is much more able than Frawley Watkins. They wouldn't tolerate what he did. Do you agree, Professor?"

"Absolutely. Of course, I don't know your judges. But from a purely constitutional point of view, you should appeal immediately. Any appellate court would overturn this travesty."

"Even in Milwaukee?" Willis said. "Dalton, what does your research show about the Milwaukee Court of Appeals?"

"There are four courts of appeals in Wisconsin. One sits in Milwaukee, and only handles cases from Milwaukee. The Chief Judge is Clarence Hochenmeister. Good reputation. Smart. Some are urging him for service on their Supreme Court. But you must remember something."

"What?"

"We've continually been surprised in this venue. The culture is aberrant. I wouldn't count on anything.

"Part of the problem has been some officers inside the Milwaukee Police Department," said Willis. "Who's the head of the police union?"

"Sebastian Raclaw."

"Sebastian Rack Claw? Look, Dalton. I'm not in the mood for bad Dickens. I said what is the man's name?"

"That *is* his name."

"Alright. I've had enough. Hawkin, make sure Holz returns to Washington as soon as he's released. I'll call you again shortly."

"Will do."

"Paul and Norman, thank you. We're done. Hawkin, call me back."

Hawkin heard their lines disconnected. He dialed.

"Listen to this," Willis said. "It's an intercept from earlier this morning. A call on a cell from the police officer, Piano, to Joe Weber. Here it is."

Hawkin recognized Piano's voice.

"They've appealed. Filed yesterday at four-thirty. Asked for an emergency release. They got to Hochenmeister on the Court of Appeals. His clerk said they're going to grant it this afternoon if we don't do something."

The next voice was Joe Weber's.

"What can we do?"

"El Futuro. I've got to talk to him right away. I'm meeting him at Webb's."

"On Farwell?"

"No. The one on Oakland."

"Do you want me to come with?"

"No. The transaction will be delicate. I'll go alone."

The tape ended.

"What the hell is that all about?" said Willis.

"I don't know. But we can't chase every half-assed comment they make. Who gives a damn who 'El Futuro' is? Abrams and Nilsson are certain that the Court of Appeals out there is sound. This is surely an aberration. It will be corrected."

"Should you go to the George Webbs? Just in case."

"And do what? Arrest him? He's an officer. Let him waste his time talking to a fortune-teller in a twenty-four-hour dive. Let's concentrate on getting Holz out."

"And more assets in."

"Right. And more assets in."

Roberto Gonzalez sat in the middle window booth of the George Webb's on Oakland Avenue, speaking on a cell phone. Coffee and toast, untouched, lay on the table before him.

Gonzalez was a community activist. He spoke for all people who were not pale and male. African-Americans, Hispanics, Hmong and Native-Americans. Labor and women's groups called on him for help. As he was fond of pointing out, the vast majority of the city was not pale and male.

Gonzalez's fee was $5,000 and he had more than 20 corporate clients. If your competitor applied for a variance, for instance, or for a permit from a city agency, you hired Gonzalez. He would appear as a citizen intervener, with a roomful of supporters, before the Common Council subcommittee hearing the matter. He had a concern, he would say. He had a sense that the committee did not have the full story. He had heard that the applicant had a bad record. On affirmative action. On free childcare. On sexual harassment. The permit would be held up, sometimes denied. Often, the applicant would retain Gonzalez for $10,000 to switch sides.

His many followers began to refer to him as 'El Futuro de la Comunidad'or the future of the community. He came to be known simply as El Futuro.

He found it convenient to conduct his business out of the Oakland Avenue George Webb's. He had no overhead, and it was difficult to serve him with process.

Jerry slid into the booth across from him, uninvited. They shook hands.

"Let me make it short," said Jerry. "I told you what I want on the phone. Judge Hochenmeister may release the man this afternoon. We want him held for as long as possible. Hochenmeister is running for the

Supreme Court. The trial lawyers already have a silver leash on his pecker. He looks good. But he can't stand trouble. He can't stand El Futuro and his buds walking up his driveway with signs. You see?"

"I see."

El Futuro drank some coffee.

"I will be equally short. Hochenmeister has been a friend. I don't want to hurt him. Of course, it couldn't hurt him to hold the man for a few days. My fee is five thousand dollars, and I will be happy to help."

He smiled at Jerry.

"El Futuro. We've known each other a long time. Joe and Bernie don't have five thousand dollars. I don't have five thousand dollars. But I have five thousand friends. The whole police force in Milwaukee. And in the suburbs. And all around the state."

El Futuro stopped smiling.

"And all the judges and their clerks. And the sheriff's deputies. All around the state."

Jerry shrugged.

"You hold a lot of demonstrations. You speak a lot in public. The rest of your life could be an unfortunate series of misunderstandings."

While Jerry and El Futuro ate and talked, Judge Hochenmeister was finishing a leisurely breakfast at his home several miles away. He smoothed out *The Milwaukee Journal*, scouring it for mention of himself. He found it. An obscure zoning case in which he had written the decision. His name in print. The race for the Wisconsin Supreme Court would be difficult. He needed all the free media he could get.

By the time he'd finished the newspaper it was almost ten o'clock. Hochenmeister had a light day ahead of him. One case even had the potential for free squeeze. The cretin Watkins had denied bail in a standard hooker-sweep disorderly. Didn't even rule on it. A no-brainer.

I'll spring the guy. Flog Watkins. Hochenmeister, the defender of liberty!

He was in a very good mood. That quickly changed.

"Honey," said his wife, "There are people in the driveway. And a camera."

Hochenmeister recognized El Futuro. Behind him were about 30 demonstrators and one TV camera, Channel 58.

El Futuro and his merry band of assholes! All they could get is 58? But maybe others are on the way?

Hochenmeister rushed out into his driveway, waving at the group.

"El Futuro!"

Hochenmeister forced a big grin.

"What a surprise. What's up, my friend?"

"Justice," said El Futuro.

Channel 58 was rolling.

"As you know, honorable Judge Hochenmeister, I represent those citizens who are not pale and male. An injustice has been done. A man named Herman Jones is in jail. He must be set free."

"Set him free! Set him free!" chanted the crowd.

Three men whipped out signs and held them in front of the camera.

"Set him free!"

"El Futuro," whispered a man sporting an earring and wearing a Bucks wool watch cap. "They want him kept in this time. It's the blond ugly one."

"Oh, right."

El Futuro held up his hand.

Hochenmeister started to speak.

"That's exactly what I will do . . ."

"No!" said El Futuro.

The crowd quieted.

"I misspoke. The prisoner is not LaShawn Jones. It is Herman Jones. He assaulted a member of the community. He sexually harassed another member. Keep him in! Keep him in!"

"Keep him in!" yelled the crowd. "Keep him in!"

The signs came down.

"But El Futuro . . ."

"We have a concern," said El Futuro. "We have a sense that you do not share the concerns of those citizens who are not pale and male."

"But I do. I do!"

"Many brothers are thrown in jail," said El Futuro. "No one releases them. They do hard time. Herman Jones must be treated equally."

Channel 58 kept rolling.

"But El Futuro, look . . ."

"We will be watching," said El Futuro.

The group walked back down the driveway.

"Give it much thought, Honorable Hochenmeister. The community does not want Herman Jones loose in society."

Hochenmeister trudged back into his house. A pig on a spit at the Kewaskum Labor Day spanfarkel had a better chance of getting free than Herman Jones. Later that day, the Court of Appeals, in an unsigned order, dismissed Herman Jones' appeal as not ripe for decision.

Chapter Twenty-Seven

A private jet landed at Mitchell Field in Milwaukee. Fifteen men descended from the side of the plane. The last to emerge was Lathrop Willis. The rest stood at the base of the stairs, waiting for him to lead them into the Signature lounge, the fueling station and reception area for private aircraft. They were all in their 20s or 30s, and very fit. No one spoke or showed any expression whatsoever.

"About twenty minutes," Willis said. "They'll be here in twenty minutes.

He made some calls while they waited. Finally, they heard another plane approach. It landed, and ten more men entered the Signature lounge. Willis waived them into the conference room inside the main door. He closed the door.

"Gentlemen, you have your instructions now. Who is assigned to Frannie's, the girlfriend's house?"

Two men raised their hands.

"And the uncle, Joe Weber?"

Three more raised their hands.

"And the mother, Sharon Weber? And the friend of the family, Shit Theory? The college computer lab? And the high school? The police officer, Piano? The professor, Frank Weber? And the father's former apartment?"

Hands shot up after each assignment.

"We have you dispersed in motels around the city. For an instant presence near any neighborhood. Any questions about where you're staying?"

No one spoke.

"Vehicles? Whose name they're in? Who's driving?"

There were no questions.

"I will be staying at the Pfister Hotel. So will Wayne Hawkin. My suite will be command headquarters. You know our objective."

Willis paused to assess his men.

"You've collectively conducted ops in every venue of importance to our country, on every continent except Antarctica."

One man raised his hand.

"I forgot. On every continent. Our mission is simple by comparison. I will remind you of it. A sixteen-year-old boy was given a stick by mistake. It contains a number of current interest that should not have been given to him. He won't return it voluntarily. He has in effect stolen extremely sensitive information, highly classified information. You will each secure your assigned area. You will find it and give it to me."

A man raised his hand.

"Mr. Willis, point of clarification. When we find him, if he doesn't have the stick on him, we're to call whom?"

Willis frowned.

"You were given instructions, and phone numbers. Two men who are already embedded here are waiting round the clock for precisely that call. They will meet you and assume responsibility. At that point, you have accomplished your objective."

"Okay. And if he is in the company of someone like the uncle, the friend, the professor. What do we do then?"

"Use your discretion. Above all, we can't be identified. You don't wade into a crowd and seize three people. But you are authorized to detain anyone with him if that's required to achieve our objective. The uncle or friend, certainly. If you're in doubt, call our command head-quarters before engaging."

There were no more questions. Willis left first. One of the men left with him and held the door as he got into the back seat of a waiting

Town Car. Willis worked his phone, ignoring the driver, as they drove into Milwaukee.

"Hawkin?"

"Right. Where are you?"

"On the highway, coming into town. Charming little place. Looks European. Can't believe it's caused us so much trouble."

"Well, the trouble's over now. You have enough men?"

"Plenty. His relatives and friends will have their houses surrounded. Starting tonight. Where is he now?"

"I don't know. They've managed to find safe houses."

"I should be there shortly. Meet me in my room. I should be checked in in twenty minutes."

The driver dropped Willis off at the front entrance of the Pfister on Jefferson Street.

"Stand by," Willis said. "I may need you."

He carried his bag to the registration desk.

Willis was splashing water on his face in the bathroom when he heard a knock. He opened to let Hawkin in.

"Well, it should be over soon. We have men all over town. We'll pick him up the minute he sees anyone or goes anywhere. His uncle. His mother. School. The computer lab. Anywhere."

Willis inspected the bar.

"Unsatisfactory, Hawkin. We must have Madeira."

He dialed room service.

"Hello?"

"Hello. Do you have a bottle of Madeira? An excellent bottle."

"Yes."

"The best you have. And a cheese. Do you have a Gorgonzola?"

"Of course."

"Send them to 1969. Two glasses. And a box of water crackers, an onion, and a knife to cut the onion."

"Yes, Mr. Swenson."

"You look tense, Willis," Hawkin said. "We'll have the stick soon. Relax."

"It's not the stick. Have you been reading the reports?"

"Yes."

"More and more evidence of Chinese and Islamic collaboration. But I can't manage to alert Congress. They yawn. Even our friends yawn and ask when I'll retire."

"Maybe they know more than we do. Maybe we're over-reacting. Give me your evidence."

"Arab investors are stepping up their presence in Africa. They work with Chinese engineers and Chinese intelligence."

"Give me examples."

"You know them as well as I do. Qatar loans Kenya three-and-a-half billion to build a port and some coastal roads. Chinese engineers and overseers will build them."

"Anything else?"

"Dubai funds a huge container terminal in a Djibouti port. Same engineers. Dubai also invests many billions in an energy sector deal in Nigeria."

"So?"

"China poured forty billion into the same area over the last decade. The result. We're shut out. And the Arabs and the Chinese start to own Africa."

"That could be consistent with simple investment decisions. Look, the Chinese also bought a trillion of our Treasuries."

"And the minute they refuse to buy more, we're in grave danger."

"But what's the strategic advantage for China, Willis? The Arabs are an unreliable and divided ally. Why do it?"

"They have common enemies. India is the historic enemy of China. And Pakistan. Russia is an historic enemy of Islam and China. Both China and Islam have fought against the United States. And the West."

"So, you think they're great friends?"

"Of course not. They'll eventually hate each other, too. But to stand by and let the East unite will put us in danger for at least a century."

"What do our friends in Congress say?"

"They don't pay attention. I need proof. And there's one thing that keeps haunting me, Hawkin.'

"What?"

"Why did a low-level Arab agent in an African country carry a number like that?"

"He was a messenger. Somebody didn't want us to know."

"I think you're not seeing it clearly. Why didn't they just transmit it electronically?"

"We'd intercept it."

"Right. But we couldn't decode it anyway. It would take thousands of years for any computer to arrive at the prime factors that code it."

"So, why did they use a messenger?"

"Because it was so sensitive that they didn't want us to know there was even contact between the sender and the receiver. A messenger is primitive. But wonderfully effective if he isn't captured. No one knows a message was even sent."

"But he was captured."

"Sure. And we can't decode it anyway. It was worth the risk."

They heard a knock at the door. Willis opened it. A young woman pushed in a small cart.

"Room service for 1969? I'm Brittney. Where shall I put it?"

233

"Over there," said Hawkin.

She looked closely at him.

"Who will sign, please?"

"I will."

Willis took the bill and scrawled on the bottom.

"Could you print your name, Sir? The hotel requires it."

Willis printed it.

"Mr. Ralph Swenson," she read. "Thank you gentlemen."

She left. Willis poured two glasses of Madeira. He cut chunks of onion and cheese and loaded them on a few crackers.

"I want you to listen to this."

Willis sipped as he pressed the button on a recorder.

"This is a phone call between Joe Weber, and his brother, Jimmy Weber, Bernie's father."

"When are you coming to see me, Joe? I have it here for you. You said you'd pick it up."

"Yeah. I will, Jimmy. Did you keep it safe for me?"

"Yup. It wasn't easy. They're always searching and stealing over here."

"I'll be over soon."

"You'll like it better than the Chinese face with the golf club."

The two laughed.

Willis clicked it off.

"What the hell is that? 'The Chinese face with the golf club.' I think they hid the stick with Bernie's father in the asylum. That's why we can't find it."

"It *is* strange."

"Go over there now. Bring a man with you. Interview Jimmy. Search him. We'll have the guards search his cell. This may be it."

"I'll leave now. Who should I take?"

"Take Chuck Dickey. He drove me from the airport. He's staffing us. He's very good."

"Right."

"I'll call him. I'll tell him you'll meet him in the lobby in ten minutes."

It takes about 90 minutes to drive from Milwaukee to Madison, home of Mendota, the principal state mental hospital. Hawkin's phone rang halfway there.

"Are you almost there?"

Willis was impatient.

"Maybe halfway."

"Chuck's driving?"

"Right. What's up?"

"Jimmy Sr.'s in a recreation room where he can receive visitors. We had his cell searched. No stick. They'll search him when you leave. See what you can get out of him."

"Will do."

"Call me when you're done."

There was no line at the front desk when the men arrived. They both passed through the metal detector. A guard walked them down a corridor to a massive door of bars. Twenty feet beyond it were more bars. Beyond that, the door was open to a room. They could hear a television playing.

"Put your hand up here."

Hawkin complied. The guard stamped his hand from an inkpad. He did the same to Dickey.

"What's that for?" Hawkin said.

"You hold it up to a light in there when you're ready to leave. If it doesn't see the stamp, the door won't open."

The guard opened the first door. They stepped inside. After it closed, the second door opened. A guard pointed to the open door.

"Jimmy's in the rec room. There's another inmate in with him. They're playing cards. Do you want to see him alone?"

"Probably. But I want him to be relaxed. Let's start out with them both, and you can come in for the other man in a while."

Jimmy Sr. and an African American man were playing cribbage when Hawkin and Dickey walked in. They ignored the television on the wall in the corner. They looked up from their card game to eye the intruders.

"Jimmy?"

"Yeah?"

"My name is Henry Jensen. I wanted to visit you to see if you could help me on something."

Hawkin stared at the black man as if he recognized him.

"Who's the other guy?" Jimmy said.

"Jim Evers. He's a friend of mine. Rode over with me. And who's your friend here?"

"Pervis."

The black man spoke quietly, identifying himself in a deep voice.

"What's your last name?"

"Pervis."

"What's your first name?"

"Pervis."

"How are you, Pervis?"

"Fair to partly cloudy."

"I play cards with Pervis," Jimmy said. "Pervis hasn't had a visitor in thirty years. He just finished three months in solitary."

"What for?"

"They say I ain't a people person."

"Did they say why?"

"They say I chew off my cellie's eyebrows."

Even Dickey flinched.

"Pervis," said Hawkin. "I've got to ask you this. Have you ever heard the name 'Wamba'? Ever heard your father use that term?"

Pervis shuddered. His enormous brown eyes, large as two small eggs, moistened. He dropped his head.

"Or your grandfather? Ever hear anyone in your family use the name? Because you have an uncanny resemblance to a man name Wamba I knew many years ago."

Pervis didn't answer. He got up and slowly started to dance in place. With perfect rhythm, he put one arm flat against his body, and flipped his hand out at a right angle. Then the other arm and hand. He jerked his head at right angles, to the right and then to the left. His feet kept perfect time to music only he could hear.

"Stop it, Pervis."

Three guards rushed in.

"No disruptions, Pervis. Sit down!"

Pervis kept dancing. A guard blew a whistle. More guards swarmed in. Pervis didn't resist. They took him two men to a limb and ran him out of the rec room.

Jimmy watched in silence and looked at Hawkin.

"Jimmy, sorry for the disruption. As I was saying, I was hoping you could help me on something."

Jimmy moved his plastic chair an inch closer but made no response.

"Your son, Bernie, did very well on a math test recently, and we want to give him a scholarship. I wonder if you could tell us where we could find him."

"Don't know."

"I understand. Part of the test was on a memory stick. I was wondering if he might have given it to you?'

"No."

"By the way. I was wondering. Have you ever heard the phrase 'a Chinese face and a golf club'? Does that mean anything to you?"

"Yes."

"It does? Can you tell me what it means?"

"I'll show you right now."

Jimmy jumped up, grabbed his plastic chair and brought it down as hard as he could at Hawkin's head. Hawkin managed to get his arm up in time to take the worst of it. The force knocked him on the floor.

Jimmy jumped on Dickey. They rolled on the floor until guards came running in, whistles blowing.

'Get him! *Get* him!"

They finally subdued Jimmy and carried him out spread eagled. Hawkin sat back in his chair, while Dickey examined his head and arm.

Chapter Twenty-Eight

"All operational heads on this call?"

Lathrop Willis was angry. He sat alone in his suite at the Pfister.

"Minor, here."

"Greene, the same."

"Peelen, also on."

"Alright. Let me give you a summary. You've already been briefed. Hawkin is resting. He managed to deflect the chair enough to spare his head. He has a dislocated shoulder and bruising on the right arm."

Willis paused. None of the men said a word.

"We have updated intelligence. Let me play a recording for you. It was a conversation this morning between the uncle, Joe Weber, and Frannie, his girlfriend.

"I'm scared for Bernie, Joe. He can't keep hiding and that. When is this going to stop?"

"Soon. The good news is he's very close to finishing it. The bad news is he needs a few more hours at the Computer Lab. Can you get him in?"

"I think so. But they'll be watching it."

"How about Saturday? It's the St. Pat's parade. Downtown will be tied up. The campus will be busy. Maybe we can sneak him in then."

"What time?"

"I don't know. I'll think about it. When it's not too busy, probably. What time does it open?"

"Eight in the morning. It closes at ten in the evening."

"All right. Let's think about it."

The tape ended.

"So," Willis said. "We know that a sixteen-year-old boy and his uncle and the uncle's girlfriend will be going to the Computer Lab on Saturday. Tomorrow. With the stick. We know the address of the Lab. And we have twenty-five men to respond. Do you think you can finally succeed in getting him? And the stick?"

He didn't conceal his sarcasm. No one thought it wise to answer.

"That's a rhetorical question, gentlemen. In case you hadn't caught on. I want twenty-five men at that lab tomorrow at eight sharp! And by ten that evening, I expect to hear that the boy has been secured, and the stick retrieved."

Still silence from the others.

"Peelen?"

"Yes, Sir."

"Minor?"

"Yes, Sir."

"Greene?"

"Yes, Sir. We'll finish this tomorrow."

"Good. That's all."

Willis hung up. He sipped a Cappucino as he read *The Wall Street Journal.* When a green light flashed on the receiver in front of him, he dialed up the volume.

"Frannie! You're still home. I had an idea. I just pulled up outside."

"I've got to go to the library, Joe. Give me a ride. We can talk in the car."

"Okay."

"I'll be right out."

The green light went off. Willis pounded his hand on the table.

Frannie locked the door. She kissed me when she got in the car, and I pulled out into the street.

"I was thinking, Joe. I got a great idea."

"What?"

"First of all, what's your idea?"

"Let's go in the evening, a few hours before it closes. We can lock the door to make it look like it closed early."

"I think it'd be too easy to grab Bernie when he walks into the lab. I don't even know who's listening to my phone, you know?"

"Nobody's listening on your phone. It wouldn't occur to them."

"Why not? You said they bugged your house. You don't even know how."

"That's different. Me, they expect to see Bernie."

"You know that Henry Jensen guy? Brittney told me after class she saw him again. In a suite with another guy, named Ralph Swenson."

"Did she get a picture?"

"No. She didn't have her cell with her. It was room service. Room 1969."

"What's your idea?"

"Anyway, Bernie can't go as Bernie. But he can go as Bernadette!"

"What the hell is that?"

"Listen to me. Pearls for Girls is taking the girls tomorrow morning to the Computer Lab. Bernie'll dress like a girl and go with. He'll do his work and leave with them. No one will know."

"That's ridiculous. What's Pearls for Girls?"

"You know what it is. We take kids from the inner-city places. To the theater. A museum. The campus. To show them there's a different life out there. I've only been doing it for a year."

"Oh, yeah. Right. But that's still ridiculous."

"It's not ridiculous. If he walks in with you and me, and there's anybody waiting for him, they'll get him. So, you and I don't go with."

"He can't go alone."

"My students have volunteered to go this time anyway. Ashleigh and Brittney and Nicole. I'll tell them to dress Bernie like a girl and bring him in the group."

"Bernie doesn't look like a girl."

"Wait til you see him in clothes. He's only sixteen, for God's sake. He'll look the part in a wig and makeup and a dress."

"Oh, God. I wish this had never started. Maybe I can get Jerry and his friends to come with."

"The Department won't assign them. He said so. And some of his friends are working overtime at the parade. Look, if no one's after Bernie there, it doesn't matter. And if they are, it'll help. They won't expect him to come in with the Pearls."

"Okay. Try it."

Frannie got out in front of her office and waved as the car sped away. She took the elevator to her third-floor office. The Department of Victimology was right next to the Spanish Department. Praisesong Brideprice's door was open.

"Praisesong!" Frannie said. "Do you want some coffee?"

She peeked inside. Praisesong was sitting at his desk, head in his hands. A woman with long grey hair tied up in a ponytail was gesturing at him as she spoke. She wore bib overalls and work boots.

"Bicycle Fish Press is interested, Praisesong. They'll publish it. When the Department Heads vote on increments, tell them I have a book offer. I want you to protect my onions."

"Coffee! Yes. Thanks!" Praisesong said, relieved to be interrupted. "Frannie, come on in. You know Cassandra, don't you? She's Vice Chair of Victimology and Professor of Women's Studies. Cassandra, this is Frannie Ferraro. Frannie's a TA in Spanish."

"Sure, of course," Frannie said.

They shook hands.

"Tell Frannie about your new book, Cassandra."

Praisesong started to gnaw his way out of the trap.

"Fascinating thesis."

"The working title is *Title Nine and Buzkashi,*" said Cassandra. *"Towards a Sustainable Afghanistan,"*

"That's the headless goat thing," said Praisesong. "They cut off a goat's head and play polo with the body."

"The thesis is that women should show up at the matches and they should demand to play," Cassandra said.

Frannie frowned.

"They'd be killed, wouldn't they? Just for showing up? Forget about playing."

Cassandra shrugged.

"We might lose a few. Martyrs to the movement. But diversity is paramount. Indigenous customs must be respected."

She bore down on Frannie.

"But that's not the main issue. The point is, let's say the University of Afghanistan has a Buzkashi team. They give fifteen scholarships. They'll have to give fifteen scholarships to the women's team also."

"I thought it was a rural thing. Do they even have a University of Afghanistan?"

"Whatever. I'll find out. But whatever they have."

"That's gross. You think any woman'll want to swat a headless goat?"

"Could be collaborative Buzkashi. They could help each other drag the goat over the goal. Look, the key insight is no walk-ons. The men's Buzkashi team can't permit walk-ons to skew the numbers. They can only have the same number as the women's team. Do you see the beauty of it?"

"They don't have Title Nine over there, do they? I mean, I doubt it."

"Have to pass it in the Afghan parliament."

"Do they have a parliament?"

"Whatever. I'll find out. They may have to start one."

"I have to cut this off," said Praisesong. "Much as I enjoy it. I'm doing the department budget. I'll be here all weekend as it is."

Frannie went into her office. She took the phone off the receiver and started to dial. Halfway through, she stopped and stared at the phone. She put it back on the cradle and walked back into Praisesong Brideprice's office. Cassandra was gone.

"Praisesong. I wonder if I could use your phone to make a call. Local call."

"Sure."

He didn't look up.

"There's a phone in the conference room if you want."

Frannie went into the conference room off the Chairman's office. She closed the door and dialed.

"Nicole? Frannie. I need a huge favor. What? You're not going to believe this. You're sworn to secrecy. Call Ashleigh and Brittney. You know Joe's nephew, Bernie. Yes, he's cute. Listen, tomorrow at seven a.m. he'll come to your apartment. Here's what I want you and the girls to do. What? Don't ask questions. It's a spoof. I'll tell you later. Here it is . . ."

Chapter Twenty-Nine

Bernie sat on the sofa at Nicole's apartment. He didn't look happy at the turn of events.

"I don't think it's a good idea, Frannie. I'm not going to look right. It won't fool anybody."

"Don't sell yourself short. Joe and I talked about this. You need a couple more hours in the lab to finish, right? It's the only way. You'll be surprised how good you look."

Nicole walked into the room in her bra and a slip. She had a couple of dresses on her arm. Bernie kept sneaking peeks at her as she held them up to show Frannie.

"Go try these on, Bernie."

Nicole gave him a hug.

"You're cute. You'll be a cute girl."

Bernie took the dresses. They heard a knock on the door as he walked into the bathroom. Brittney and Ashleigh came bursting in.

"Where's Bernie? He's so cuuuuute! Where is he?"

"He's changing."

"That's so neat! What about his hair?"

"I have a wig from the theater department."

Bernie walked morosely out of the bathroom in an ankle length blue dress with puffy sleeves. He slunk into the living room for inspection. The girls squealed with delight.

"You're so cuuute, Bernie!"

Ashleigh hugged him. Bernie cheered up considerably when Nicole gave him a hug, pressing her large breasts against his chest.

"Did you bring the wig?"

Brittney pulled a blonde pigtail wig from a shopping bag. Nicole wrinkled her nose.

"That's like Heidi meets the Von Trapps. It doesn't look real."

"No problem. It'll be fine."

Brittney stuck it on Bernie's head. She took off her pink, Green Bay Packers hat with the long bill and put it on the wig.

"See."

The others circled Bernie, inspecting her work.

"Maybe. Maybe. But the shoes'll have to go."

Nicole darted into her bedroom and came out with a pair of pink Nike's.

"Try these on."

Bernie kicked off his shoes and tried on the sneakers.

"Not bad. Not too tight."

"I've got big feet," said Nicole. "Bernie, you're the cutest girl!"

They gathered around him pinning the wig, straightening the dress, and adjusting the cap.

"Now remember, don't talk too much."

Nicole shook her finger at him.

"Your voice is kind of deep for a girl."

"You'll say he has laryngitis," Frannie said. "Okay, Bernie. Now, practice walking."

Bernie lumbered across the living room.

"Not like that, Bernie."

Ashleigh walked slowly across the rug.

"That way. See?"

He practiced more while Nicole and Brittney offered encouraging words.

"Good. Now what exactly are you doing this for?"

"We're trying to fool some guys for a while. The Pearls for Girls are supposed to have the lab this morning. I've got to be there."

The three girls fussed over him some more. Ashleigh put on some makeup. When they were done, they gave him a group hug.

"Let's go, girls," Frannie said. "I'm going to my office. Bring him there when you're done."

They walked toward the computer lab. Nicole and Brittney walked at Bernie's side, with Ashleigh directly behind him. Other girls streamed in with them. Junior high and high school students, some in dresses, some in jeans, flanked by volunteers from the Pearls for Girls Board. They were mostly African American, excited and bright eyed.

A man on a ladder was cleaning the gutters near the front door. Another man stood at the foot. Both wore Community College work shirts. They watched as the girls filed in.

The girls began to take seats in front of computer screens in the main room. Men in jackets and open collared shirts walked through from time to time. Nicole showed Bernie to a large screen in an office, off the main floor.

"The chairman of the Computer Science department said Frannie could use this," she said. "It's the fastest one they have and the most powerful."

"I'm near the end," Bernie said. "I just have to test it now. This should be it."

Three men stood in the front of the room. One was short, balding, in his mid-forties, dressed in a sweater and khakis. The other man was in his mid-thirties, tall, wearing sport jacket and dark slacks. A third man with a sad face stood next to them. He tapped a glass on the table until the room grew quiet.

"I want to welcome Pearls for Girls," he said. "My name is Peter Curran. I'm an assistant professor of Computer Science. It's my

247

pleasure to introduce two distinguished guests. State Representative Mike Porco of Madison, the Chairman of the Budget Committee, and State Senator Blaise Nuckles of Alma, the Vice Chairman. They are responsible for drafting the budget. Of course, we deeply appreciate their support."

Curran was a man unaccustomed to lying. He choked slightly as he praised them.

The short man grinned at the girls, like a minor British functionary inspecting an African village in the 19th Century.

"Thank you, Professor. Thank you. Senator Nuckles and I have heard all the horror stories about Milwaukee Public Schools. And of course, all the stories about women and science. Too few women, and too little science."

He paused to let them ponder the depth of his remarks.

"Well, Senator Nuckles and I are here to make a statement. Yes We Can! Math! Yes We Can! So, please start your assignments, and the Senator and I will inspect your work."

Not a single girl clapped. They stared at him, then turned to their screens. The pair of woolybacks strutted down the front aisle of girls at work. The scoundrels enjoyed their yearly stumble, burping and yawning, into Milwaukee, the state's revenue engine, to pity the people who fed them.

Porco and Nuckles stopped behind the girl nearest to Bernie. She was about 12, neatly dressed, with neatly braided hair and glasses.

"What are you working on, young lady?" said Nuckles.

"Stuff."

"What's your name?"

"Latisha."

"Way to go, Latisha," Porco said. "Let me give you a test. Two times X equals four. What is X?"

"No problem. Write it down."

Porco wrote it in her notebook.

"Two," she finally said.

"Very good, young lady."

Porco patted her on the head.

"We don't get that stuff til next year," she said. "I taught myself it."

"Very good."

Curran guided Porco and Nuckles over to Bernie. Bernie was hard at work. His bodyguards, Ashleigh and Brittney and Nicole, parted to let them in.

"What's your name, young lady?" said Nuckles.

Bernie didn't bother to look up. He kept on working.

"It's Bernadette," Ashleigh said. "She has laryngitis."

"Bernadette, that's a pretty name. What are you working on? My, there're a lot of numbers on the screen."

Bernie continued to ignore Nuckles.

"School stuff," said Brittney.

"Way to go, Bernadette," Porco said. "Let me give you a test. X times X equals a hundred. What is X?"

Bernie rolled his eyes. He whispered to Nicole.

"Bernadette says ten and minus ten."

"Bernadette."

Porco smiled tolerantly.

"There can only be one answer. X can be only one number. There's just one X. Just like there's only one Bernadette. You aren't two people, are you? A boy and a girl? Well, X isn't two things either."

Curran was mortified. He tried to hurry them on.

Porco dropped to one knee.

"The answer's ten. Bernadette, I solemnly swear to provide the funds necessary to get you math literate. To ease your phobia. What do you think of that?"

"Okay," said Bernie, in a fake whisper.

Curran pushed Porco and Nuckles to the next station.

At 10:30, Bernie sat back in his chair.

"I'm done," he said to Nicole. "I've got the factors."

He held up the stick and another flash drive.

"Here's the original number. And here's the answer."

"Way to go, Bernie!"

The girls hugged him.

"Let's go."

"I've got to go to the bathroom."

"Go ahead. Then, we'll leave."

Bernie walked out into the empty hallway. He pushed open the door to the men's room. A man in a jacket and no tie was washing his hands.

"Wrong room, little girl."

Bernie turned immediately and left. The man dried his hands. As he left, he saw Bernie disappear back into the Computer Lab.

"A guy saw me," Bernie said to his bodyguards. "In the men's room."

"We should have taken you to the ladies' room. Are you ready? Let's go."

"He'll see us."

"We'll go out the side."

All four hurried out the side door. They saw two men walking slowly behind the building. The man in the hallway pulled out his cell.

"Mr. Willis? Minor here?"

"Yes. Is he there?"

"I don't know. It's been all girls this morning. A group called Pearls for Girls. But one of them walked into the men's room. She left when she saw me. Then, I saw her walk back into the Lab. Not into the ladies' room."

"What? Go back in the Lab immediately! Identify her position. Have the team move in immediately. Seize her when she leaves the room again."

"Yes, Sir."

The man walked back into the Lab. He walked slowly down the aisles. No one paid attention to him. He called again.

"Sir. Bad news. She's gone."

"What?"

"She's not in the Lab."

"Wouldn't you have seen her leave? She may be hiding."

"There's a side door. Fire exit. She must have left there."

"Damn it, man! Here's what I want you to do. Leave half your men at the Lab. It's not certain she's . . . he's our target. She may still be on campus. Send a man to Frank Weber's office. You go to the girlfriend Frannie's office. You have the map of the locations?"

"Yes, Sir."

"Scatter the rest of the men. Send them to the mother's. The uncle's. Shit Theory's. The police officer, Piano's. And then, the father's old apartment. Send them now!"

"Yes, Sir!"

Minor went into action. Within minutes, men hurried from the building to their assignments. Minor left the Lab. He walked the long diagonal path to Curtin Hall.

The light was on in Praisesong Brideprice's office when Bernie and his Angels got to the floor. Frannie was in Praisesong's office talking with him.

"Budget. Goddamned budget," he was saying.

They heard voices from the classroom down the hall.

"Who's having class, Praisesong?" Frannie said.

"Cassandra. Grad Seminar. Meets Saturday morning. 'Pre-Enlight-enment Victimization.'"

They went into Frannie's office.

Nicole looked excited.

"So, what's going on, Frannie? Really? Who's after Bernie?"

"I think like industrial spies and such. They think Bernie's onto something they can steal."

"That's so neat!"

Ashleigh squealed as she gave Bernie a hug.

"You're so cute, Bernie. You're so smart!"

She hugged him again.

"Easy, honey. He's sixteen."

"What are you onto, Bernie?"

Bernie didn't answer. He turned back from the window.

"Frannie, he's coming up the path. The guy in the men's room. He's coming here."

The Angels swung into action.

"Lock the door," Frannie said. "You stay here with Bernie. I'll get Praisesong."

Frannie ran into his office.

"Praisesong, I'm in trouble. I need your help."

"What is it?"

"Joe's niece, Bernadette. Some men are after her. I have to get her out of here. One of them's coming into the building. Now!"

Praisesong jumped up.

"No problem. I've got my Harley downstairs. I'll get her out of here. You call the police."

"But this guy'll see you. He'll stop you."

"I'll get Cassandra. These goddamn child molesters. Cassandra's into that big time."

Praisesong and Frannie ran down the hall. They hurried through the open door. Cassandra was gesturing while she read from a book.

"Chairperson Brideprice!" she said. "What a surprise! To what do we owe this honor?"

"Can I speak to you?"

He took her aside.

"Let me put it in ducks and bunnies. A child molester is in the hall-way. He's after Frannie's niece. A virgin bride thing. Like a Warren Jeffs thing? You know? I mean just an example."

Cassandra was all over that kind of talk. All over it. This was meat to a wolf. Her ears seemed to flatten against her head.

"We need to rescue her. He's got to be stopped. Could you, you know, you and some of your, uh, burlier students go out and confront him. I'll call the police and get her out down the stairway."

Cold lasers shot out of Cassandra's eyes as she turned to her class.

"A teenage girl in trouble out in the hallway. A man from Warren Jeffs's compound is in the building to kidnap her. They want a virgin bride. We are going to stop him. Now!"

This was taking a blowtorch to dead branches after a drought.

How sweet does it get? Thank you Jesus! Every demon from hell in the hall outside of Pre-Enlightenment Vic, and Cassandra leading the platoon?

The whole class scrambled for the door. Minor was coming down the hall. It was bad enough that he was the only white man in sight. And then Frannie fingered him.

"It's *him*! Warren Jeffs's son!"

Impressions from a dozen lifetimes of insult and abuse flooded their brains. *Warren Jeffs sent a man to get a teen bride in Milwaukee? I thought he was in jail. His son was there to kidnap the bride? To get a virgin bride. The last virgin at Community. I don't think so!"*

"Buzkashi!" said Cassandra.

"Buzkashi!"

The class roared back, without the slightest idea what it meant. They advanced on the goat. Minor stopped. He started to back up slowly, as they bore down on him, wall to wall. Praisesong peeked around his office door.

"Let's get the hell out of here, Kid."

They ran down the stairs to the first floor, out to the bikes. Praisesong's Harley was parked near the building.

"It'll be a little chilly, Kid. We're not going far."

"Where are we going?"

"The museum. We can hide there."

Praisesong opened it up. The bike skipped off the sidewalk into the street. They sped south on Downer Avenue to the downtown. They stopped for a light at Brady and Farwell. Praisesong looked around at his passenger.

"What happened to your hair?"

"My wig blew off."

"You ain't a tranny, are you?"

"No. I'm in disguise."

"What's your name?"

"Bernie."

"That's all right, then."

Praisesong was down with that. He himself had been in disguise his entire life.

Chapter Thirty

Lathrop Willis' phone rang.

"Who the hell is this?"

"Minor, Sir."

"Where are you, Minor?"

"Outside of Curtin Hall."

"Did you get the girl?"

"No. A bunch of students came running at me in the hallway. I saw the girl run down the stairs with an Indian while I fought them off. Someone outside told me they went off on a motorcycle."

"The girl got away with an Indian while you were fighting students in the hallway. Minor, what the hell are you doing? How did any of the students even notice you?"

"I don't know, Sir."

"We monitored the police scanner. They reported a motorcycle speeding downtown. It stopped at the museum. Take your men down there now."

"Do we need to worry about the police?"

"They're tied up at a parade. Shouldn't be any at the museum. Take some men to the museum. Leave a detail at the computer lab."

"Yes sir."

Bernie and Praisesong pulled up behind the museum on Wells Street. Praisesong parked by the back door.

"We'll go in this way."

"Will they let us in?"

"I keep a key. I used to work here stuffing animals."

The back rooms were empty. Praisesong paused in a room with stuffed animals. He picked up a bobcat.

"I stuffed this damned thing. It's bad work, Bernie. Don't do it. Get some college in."

Bernie lifted the bobcat.

"Is this heavy, hey! I thought it'd be empty. You know. Just the fur and the skin and that.'

"It's the base. They weight it pretty good."

They passed through more rooms until they got to a hallway.

"Who's that a picture of?" Bernie said.

"Owen Gromme. You ever heard of him?"

"No."

"Famous painter. Wildlife. He worked here for forty years."

"Will we meet him?"

"He's dead."

Praisesong pointed out in the hallway.

"There's the back of the exhibits. You know, the early Norwegian immigrant household, and that? Irish household? Indian camp?"

"Yeah."

Bernie walked up to one and peeked through the curtain. It was the early German household. A realistic statue of a woman in a dirndl was bent over, placing a loaf of bread in an oven. All of the furnishings and kitchenware were mid-19th century. A handful of people walked slowly past it on the other side of the glass in the public hallway.

"Hey Praisesong?"

"Yeah?"

"How are we going to get out of here?"

"We'll wait a little bit, and then I'll take you home. Where do you want to go?"

"I'm staying by Nicole's. In Brewers Hill."

"No problem."

They roamed through the back rooms for a while. Bernie poked his head through a curtain again to see the early Polish household.

"Praisesong!"

"What?"

"I saw him. The guy in the hallway near your office. He was just walking by."

"Let's get the hell out of here."

"What if they're out back, too?"

They heard men's voices in the room near the back door. The voices were getting nearer.

"Bernie! We gotta hide. Follow me."

They ran down the hallway and around to the end. There were cardboard boxes in the space behind the last curtain.

"This is the Indian Village."

Praisesong reached into a box. He pulled out two headdresses. He handed Bernie one.

"This one's for a kid. Put it on."

Praisesong put on the other one. He peeked through the curtain. No spectators were in sight. He pushed through the curtain. Bernie followed him.

A statue of an Indian was lying asleep by the embers of a fire. A teepee was next to him.

"Get in the teepee," Praisesong said.

"I can't fit. They'll see my dress."

"Stick your legs in up to your neck. With just your headdress sticking out. Don't move til I tell you."

They heard a woman's voice coming down the hallway beyond the glass.

"Quick."

Bernie got into the teepee. Only his head stuck out. He closed his eyes. Praisesong yanked the blanket off the statue of the sleeping Indian. He lay down next to it and pulled the blanket up to his neck. Only his face and headdress showed. He closed his eyes.

An attractive woman in her mid-thirties with her four-year-old daughter stopped in front of the Indian Village. The little girl had a headful of blonde curls. She peered into the exhibit.

"Those are Indians, Honey. They're sleeping."

"Mommy?"

"Yes?"

"Why are they sleeping?"

"Cause they're tired, Honey."

Minor walked up beside them. He glanced into the exhibit, then down the hallway at the people walking past the other exhibits.

Praisesong's nose started to run. He turned it slowly against his arm to clear it.

The little girl pointed into the village.

"Mommy, the big Indian is waking up."

Her mother chuckled.

Minor looked at them.

"She has such a vivid imagination," the woman said apologetically. "Honey, he's a statue. Do you know what a statue is?"

The girl with the golden curls nodded emphatically.

"But he's waking up, Mommy!"

"Where, little girl?" said Minor.

The girl pointed at Praisesong. The mother laughed again.

"She has such an imagination."

Praisesong could hear the conversation. He opened his eyes to see Minor pressed against the glass. Praisesong jumped up.

"Let's get the hell out of here, Bernie!"

The mother fell back against the wall, holding her chest. Minor ran toward the door at the end of the hall.

Bernie and Praisesong ran down the back hallway. They almost got into the room near the backdoor when they heard voices. Two men were halfway up the stairs into the basement.

"Jump on the bike, Kid!"

Bernie ran through the back door and got on the Harley. Praisesong picked up the bobcat. He threw it down the stairs at the men. They fell onto the landing. He ran out the door and jumped on his bike. As they came bursting through the door, the bike jumped over the curb into the street. The men jumped into a car and sped after them.

When Praisesong got to Wells Street, he took a sharp right going west against traffic on the one-way street. A car swerved to miss him. Praisesong jumped the curb again and continued west on the sidewalk up to the Marquette University campus. The men in the car pulled over to avoid the oncoming traffic.

A Coast Guard chopper hovered 500 feet above. Lathrop Willis' phone rang again at the Pfister.

"Mr. Willis?"

"Yes."

"Sturdevant, here. Chopper pilot. The Indian and the girl. Uh, is it a girl?"

"Don't know. Where are they?"

"On Wells. Going the wrong way."

"Follow them. Phone location to Minor. How crowded is it down there?"

"Pretty crowded. There's a parade starting."

"Follow them. When they leave the downtown, Minor's men will get her."

"Yes, Sir."

"How long do you have the copter?"

'That's all arranged. No deadline."

"Update me with her location."

"Roger. Out."

The chopper headed south as Praisesong turned onto 17th Street.

"Praisesong."

"Yeah?"

"I just called Joe. He says go to the start of the parade route. Jerry Piano's there. He said stay with the parade a while in the middle of the street. Don't let anybody grab me. Then take off for Nicole's."

"Where does it start?"

"He says Tenth and Wisconsin."

"No problem."

Praisesong turned east on Wisconsin Avenue.

A substantial Green crowd had gathered at Tenth Street for the St. Patrick's Day Parade. Green plastic hats and boas. Green and Orange sashes. Men dressed like leprechauns in green suits, green shirts, and green shoes. Green stocking caps. Green shamrocks stamped on bright red cheeks.

A unit walking Irish Wolfhounds gathered on one side. The finalists in the red hair and freckles contest gathered on the other. Bernie saw Jerry Piano waving at them from the middle of the crowd. Praisesong guided the bike slowly towards him.

"Over here."

Jerry gestured to a unit just beyond him.

"Joe called. Here's the plan. You'll march with Labor. They said it's Okay. Slip your bike in here."

Two men walked over to join them. Jerry introduced them.

"This is Rick Michalski. He's the President of the Machinists. And this is Marc Nordberg. He's the President of the Sheetmetal Workers."

They all shook hands. Michalski had won the Silver Star and two purple hearts in Vietnam. He was powerfully built, with bright friendly brown eyes.

Nordberg was younger and much taller. He had played defensive tackle at Random Lake High School. Their defensive line weighed more than the line at the University of Wisconsin during the years he played. The players spent much of their time at their families' farms throwing bales of hay into and out of lofts. Most opposing players did not enjoy running against the Random Lake defensive line. Especially against Marc Nordberg.

Bagpipes started to play. The car of the Parade Marshall, Jeremiah Haggerty, started slowly down Wisconsin Avenue.

"We're next," Michalski said. "Pull up here."

Praisesong nudged his bike forward into the middle of the Machinists. They started down the Avenue. The crowd cheered each unit as it marched by.

Willis' phone rang again.

"Minor, sir. We have men on both sides of the street. The boy's on a motorcycle in the middle of the parade."

"Are you sure it's him?"

"Sure of it. He had a wig on before. We confirmed it through photo identification."

"What's the best way to get him?"

"We could try at Fourth and Wisconsin. The crowd's really skimpy there. We could move in and take him. Might be better to wait until the end. Take him as he goes home."

"Be discreet. If you can take him now, fine. But don't create a scene. You'll have more resources after the parade."

"What are they?"

"I've arranged for the FBI to infiltrate the crowd at the end. They have full arrest powers. They trump the Milwaukee Police."

"That's great."

Praisesong pushed along slowly among the marchers. As they came up on 4th and Wisconsin, a man walked over from the curb toward the motorcycle. He pushed by Nordberg.

"Can I help you?" said Nordberg.

The man ignored him. He approached the motorcycle. Bernie shrank to one side and buried his head behind Praisesong.

Nordberg grabbed the man's arm. The man tried to pull away. Nordberg crushed his hand around the man's elbow.

"You listen to me."

He walked the man along as he spoke.

"This is a private unit. Get the hell back to the curb. Don't come out here again."

He shoved the man beyond the marchers. The man stumbled, then blended back into the crowd on the sidewalk.

The crowd cheered as the parade turned north toward City Hall. They could see the reviewing stand, two blocks away, covered with American and Irish flags. Mayor Nuedling and the Common Council stood on the sidewalk, waiting for the marchers. The County Board stood right behind them.

Bernie tightened his grip.

"How are we going to get away from here, Praisesong? There's a lot of people there."

"I'm thinking. What's going on here, anyway? We got a helicopter over us. Guys at the museum. A guy comes out from the crowd. Why do they want you?"

"Frannie'll tell you. But how do we get out of here? They'll be there at the end waiting for me."

"Here's what we'll do. I'm going to open it up right through the damned crowd. I'll head north on Third. They'll follow us. When I get to Brewers Hill, I'll cut through an alley. You jump. I'll head north. I'll leave it all on the concrete. You run like hell to that girl's apartment."

"Thanks. I don't want to get you in trouble.'

"No problem. I got points to play with."

City hall was a half block away. Nuedling stood in front of the crowd wearing a green tie. Turnpaugh and Fieblewicz and all the Council and Board and their staffs stood just below the TV cameras, trying to get picked up as background. And men in dark suits with earpieces walked through the crowd without talking to anyone, eyeing the oncoming marchers.

Praisesong got about twenty yards away.

"Stand by Bernie!"

He inched along.

"Geronimo!"

He shouted and opened up his Harley. He gunned it straight for the crowd.

Nuedling hit the deck. Turnpaugh and Fieblewicz stumbled and fell to get out of the way. Praisesong swerved to avoid them. He saw daylight on the sidewalk and went up over the curb.

"Look out! Get out of the way!"

People screamed as he gunned it down the sidewalk, north to State Street. The men with the earpieces scrambled to jump into their cars. The helicopter flew directly overhead. Praisesong turned west on State Street to Third and turned north.

"Stand by Bernie!"

They could hear sirens a few blocks behind them. Praisesong looked up at the helicopter.

"Stand by! We're cutting tight here."

He took a hard right on North, and then a left into an alley.

"Jump, Bernie! Jump! Run like hell!"

He slowed enough for his passenger to jump off. Bernie ran between two buildings and was gone. Praisesong sped north to Locust, and down the entrance ramp to I-43. He sped north wide open.

Willis's phone rang again at the Pfister.

"Sturdevant, Sir."

"Where are you?"

"Following the Indian, Sir. He's on the Interstate. Pushing a hundred. He'll be in Green Bay in an hour."

"Is the boy on back?"

"Negative. Nothing on back. Just an Indian on a Harley going north like a bat out of hell."

"Return to base!" Willis slammed the phone onto the desk.

Chapter Thirty-One

I dialed the Pfister Hotel and asked for Ralph Swenson.

"Hello?"

"Is that you, Ralph?"

"Who is this?"

Willis sounded as if he wanted to reach through the wires right then and there and strangle me.

"Joe Weber. And you must be Ralph. Did you know you also sound like a man I met a little while ago? Lathrop Willis. Is he related to you?"

I could picture wormy red veins pounding in Willis' head.

"What do you want, Weber?"

"I have something for you. The stick that Mr. Barnes gave Bernie. I want to give it back to you. Now."

There was complete, profound silence.

"That will be fine," Willis finally said. "Where are you? We'll come and pick it up right now."

"That's not the way I want to do it. Your homies are packing. I don't want them near me. If you want the stick, you can meet me at Three Brothers at four p.m."

"I'll be there."

I hung up and dialed again.

"Hey, Jerry."

"Yeah."

"I need some guys at Three Brothers. Bernie needs backup. Four p.m. This should be the last time. We're giving them what they want."

"I'll see what I can do."

"I really need it this time. I need bodies. I need squads."

"Okay. We'll meet at Clyburn. Near Van Buren. At ten to four. We'll caravan to Three Brothers. Is Bernie coming with?

"No. He's safe."

I spent some time working the phone. When Frannie and I got to Clybourn, eight squads were lined up. Officers walked down the line talking to each other. Ernie Doggs drove point. Jerry's squad was right behind.

Ashleigh's canary yellow VW with the daisy painted on the back was the first car behind the squads. She and Nicole and Brittney were talking with two officers. Frank and Terry sat in Frank's '92 Buick Park Avenue right behind them, waiting for orders.

"Okay."

Jerry raised his hand.

"We drive in formation. When we get there, park on both sides of the street. Double park if you have to. You won't get no ticket. Ernie, let's go."

E.R. "Ernie" Doggs pulled slowly out into the street, lights flashing. Jerry and Frannie and I pulled out behind him. Then the other squads, then Ashleigh, then Frank. We hooked around onto the Hoan Bridge, eight squads driving in a line, lights flashing, with a yellow VW and a '92 Buick bringing up the rear.

There were a dozen black Lincolns lining St. Clair Street outside of Three Brothers when we got there. The squads parked in the middle of the street, lights on. Ashleigh and Frank parked behind them. It was a strange sight. The blue-striped, white cars with lights surrounded by black sedans on the curbs.

A group of men stood at the door.

"Who are they, Jerry?" I said.

"Couple of FBI. I don't know the rest."

Marc Nordberg was standing near the front door with four sheet metal workers. El Futuro stood off to the side, unfee'd and unhappy, surrounded by a small posse. Michael stood apart, dressed up in a nice raspberry suit, white hat, black shirt, and lemon tie. He smiled broadly at me, his gold front tooth shining in the afternoon sun.

"It's the best I could do."

Jerry was apologetic.

"It's good," I said. "This is just right."

The stone-faced men in front of the door didn't seem to be paying attention to anyone, until the girls got out of the VW. Ashleigh dropped her purse as she stepped onto the sidewalk. A dozen eyes watched her spend a lot of time bending over to pick it up.

Jerry called Nordberg and El Futuro and Michael over to the curb.

"Marc, you and your men go in first. Hang by the wall on the right. El Futuro. You and your men stand over by the bar. Don't say nothing."

"And what am I supposed to do?"

"Nothing. Not a goddamned thing. You're a witness."

"To what?"

"To nothing."

El Futuro looked even more unhappy. He shrugged and waved his men behind Nordberg.

"Michael, you fall in behind El Futuro. Ernie and I'll go in next. Joe, you and Frannie walk between us. I want the rest of the officers to follow us. Girls, you follow the officers. Frank and Terry, you follow the girls. Any questions? Go!"

Marc Nordberg pushed open the door to Three Brothers. His men followed. The rest of us marched in like Jerry said.

The curtains were drawn in the restaurant. The lights were low. The sheet metal workers were standing at the wall to the right, mixed in with men in suits. No one spoke. El Futuro and his men stood across from them at the bar.

I could hear Pirate Jenny playing on the jukebox.

"Meine Herren, heute sehen Sie mich Glaser abwaschen . . ."

Lathrop Willis and Wayne Hawkin sat facing the door. A dozen other men were seated throughout the restaurant. Michael had stones. He sat in a chair across from Willis and Hawkin, grinning at them. Branko came hurrying up to the door to greet us, rubbing his hands. His beret was tilted a little too far. He looked uneasy.

"To what do we owe this honor?" he said. "The MPD, some very important gentlemen who are unknown to me, a request to open early. For some reason this reminds me of Belgrade in 1944. Not pleasant memories. No?"

Jerry didn't say anything.

"We open at five," Branko said. "I'm sure that there will be no unpleasantness. Nothing to disturb my customers? If they come a few minutes early, and see . . . what?"

Branko looked anxiously at Nordberg, then at El Futuro, whose lieutenant flashed his grills. Branko winced from the sparkle caused by the diamond on his front tooth.

Willis eyed the crowd with distaste and looked at Michael.

"What's your name?"

"Mr. Claude Balls. Who you?"

Willis ignored him.

"We'll make this short," I said to Branko.

I walked up to Willis and Hawkin. Willis gestured to a chair, but I stayed standing.

"To whom am I speaking? Henry Jensen, Ralph Swenson, Lathrop Willis, or Wayne Hawkin?"

Willis smiled, but only with his lips. The man was unshakeable. He looked past me and Michael at the Milwaukee police officers, the sheet metal workers, El Futuro and his posse: Ashleigh, Brittney, Frannie and Nicole, Frank and Terry.

"What's in a name? A rose by any other name is just as sweet. Where is the stick?"

"Which one?"

"What do you mean, which one?"

"The one with your number? Or the one with its prime factors?"

Willis was stunned. Probably for the first time in his life. He didn't speak.

"I have two sticks in my pocket," I said. "I'm going to give them to you. And when I do, you'll never return to Milwaukee."

Willis kept silent.

"And the thief with the gun? He's gone, right? Forever?"

Still silence.

"And these guys with the stone-cold eyes. They're out of here?"

"Where are the sticks?"

I handed him two packages.

"Here."

"If you're lying, we'll be back."

"I'm not lying. And if you come back, you'll be lying on a cot in the county jail."

The music filled the silence.

"Und das Schiff mit acht Segein . . ."

Branko rubbed his hands even harder.

"Gentlemen. Some people may arrive early. They are in the mood for wine. For music. For burek. For raznichi. Not for trouble, you see. Not for politics. I am a peaceful man. What the hell is this?"

Willis put the packages in his coat pocket.

"If they are what you say they are, we will not come back. We will have no need to. But if the number is not here, we will assume you stole it. And act accordingly."

"The stick is there. And more."

I turned to leave. Jerry started to wave the rest of our side toward the door.

"One more thing," Willis said. "I'm tired of your fake programs. If what you say is true, it means there's a student in a Milwaukee school who makes Archimedes, Gauss, and Riemann look like accountants."

"They're dead," I said. "He's alive. And he's going to stay that way. Don't come back."

We all got back in our cars.

"Hit it, Jerry," I said.

We pulled off of St. Clair Street, lights flashing, siren blasting, and headed back to the Hoan Bridge.

Chapter Thirty-Two

A curious two-story stone building stands at the corner of Wall and College Streets in New Haven. It has no windows. Two massive bronze doors with brass studs face the street. Stone arches with contrasting stone stand where windows should be. A low iron fence surrounds the building. The landscaping is immaculate. Beautifully trimmed shrubs are carefully laid out on the lawn around the building.

Two men opened the low iron gate and walked up the path in the dark to the building. They each walked up separate stairways that flanked the stone porch. One of them pulled on the brass ring hanging from the right door.

It opened. They closed the door behind them and stood in a dimly lit entry hall. One of them carefully banged the round brass knocker on another massive door. One knock. Then two in quick succession. One knock. Then two.

A small sliding panel opened in the door.

"Pocula elevate."

"Nunc est bibendum," one of the men said.

The door opened. A handsome black man, about 75 years old, stood in front of them in a room with a 15-foot ceiling and marble floor. The carved woodwork was dark and highly polished. Murals of medieval court life covered the walls.

"Wamba!"

Lathrop Willis and Wayne Hawkin hugged the man.

"Z's! I thought you might be back. For the reunions."

"Are they in session?"

"No. I was just leaving. May I get you some sherry?"

"Two sherries from the poculum. We'll be up in the library. It's good to see you, Wamba."

"And you sir."

"And leave the decanter with us."

"Yes sir."

Willis and Hawkin walked up a dark wooden stairway to the second floor. They sat in wine dark leather chairs in the library. The ceiling fifteen feet above them was plaster, intricately patterned. Willis looked at the books on the shelves, all identically bound in calfskin.

"It's all there, Hawkin. Every speech from every Z session. All of Volero's Polyps. The speeches from every session for every pont."

"The number. You are going to tell me about the number. You said you wanted to tell me here."

"Yes. The number."

"Well?"

"The boy told the truth. He found the prime factors. Once the prime number screen was lifted, Gieck's men broke the code that remained."

"And?"

"It's everything I feared for most of my career."

"What is it?"

"The Chinese are far advanced in cementing an alliance with the Islamic street that will shortly overwhelm their countries."

"The message could have hardly said that. What did it say?"

"It announces Chinese funding for Al Qaeda in Yemen and also in Somalia."

The two men sat in silence.

"There's also reference to a cell in New Delhi. We hadn't even known about that."

"Here you are, Gentlemen."

Wamba held out a tray with two glasses and a decanter.

"Thank you, Wamba."

Willis put the tray on a small walnut table next to his chair. He poured two glasses and handed one to Hawkin.

"I'll be going," Wamba said. "Do you need anything else?"

"No. Thanks."

They watched Wamba leave. Willis raised his glass.

"Pocula elevate, nunc est bibendum."

"Bibemus."

They drank.

"That's absurd," Hawkin said. "We can't send Chinese Uighurs from Guantanamo back to China. They'd be shot. We have to send them to Bermuda, for God's sake. How can the Chinese fund Al Qaeda and get away with killing Chinese Muslims?"

"The Muslims are disorganized, corrupt, and divided. They hate each other. The Chinese Uighurs are Sunnis. The Shia don't care about them. Arab Sunnis don't care about the Uighurs. And they all give the Chinese a pass to gain a powerful ally."

"But the Saudi royal family would kill Al Qaeda if they got their hands on them. So would most other Arab governments."

"The Saudi royal family has a generation left. The one's who don't get to Zurich in time will get what Louis XVI and Charles I and the Romanoffs got. Same with the other governments. The street is boiling. The explosion is near."

"But how can they think this won't be discovered? They own our treasuries. We educate their students at Cal Tech and MIT."

Willis drained his glass.

"They're keeping us off guard. Driving us into second place."

He poured himself another.

"There's still time. I *think* there's still time. I *hope* there's still time. I've spoken to a few friends in Congress. Some of them may grow a spine and deal with the Chinese."

Willis stood up. He walked around the room, looking at silver from the mid-nineteenth century.

"It's what I've always feared, Hawkin. An alliance of the Caliph and the Emperor. The East can't be allowed to come together. When Achilles killed Hector at Troy . . . magnificent. And have you read the Persians recently? Magnificent. The Greeks put a stop to them. Then the Khan came back in the twelfth century. Took our ancestors a damned long time to drive them out."

"Willis. Do you think other people think the way we do? I mean, in America."

"I hope so."

"I don't think they do. You and I read Homer and Aeschylus in Greek. No one else reads them in English. Most people never heard of them. They'd think they were television characters."

Willis seemed not to hear.

"If they're funding them in Yemen and Somalia, they're funding them elsewhere, too. In Mali. In Iraq. In Afghanistan. Let's go into the templum, Hawkin."

They walked into a small room beyond the stairway landing. A curious room. A throne with carved wooden arms lay on the east wall. The arms ended in two carved lion heads. Over the throne, the arms of Zanoni. "Hear and Obey" above an eagle with lightning bolts shooting from its talons.

Flanking the throne of Zanoni were two smaller thrones, set at an angle. Twelve high backed small wooden thrones were arranged six on a side along the north and south walls, connected by a common wooden platform. Over each throne stood a shield with the arms of the other ponts, Periander, Eumenes, and the rest.

A marble fireplace, unlighted, lay along the west wall. Paintings from mythology covered the ceiling and upper walls. The lower walls were carved wood. The floor was marble.

The room was empty. Willis sat in the throne of Zanoni and then he motioned for Hawkin to sit next to him.

"Why should you sit there?"

Hawkin was joking.

"I'm Z also."

"I'm senior. Sit on the throne of Anselmo. He was the second in command."

Hawkin sat down.

"You know, Hawkin. I was happiest here at Scroll and Key."

Willis looked around the room.

"We were twenty-one. Every Thursday, we sat here after dinner and port. A different pont would read his essay. Zanoni in his black robe. Anselmo and Arbaces next to him in white robes. The other ponts in red robes. A splendid fire. We would criticize and discuss."

"We were spoiled. All of this for fifteen college brats."

"Yes. Fifteen men. But out of it came patriots. We lost men in every war. In the civil war, on both sides. The best America had to offer. And many came to the Agency. Tracy Manning. Me. You. Allen Barnes. And many others. We're vigilant. And we won't be overwhelmed."

"By the way," Hawkin said. "The boy. We'll need him. You've considered the implications for our own cryptography?"

"Of course."

"I mean you can't kidnap him and waterboard him every time you want him to solve a math problem."

"I must make a confession."

Willis drained his glass.

"I called the boy myself."

"What? What did you say to him?"

"I said he deserved our country's thanks. He saved many lives."

"His discoveries will get out. When they do, they'll read our codes."

"We'll have to learn to encrypt them differently. The race will continue like it has since the first hominid made a stone knife."

"What's your plan with Congress?"

"Congress is naïve and impotent. But congresses come and go. We persevere."

"What do we do?"

Willis stood up.

"We do what Keys men have always done. We stood fast in the most evil times. Hitler, the Soviets, now the Caliph and the Emperor. We're going to stop them. Europe and America *are* civilization. And we won't surrender it. Ever."

The two walked down the stairs to the front door. They heard a knock. Then two knocks in quick succession. A knock. Then two in quick succession.

Willis opened the sliding panel.

"Pocula elevate?"

"Nunc est bibendum," said a voice.

Willis opened the door. A pretty black girl, about 21, with cheerful eyes and a red, black and green bandana, stood at the door.

"Are you here to help Wamba?"

"No, actually."

"Who are you?" Willis said.

"I am Zanoni," she said.

Willis stood frozen. The muscles in his arms trembled.

"And who are you, may I ask?"

"We're alums," Hawkin said. "Back for the reunions."

He and Willis walked slowly down the stairs outside and into the New Haven evening.

Chapter Thirty-Three

Some Bob Marley music pounded through the room.

'Is this love, is this love, is this love, is this love that I'm feelin . . .'

Terry Shit Theory Norris chugged a Miller. Jerry Piano, Ernie Doggs, and some of the other coppers talked with Ashleigh and Nicole and Brittney. Frank, El Futuro, Michael, and El Futuro's running dogs stood talking with Frannie. Sharon, Bernie and Jimmy Jr. sat on the sofa drinking soda. Jimmy was home from Fordham on spring break.

Praisesong and Supreme Star Hussein stood in a corner, Praisesong listening gravely to Supreme's theory of everything. The Machinists and the Sheetmetal workers were in the next room, talking with Karen Dudek and other girls from Frannie's class. Michael sat in a corner smiling, gold tooth flashing, pulling on his third can of beer. Branko sat next to him.

"Food's ready!"

I checked the drinks again. Ten cases of Miller in tubs full of ice. Twelve bottles of Phat Bastard Merlot, cooling on ice in another tub.

I checked the food. Onion dip and pretzels. Slices of sausage on saltines. Cocktail wieners. Four dozen bratwurst cooking on a grill on the back porch. And bowls of buns, chopped onions, sauerkraut, and pickle relish. Plenty of mustard and ketchup, too.

I normally wouldn't spring for rations at that level, not for so many people. And it's safe to say that this was the first time that these citizens were all at the same party. But we were celebrating Bernie's freedom.

"A toast!"

Jerry Piano was on his feet with some beers already in him. Ashley touched his arm, her fingers lingering a little longer than necessary.

"To Branko!"

Jerry bellowed.

"The man's stone cold. Love the beret, man. You put up with some shit at the Brothers, man."

Branko bowed to the loud applause. His black eyes beamed.

"To Terry Norris," said Frank. "The Brewers need you, Terry. You caught the man between the shoulder blades with that can of peaches."

Norris bowed to violent applause.

"Did a little pitching at Tech. Had a little bit of a fastball. And if any of you's need a roof, you're not getting it tonight."

"Bernie, you're cute."

Ashleigh was a little tipsy. She held onto Jerry's arm and raised her beer.

"How'd you get so smart?"

Bernie turned red, but he didn't say anything. He looked relaxed, sipping a coke on the sofa.

"And hey, Jimmy," Ashleigh said. "Spring break next year starts March twelfth. What day is it?"

She cupped her ear.

"Friday," said Jimmy.

That brought more violent applause.

The phone rang. I walked into the kitchen to get it. I could hear Jerry on the next toasts.

"To the stove-bomber, Frank, and to Supreme Star Hussein. I have to say, outstanding work, man. But you ain't parking no squads, man. And Frank . . ."

I could hear everyone laugh as I picked up the phone. It was Elmer. He'd been here earlier but must've slipped out on patrol.

"Frank. I think one of them's back. Just parking his car."

"Got it."

I ran back into the living room.

"It's Elmer. They're back. Sharon, take Bernie and Jimmy up to the bedroom. Jerry, you and your guys stand by the door."

They all jumped up. Sharon hustled her sons up the stairs. Frannie and Ashleigh and her friends stood along the wall. Jerry and his men flanked the door.

Frank, Terry, Branko, and Praisesong backed Jerry up. So did the sheet metal workers and the machinists, and Michael and El Futuro and the rest.

The doorbell rang. I opened it. Allen Barnes stood on the porch.

"Joe. I need to speak with you."

"I don't need to speak with you. I told the others never to come back. We're not putting up with any more shit."

"I'm not with the others. They let me go. I'm all alone. I need to talk with you."

We stood in silence. Jerry looked at me.

"Okay," I said. "You can come in. We'll talk in the kitchen."

I had my hand firmly on Barnes' shoulder as I guided him to the kitchen. Some excellent Marley kept pounding. Jerry, Frank, Terry and Marc Nordberg followed us in.

"What do you want"?

"I need Bernie's help on something."

"You're not getting it. You scared the hell out of him. You chased a kid for three months. It stops now."

"It's not what you think."

Barnes looked absolutely dejected.

"Look, Joe. I have nothing. They fired me. Forced retirement. They don't take my calls. I'm an embarrassment to them."

I started to feel bad for him. He looked so damned sad.

"I want to tell you how this happened. They gave me a number to decode. They said our cameras picked it up on one of Jupiter's moons."

"Hey," I said. "There's a Nigerian oil minister stole two hundred million and wants to share it with you. They tell you that, too?"

Barnes ground his lips.

"I know what they were doing now. I didn't then. But the camera did pick something up."

"So?"

"There was a mistake, and Bernie got the wrong number. That's what started all this."

"So?"

"I want Bernie to look at my number."

"Why? If it's bullshit, why?"

"Because I don't know if it's bullshit or not. In my mind, it's open. I want to close it."

The thing about Barnes, he was totally honest. Crazy, but honest.

"Go outside," I said to Jerry. "Take some men. If there's anyone else out there, arrest them."

Jerry left.

"If you're alone, like you say, I'll let you talk to Bernie. If you're not, the MPD's taking you downtown."

Barnes relaxed. I knew he was alone.

Jerry came back in a few minutes.

"There's no one else. I left two men outside. Your crazy neighbor is prowling on the curb.

"Okay. Frank, can you bring Bernie down?"

The music was turned up loud. The others were hitting the Miller and the Phat Bastard pretty hard. Jerry'd told them it was okay.

Frank returned with Bernie and Jimmy.

"Bernie, this is Mr. Barnes. He has one more number to show us. To see if it means anything. Where's the number?"

Barnes pulled a piece of paper out of his jacket pocket and unfolded it. The number filled most of the page.

"What does it mean, Bernie?"

Barnes' eyes were exceptionally shiny.

"They told me that the first sixteen numbers were found carved on a bone in Africa twenty thousand years ago. If that helps."

Oh, a bone in Africa, is it? Well, that explains everything. Christ, I'm getting tired of this. How did they get into power? That's another thing I love about them. Not a lot of warm-up. A gun in your kidney in a Serbian restaurant. Here's a long number, give me the answer. Now!

Bernie and Jimmy and Terry looked at it. Bernie frowned.

"It's not a prime number," he said to Barnes.

"Why not?"

Bernie looked at him with a hint of resignation.

"It ends in a zero. No prime number ends in zero."

"You've got to help me," Barnes said. "It's got to mean something."

"Why?"

Bernie was pretty matter of fact. I was feeling bad for Barnes again, but Bernie was very cool.

"Well, because. There's got to be a reason for everything."

Bernie shrugged. He looked at it again.

"Well, there is one thing."

"What?"

Barnes leaped on it like a starving cat on a saucer of cream. Bernie looked at it some more. He was reading the whole number pattern.

"Let's say you disregard the first sixteen numbers. The ones that you said were carved on the African bone and that."

"Yes!"

Barnes' eyes were gleaming. They could've melted the glass in the kitchen window.

"If you start at the seventeenth number and go in groups of four?"

"Yes!"

"Most of the groups are prime numbers. Like the first one is 2,791. See that? And the next one is 5,641?"

"Yes! Yes!"

"They're both prime. And so are most of the rest. See? 9,769. 4,157. 3,331. 8,669. But there're five left over at the end. And they're not prime."

"What are those?"

"10120."

Bernie might just as well have been talking Chinese characters to Barnes.

The sign for the cat and the dog are there. But I don't know the last five characters.

Barnes just wanted results.

"Yes! Yes?"

He was begging.

"What is it?"

"I don't know."

Bernie shrugged.

"Nothing, really. You can always make some prime numbers out of a long sequence. Plus, these are just random anyway."

Terry wasn't paying any attention. He kept staring at the number.

"Joe, I want to talk with you."

We stepped outside onto the back porch. Jerry'd already taken the brats into the living room.

"What is it?" I said.

"We've got to get rid of this guy, right?"

"Right."

"I mean they'll be out here all the time if we don't do something."

"Not anymore. This is it. I felt bad for this guy. It was stupid of me. It won't happen again."

"But we've got to get rid of him. He needs a sign. A dream. I got an idea."

"What?"

"This'll get him. Remember I told you me and your brother were in school together?"

"Yeah."

"We took a seminar. One of the problems was how many chess games were possible if every piece made every possible move."

"So?'

"So, a seasoned numbers dick at Bell Labs proved that the possible combinations were 10 to the 120th power. If every piece made every possible move."

"So?"

"So, this is it. The last five numbers Bernie said were 10120. See? The number for the total chess games. He listens to Bernie. So, make something out of it. Give him something to chew on so he'll get the hell out of here."

"That's ridiculous. The goddamn number covers a page."

"Okay, we just need to get rid of this guy, right? Bernie narrowed it down. He believes Bernie. So, use it."

"This is all bullshit. Probably doctored by Willis."

"Yeah? Who cares? Tell him it's a sign. A number screen. Throw out the numbers on the gorilla's pecker or whatever the hell they were, and Bernie's primes, and you're left with the message. I got to sneeze."

Terry sneezed.

"What message?"

"How the hell do I know? Make something up. The guy wants meaning. That's your department. You give good meaning."

"Okay."

We went back in. Bernie and Jimmy were staring uneasily at Barnes, who kept shooting tucked little smiles at the boys and Jerry and Marc.

"We've cracked it," I said.

Barnes looked at me with disdain.

"Who cracked it?"

"Bernie and Terry."

"What do you mean?"

"Bernie," I said. "Is it true that this number has sequential four-digit prime numbers from the beginning until the last five, and if you throw out the number on the gorilla's . . . I mean, the African bone at the beginning?"

"Yup."

"And if we screen out the four-digit prime numbers and the bone numbers, what number is left over?"

Bernie looked at the page.

"10120."

"Okay. Terry, what does that number mean?"

Terry Shit Theory Norris nodded gravely. He didn't crack a smile.

"It was proven at Bell Labs in the 1940s. 10 to the 120th power is the number of possible chess games, if every piece made every possible move."

"That's a number bigger than all the atoms in the universe," Frank said.

I glared at Frank. He wasn't helping me close the sale.

There was absolute silence in the kitchen. Jerry and Marc Nordberg remained stone faced. They sniffed the scam, but to them it was still Sanskrit.

"So, what do we do with all this?" Barnes said.

"I don't know," I said. "You know anyone at NASA?"

"I know the head of it. He was a classmate of mine. Guelph."

Jerry wanted to jump Ashleigh's bones, not talk NASA's Guelph.

"I'll be inside," he said. "Call me if you need me."

Marc Nordberg followed him out.

"Guelph," I said. "What kind of name is that?"

"That was his name in a group I was in. What should I tell him?"

"Tell Guelph to beam a message into space. E4."

"What's that?"

"The standard chess opening. White moves his King's pawn two spaces. It's expressed as E4. If something's out there, they'll know how to answer."

Barnes looked more excited for the first time all evening.

"Why not? Why the hell not? I'll go down and see him myself."

"There you go."

We headed back into the living room. Barnes just stood staring at the people, the dancing, the scene. The music had changed.

"It's a strange world we live in Master Jack," filled the room.

It bothered me to think he'd just go out into the night by himself.

"Look," I said. "You can stay and have a beer and a brat if you got nowhere to go. We've got plenty of food."

Barnes looked with excitement around the room.

"I think I will. Thanks."

He grabbed a Miller and sat down on a chair near the tubs. I left him to see how everyone was doing. I grabbed a beer for myself.

Frannie waved at me.

"Honey, can you get me some wine?"

"Sure."

I went to get some Merlot. I could hear Barnes chanting in a sing-song voice.

"Thales, Prasatagus, Eumenes, Arbaces, Mago, et Nichao, Periander, Glaucus, Anselmo, Volero, Belus, Guelph, Pironis, Chilo, Zanoni, Collegium Conservet Jupiter."

Naturally, no one came near him. I grabbed the bottle and a glass and went over to Frannie.

"Let's dance," I said.

Frannie took my hand. I put the bottle and glass down on a table. We walked by Barnes again. He was staring with a big smile at the girls dancing with the cops. I can still hear him singing softly.

"Gaily the troubadour touched his guitar, as he was hastening home from the war. Singing from Palestine, hither I've come. Lady love, lady love, welcome me home."

I smiled and took Frannie in my arms.

About the Author

Matthew J. Flynn is a prominent lawyer, politician, and former Naval Officer. His career in politics and service in the Navy have given him an insight into how our government and our enemies operate. He uses this perspective as an inspiration for his thrillers. Flynn lives with his wife in Milwaukee.

Upcoming New Release!

Matthew J. Flynn

AMERICAN DAWN
Revenge Series
Book Two

Hell has no fury like a woman scorned.

Beautiful Dawn Rybarsky, a college girl, falls in love with a powerful politician, Dan Race, who is managing a crooked Senate campaign to destroy the opposing candidate. He exposes her to a world in bed and in politics that she had never imagined.

Race makes a bet with an evil campaign consultant that they will share Dawn sexually if their candidate wins. He does win. But when Race sets a trap for Dawn to lure her to join them, hell has no fury...

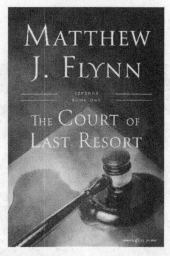

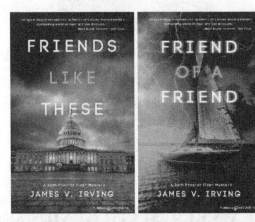
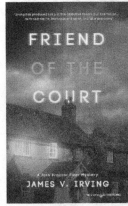

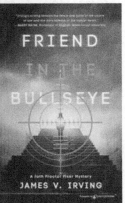

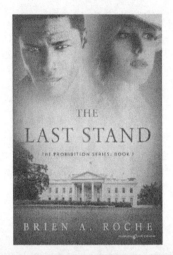
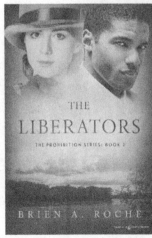

Made in the USA
Monee, IL
26 November 2024

71386439R00177